Smiley

By
Michael Ezell

Cover design by Valdas Miskinis.

ISBN: 978-0-692-94477-6

Thanks to the wife-with-endless-patience. April, I love you for putting up with so much more than the time I spent in the writing cave.

Thanks to Christopher J. Valin and Steve Barr, who along with a missing quarter of our group made me a better writer. (Chris gets 2x the Thanks for helping me format this book!)

Thanks to the Two Dans, who each enriched my life in different ways. Daniel Fraembs and Danny Grossman. The world is a lesser place without them.

Evil is unspectacular and always human, and shares our
bed and eats at our own table.
- W. H. Auden

1

West Virginia Route 45 - Midnight

Unaware she was experiencing the last few moments of freedom she would ever know, Taylor stuck both middle fingers in the air.

"You fat asshole!" The cold air burned her throat, but it was worth it to scream her rage at the sonuvabitch truck driver. Not that he heard it. The eighteen-wheeler's taillights were already a good quarter mile away, headed back toward the highway onramp.

Needles of freezing rain hissed against the frozen black pavement and made a dull drumming sound on the hood of her parka. Taylor had screwed seven truckers to get the money for the puffy Gore-Tex coat. It made her look like a bright blue teddy bear.

This last asshole had waited till he drove her up here to the rest area, and then tried to talk her back on her price. Screw him. She'd rather walk the mile back to the truck stop than let his flabby ass wallow around between her legs for a lousy twenty bucks.

She started back down the access road to Burton's Truck Stop. Not all her goose bumps came from the cold.

This time of night, she knew there wouldn't be much traffic. Just her, the empty dark highway, and the black woods out to her left for the next mile. She flinched when some freaky bird let out a high-pitched cry among the tall trees. Wide wings beat the air once, twice... then nothing. Taylor noticed she'd stopped walking.

She set off again at a jaunty pace, following the highway boundary line down the mountain, the clack-clack-clack of her high-heeled boots as good as whistling past the graveyard.

Something out there in the still woods went *pfffap*!

When the silver dart hit her in the thigh, Taylor let out a little shriek. She blinked at it, trying to comprehend how it came to be there. Her brain told her to snatch the shiny thing out of her leg, but... her arm seemed to move in slow motion. Her fingertips brushed the dart and she fell face down in a snow bank the plow had piled beside the road.

It was like being smothered with a frozen pillow. She couldn't breathe, couldn't move. She felt panic rising in her throat— Panic turned to sweet relief when someone rolled her over. The relief lasted a few fleeting heartbeats.

The burning hatred in the man's pale blue eyes made Taylor wish she *had* suffocated in a downy bank of snow. And it wouldn't be the last time she wished that wish upon a star.

***

"Michelle is dead and buried in California and there is nothing I can do about it."

Garrett Evans knew one day he wouldn't need to say his mantra before he got out of bed. Today wasn't that day.

It took him exactly twenty-five minutes to get out the door with a travel mug of coffee. He took his time driving to the office. Nothing pressing. Not today, not yesterday. Hopefully, not ever. The quiet had drawn him back here more than anything.

Artemis, West Virginia was about as rambunctious as an Amish funeral. Red brick storefronts that hadn't changed since voters liked Ike, quiet streets with American flags hanging from the eaves of most houses, rundown farms that didn't produce much more than tumbleweeds and eviction notices these days.

Not exactly a one-horse town at around nineteen hundred residents, but in the early morning quiet like this, you could almost believe you were in an abandoned outpost in some zombie movie. It definitely made for a different commute than sitting bumper to bumper in the filthy morning air of Los Angeles, headed into Rampart for another day of dealing with gangsters, dealers, crackheads...

Just thinking about LA made his chest start to tighten. Leading edge of a panic attack. He took a deep breath through his nose and blew it out through pursed lips.

"Calm and focused," he said.

His therapist didn't teach him that one. Garrett read it in a book somewhere, and while it didn't always work, he found saying something aloud helped break a negative chain of thought.

He parked in front of May's Diner and got out. He put on his jacket to cover his .45, even though he had his badge on his belt. The city gave him a uniform, but the stars on the collar made him feel like he was doing a bad impression of George C. Scott in "Patton." His old man

3

had worn the official uniform for the 4th of July parade and funerals. It stayed in the closet otherwise. To Garrett's knowledge, the only "uniform" Chief Lamar Evans ever wore at work, rain or shine, winter or summer, was a white button-down Western style shirt, a clean pair of jeans, and hiking boots. Garrett's shirt was blue, but everything else was the same.

On the way into May's, he saw Melvin Davis, Earl Hunsacker, and Poor Boy Willis sitting on a bench outside Davis Hardware. (The only business in Artemis older than May's.)   Collectively, the old boys were about 290 years old.

"Mornin', boys," Garrett said.

"Mornin', Johnny Law," Earl answered.

Earl probably had this same conversation with Garrett's dad for thirty years.

"Every time I see you get outta that car, it reminds me of your daddy when he first started here," Melvin Davis said.

"Yes, sir," Garrett said. "People always tell me I'm the spittin' image."

For years, Garrett pretended he didn't see it. More out of rebellion than anything else. He'd finally grown old enough to admit he had the old man's square jaw and the tendency to knit his brows in a scowl when he was thinking. But the green eyes and sarcastic wit came from Mom.

Garrett noticed Poor Boy going out of his way to ignore him. He grinned and said, "Gettin' pretty dang cold at night. Poor Boy, you might wanna think about shutting down the still for the winter. You break a hip out there, we won't find you till Spring thaw."

"Don't know what you're talkin' about, Revenuer," Poor Boy said.

The first month after he moved back home and took over his dad's spot as Chief of Police, Garrett had a long discussion with Poor Boy about the difference between Federal Agents and the local law. It didn't take. To Poor Boy, anyone with a badge was a "Revenuer," out to shut down his still.

Major corporations sold moonshine openly in grocery stores, licensed and all, so Poor Boy had fallen behind the times. Kind of like the town.

Garrett strolled into the diner and saw a few of the old gray heads he normally saw, making their way through chicken fried steak and eggs, grits and sausage, and May's specialty, the Allegheny Mountain Omelet. Garrett had never seen anybody finish one.

These would be the only customers for most of the day. Everyone ate lunch at the new buffet place out by the highway. Cheaper, wider selection, and to the younger people, not the tired old place their grandparents ate breakfast.

Misty Heideman placed three disposable aluminum pans on the counter. Her blonde hair already frazzled by the kitchen heat, the young woman gave Garrett a tired smile. "Scrambled eggs, three chicken fried steaks, gravy on the side, and hash browns. Anything else, Chief?"

There was never anything else. But small town folks have to talk about something, don't they? "Nope. That'll do, Misty. How's Angela?"

"She's getting too big for her britches."

"We all do sooner or later, don't we?"

Garrett paid for the food and over-tipped Misty as usual. Single mothers struggled everywhere. A single mother in Artemis, West Virginia struggled harder than most. They'd long ago gotten past her halfhearted refusal of the tip.

On his way to the station, the radio crackled with Shirley Rankin's voice. "Chief, we got a call of a deer down in someone's front yard out on Fourth Street. Smiley's already out there."

"Sounds like everything's under control, then. I'm on the way with breakfast." Garrett hung the mike back on the dash, but he turned around and headed toward Fourth Street. He knew Shirley never called him on the radio without a good reason.

"Smiley's asking for you. I'll warm up the breakfast for the boys after you get here."

Garrett grinned and double-clicked the microphone. His way of acknowledging the call. He cut through the parking lot of Sanderson's Bows 'N' Bullets and drove down the alley for two blocks before turning onto Middleton and heading north toward Fourth Street. He smiled, remembering using the alley as an escape route after toilet-papering the house of his first big crush, Mary Schaeffer.

By the time Garrett made it to Fourth Street, Smiley's winch had dragged the deer carcass up a wood plank and into the back of a faded white pickup with the County badge on the doors.

Jebediah "Smiley" Carmichael cut a tall, lean figure in his khaki uniform and shined cowboy boots. Almost like an Old West gunslinger, except for one thing. His quick laugh and infectious smile were legendary around these parts, and had earned him the obvious nickname way back in grade school.

Smiley wore a Smith and Wesson Model 586 .357 Magnum clipped to his belt in a leather holster older than Garrett. Technically, he wasn't supposed to carry a piece within city limits. But to Garrett's knowledge, Smiley had never taken the gun out of its holster. And since Dad always let him carry it, Garrett never said anything about it. Everyone else just assumed because Smiley wore a uniform, it was legal.

When he didn't get the trademark goofy smile, Garrett smelled something bad in this. But he'd begun to assume these "gut feelings" were just the PTSD making him instantly wary of every little thing. This time he ignored it.

Garrett looked at the dead deer in the truck bed and saw the bloody spot over the white belly fur.

Contrary to his nickname, Smiley looked highly pissed off. He didn't even say good morning, just started right in. "Somebody who wants to stay anonymous said they saw an old green Dodge pickup parked back along the road last night. And that hole in the belly is from a broad-head. You know what dirty son of a bitch did this, right?"

"I probably do. And you and I both know we need more evidence than a broad-head hole in a deer's belly to arrest him," Garrett said.

"He still ain't got any better with his damn bow. Poor thing wandered around gut shot and miserable." Smiley stroked the deer's face. The deep lines and fine blue veins on the back of the old-timer's hand reminded Garrett that Smiley reached retirement age years ago. Probably taking everything personally to hang onto it for a while.

"Well, I guess at the very least I can go out and talk to him. Maybe put the fear in him," Garrett said.

"Wouldn't do no good. He'd just look you in the eye and lie to you. Whole family's never been worth a damn, and they always been proud of it," Smiley said.

One of the more basic rules of small town life. If

your relatives have done something bad, your whole family isn't worth a damn. Garrett started to make a smartass comment about it, but he got a sideways look at Smiley and thought better of it. He could probably warm his hands in the heat coming out of Smiley's pale blue eyes right now. You had to work pretty hard to piss off a man who would laugh at a kid's knock-knock joke so hard he nearly wet himself.

The more Garrett thought about it, the more he figured, what the hell? He didn't like Robert Lee Withers much anyway. He'd cheer Smiley up and serve notice to a poaching asshole at the same time.

"Wouldn't hurt to talk to old Robert Lee. Maybe it'll make him settle in for the winter," Garrett said.

Smiley shook Garrett's hand with a strong grip. "Thanks, Garrett. I appreciate that. Your dad would've done the same."

"Dad probably would've driven out there and whooped his ass."

At last, a brilliant smile creased Smiley's weathered face, showing perfect white dentures he'd had since he got his teeth kicked in by a horse as a kid. "They call that police brutality, these days. Prob'ly wind up on the WhoTube, if you ain't careful."

Smiley climbed into his County pickup and Garrett watched him drive away. Some of his earliest memories were of hunting and fishing with his dad and Smiley. In fact, Smiley reminded Garrett of his dad in a lot of ways. Including the angry heat from his eyes.

***

The rutted road leading to Robert Lee Withers' place beat the hell out of the Crown Vic's suspension and sloshed eggs and hash browns around in Garrett's belly. The police special had been engineered for pursuits on streets and highways, not four-wheeling down old country roads. Garrett hoped the ruts would break something vital so the city would finally have to buy a new Chief's car.

Tom Poston followed behind him in the city's newest police car, which had a hundred thousand miles on it. Tom probably wished the same calamity for his car's suspension.

On the outermost edge of the actual city limits, the Withers family had long considered themselves beyond the local law. They were farmers at one time, producing hay for the surrounding dairy farms. But somewhere around the mid '70s, they gave up on hay and settled on being minor criminals. Moving stolen farm equipment, dealing the occasional pound of weed they grew behind the barn, and poaching anything that would stand still long enough to be shot.

The wide dirt yard in front of the Withers place doubled as a parking lot for various rusting hulks, an archeological record of the US automotive industry buried under the thick white sediment of winter. Garrett drove around a long dead '59 Buick and parked next to a green Dodge pickup. A quick peek into the bed. Garrett saw dried blood and telltale bristly hair that could only belong to a Whitetail deer. Too fresh to be leftover from deer season.

He hit the thumb snap on his holster, loosened his Colt Commander just a bit. He'd dealt with Robert Lee before and knew he'd be wearing a gun. Perfectly legal on his own property, and Robert Lee had never threatened anyone, but in his time with LAPD Garrett had attended too many cop funerals. He didn't take chances with anyone.

"Hey, Tom, just flank out wide of me on the right, okay?"

A senior patrolman who grew up under Garrett's dad as Chief, Tom only arched an eyebrow. He didn't have to ask the question.

"Just being cautious," Garrett said.

Robert Lee had heard them coming from the proverbial mile away, of course. Garrett could see his outline behind the screen door. Waiting there in the dim house, under the shadow of the sagging covered porch.

"Robert Lee, can you come out and talk to us for a second?"

"What about?" A drunken slur. Not the best time to talk to Robert Lee, but then, there rarely was a good time.

"About a deer that wandered onto Fourth Street and died in somebody's front yard. Smiley figures somebody shot with a bow, and a witness saw a green Dodge—"

The screen door slammed open and Garrett's suspicions were confirmed. Robert Lee had a wide leather belt stretched under his ample belly. A Ruger Redhawk .44 mag sat snug inside the belt on his right hip, no holster. Gun people called it the Mexican Carry.

"You tell that old son of whore he can stop pointin' the damn law at my house every time he finds a dead deer! He done the same thing to my old man, harassed him to death, wore his heart right out."

Garrett didn't bring up the fact that old man Withers died of a heart attack climbing into a tree stand. And not during deer season.

"I think you and I both know Smiley doesn't have to point me out here. I could probably stretch the blood and hair in your truck into a probation violation. But I don't want anything like that. I just want you to shut her down for the winter. Maybe think about getting yourself a hunting license like everyone else next Fall, when you get off probation."

Robert Lee's eyes got squinty and his face went red. Spit flew from his lips when he screamed at Garrett. "If you got somethin' on me, then take me to jail. I don't like you Garrett Evans, and I ain't gonna pretend I do. Come back here with college behind ya and think you're smarter than all us hicks."

"Not true at all, Robert Lee. I was born here just like you. And I didn't finish college, so it really doesn't count for much."

That seemed to dampen the fire in Robert Lee's belly. He wobbled to the left and had to catch a porch column to stay upright. He opened his mouth to say something, but caught movement to his left. Swaying like a sailor on a rolling deck, he faced Tom Poston.

"You sneakin' up on me, Tom?"

"Nope." Tom said nothing else. Garrett had trained his guys on Contact and Cover. Right now Garrett was Contact, which meant he did all the talking.

Garrett showed his empty hands, but kept them close to his waist. "No one's sneaking up on you, Robert Lee. We drove right to the front yard in the open. We just want to talk, that's it."

Robert Lee's cheeks still held a high red color. His labored breathing huffed into a more rapid pace. Garrett had seen the look before on many, many drunks. Working himself up to do something. So Garrett decided to short-circuit the process if he could.

"Tell you what. We've had our say, and I think we can understand each other like two grown men, can't we?" Garrett said.

"I guess," Robert Lee said. His eyes stayed narrow, though, suspicious.

Garrett smiled. "Good. Then Tom and I can just leave. Fair enough?"

"Yeah, you do that."

Tom and Garrett both backed toward their cars, still watching. Robert Lee opened his front screen to go back inside—

And Tom tripped over a corroded bumper and sat down hard.

Later, Garrett would run it through the theater of his mind over and over. Freeze-frame on the beginning. No loud noises. Nothing threatening. A cop just tripped and fell on his ass.

Robert Lee spun at the sound, the Ruger suddenly in his hand. The .44 *boomed* over the snow-covered yard and Tom Poston flopped back like a discarded doll, shot through the head.

The Colt leaped into Garrett's hand and the front sight found Robert Lee's chest before Garrett mentally registered the action. Two loud thunderclaps from the .45 and Robert Lee dropped just as fast as Tom had. Garrett's pulse hammered in his neck, bright dots swam across his vision.

"Ah, fuck," Garrett said.

In the hushed silence of the snowy yard, only rusting cars and two dead men heard him.

2

Taylor smelled hay and clean earth. And blood.

The blood came from various places on her body. The man had been at her twice so far, working with a scalpel and a piece of hot steel he heated with a torch. Strapped into the special chair, she couldn't tilt her head down to look at her ruined body. Whatever he put in the IV in her arm turned the screaming white pain in her breasts into a dull throb. She had no way of knowing this wasn't a kindness, but the cruelest sort of relief, meant to keep her from going into shock and dying too soon.

The trapdoor hiding this place opened, smooth and silent. This wasn't some old doomsday shelter thrown together and neglected. This underground room had thick support and crossbeams, and a tidy, dry dirt floor. Like the workshop of a meticulous man.

He came down to her on handcrafted wooden stairs that would have looked right at home in a multi-million dollar house. Same as the last two times, he wore a rubber butcher's apron and nothing else. Taylor hoped he wouldn't try to screw her again. His last failed attempt drove him into a special kind of rage. The scalpel and hot iron hadn't been enough. He'd used pliers and laughed in her face when she screamed.

"Well, the little whore is awake," he said in a soft drawl.

Taylor saw the bone saw in his hand and screamed and screamed.

The cold mask he wore when he started on her ankle never changed expression. If someone had told Taylor this blue-eyed monster's nickname was "Smiley," she would have told them they were fuckin' crazy.

***

The station house felt like the family room at a mortuary. Silent. Bereft. Stunned. Foil-paper letters hung on a string said *Happy Anniversary*. Garrett snatched the sign down, rolling string and letters into an angry ball and slamming it into the trashcan.

The State Police interview had been short. Pretty cut and dried Justifiable Homicide. But Garrett still had a pounding headache. It started when he drove to Tom Poston's place and told his wife he'd been killed. The kind of headache no pill could fix. He thought maybe half a bottle of Jack and a night of self-loathing might take the edge off.

Harley Merriman manned the radio in Shirley's absence. Shirley had stayed on the radio long enough to settle everything down. Then she went home and alternately cried and drank herself to sleep. She'd known Tom for better than forty years. He even took her to a school dance when they were in Junior High.

Garrett waved through the window of the dispatch center and Harley gave him the "hold on" signal. He hurried to the door and peered out toward Garrett's office, like some horrible secret waited down there.

"There's a fella here to see you, Chief."

"State or County?"

"He's...a black fella. That is to say, not that he couldn't be a State or a—Well, anyway, he's neither."

Times change, but slowly, slowly.

In Garrett's office, the stranger sat on a couch the City Council bought in 1979, when Lamar Evans first became Chief. Orange plaid and pleather. Oddly enough, the man looked right at home in 1979, with his long leather coat and flawless Afro.

"Can I help you?" Garrett said.

"Chief Evans?" The man looked surprised.

"Yes?"

"Sorry, you seem young for a Chief."

"I get that a lot."

The man stood to shake hands and Garrett took the measure of him. Two or three inches taller than Garrett's six feet, and about forty pounds heavier. Thick through the neck and chest, with big hands and scarred knuckles.

"The name's Chester LaSalle. I understand you had some trouble this morning."

"Yeah, so... I was just stopping back by to check some messages. Technically, I'm not on duty. I have to be cleared by the State investigator—"

LaSalle flopped back down on the hideous couch. "How long you been at this?"

Garrett shrugged and sat behind his dad's desk, a flawless cherry-wood piece of art crafted by Smiley Carmichael himself, with the tracks for all the drawers so ingeniously recessed you could hardly see the part line where the drawer and desk came together.

"I've been on the Job thirteen years now. Twelve in LA," Garrett said.

LaSalle's eyebrows went up a millimeter. "Then

you know there's no way in hell of telling what a drunk's about to do. No making sense of it."

"You a counselor?"

"Nope."

One thick hand laid a flier on the desk.

A smiling young girl stared up, forever frozen in a moment of joy at a seventeenth birthday party according to the candle on the cake. Blonde, straight teeth, two piercings on her right eyebrow.

LaSalle said, "I've been looking for her for two years. Finally talked to a trucker who said he dropped her off near this town. I hear there's a truck stop around here that lots of young girls frequent."

"Only certain kinds of girls," Garrett said.

"I'm not looking for a saint. Just a missing girl."

"Private eye?"

"Got some credentials if you wanna see them."

The corners of the laminated ID were creased and bent. He'd had this out quite a few times in quite a few police stations, most likely.

"New York State, huh?" Garrett said. He handed it back. "You probably already found out New York or LA anything doesn't really impress out this way."

"That I have. I'm sure it's just the New York thing."

Garrett put the Cop Eye on LaSalle. The vibe coming off this guy was *not* Private Investigator. Didn't make him bad, necessarily. Not yet.

"You specialize in Missing Persons?" Garrett said.

"No. The grandfather is an old friend of mine."

Garrett took another look at the flier. Girl's last name was Santini.

"Blonde Italian girl?"

"Miracles of modern chemistry. Would you mind

if I asked around the truck stop, see if anyone remembers her? I'll probably be around for a few days, try to talk to as many truckers as I can. I always make a point of checking in with the local law," LaSalle said.

"No problem. For me, anyway. You may not get the warmest reception out there."

"Maybe you'll come along. Help warm up the atmosphere a little." LaSalle stood and headed for the door, walking on the refusal he'd probably gotten in every little town he visited.

Garrett didn't know why, but he already liked the big man. Very matter-of-fact and self-sufficient, he didn't really care if Garrett went along or not. He'd promised someone he'd find their girl and that's what he would do. Garrett could respect that.

"Tonight?" Garrett said.

LaSalle stopped and looked back. His turn to take the measure of Garrett.

"Nah, I wouldn't ask that. Not after today. I'm staying in room fourteen at that little motel on the edge of town. You know the one?"

"You mean the Lazy Eight, a.k.a the Artemis Hilton?"

"That would be the one."

A business card appeared. Plain and white, perforated on the edge, likely from a sheet of home-printed cards. It just said *LaSalle* and gave a cell phone number.

"Give me a call when you're ready. I also have someone local I'd like to talk to, if that's okay with you," LaSalle said.

"Who would that be?" Garrett said.

"Lady by the name of Nadine Pearson. Somebody told me she likes to minister to the girls out at the truck

17

stop."

"Good luck with that one. I know you want to chase down every lead, no matter what, but just bear in mind Nadine lives with her nose against her window and sees the worst in everyone."

"Sounds like a lady after my own heart," LaSalle said.

***

Garrett knew he would dream that night. It had taken months to get past the dreams of Michelle, and he hadn't even been there when she died.

In this dream, the Robert Lee Withers incident went down pretty much the same way, except Michelle went on the call with him instead of Tom Poston. They rode together in Garrett's warm car, him in his ridiculous Chief's uniform, her in LAPD blue, chitchatting all the way about whether painting a baby's room a particular color really affected the child later in life.

The snow pattered against the windshield and her perfume made his heart ache.

And then they were standing in Robert Lee's front yard and it all happened again, but this time Garrett's gun wouldn't work. He crushed the trigger until tendons stood out on his forearms, but the Colt refused to fire. Robert Lee just kept shooting and Michelle just kept screaming.

In the morning, Garrett sat up in bed and didn't move for an hour, staring at the wall and thinking about nothing. By the time he mentally checked in, his Mustang rumbled down the empty highway. Not the greatest car for winter roads in West Virginia, but he'd driven the damn thing all the way from Cali, and he kept it as a tiny reminder of what might have been. His therapist said he should sell it.

He punched in LaSalle's number and hit Speaker. It rang once. "LaSalle."

"Hey, it's Chief— Uh, Garrett Evans. You feel up to taking a ride?

3

"Yep. I remember her. Poor thing."

Nadine Pearson looked sorrowful, but then she often did. She'd worn old maid style high-collared dresses since high school. Maybe the life of the senior citizen spinster she would become loomed before her even then. She outlived all her family and took possession of this three-story monstrosity out on the end of Main Street. When the new county roads, and eventually the highway came in, it made the top floor of Nadine's house a perfect crow's nest to see all the comings and goings in Artemis. And she took full advantage.

She tapped LaSalle's flier with a nicotine-stained finger. "She said she was from New York. Ran away because her pa wouldn't let her date some young fool she fell in love with. Look where it got her. Men are always looking. They get what they need, and it ain't ever enough. So they go looking again."

She didn't add "No offense." She adjusted red-framed glasses with no lenses in them and glared at Garrett and LaSalle.

They sat smashed together on a love seat probably made the same year Thomas Edison patented the incandescent lamp. One of those overwrought Victorian things with high backs behind the occupants that swooped down to a low center. The wood frame creaked every time LaSalle shifted.

"Ma'am, as the son of a single mother, I can't really argue with you, there. You'd be talking about Jerry Conway. I, uh... spoke to him a couple of years back. They parted ways in Georgia. What I'm trying to figure out is how she got to your pretty little town."

Garrett noticed LaSalle kept a smile in his voice when he spoke to Nadine. He had an easy way with people. It probably made him great at his job.

Nadine lit a cigarette and smoke curled up past a ceramic praying Jesus mounted on the wall behind her. Even our Savior bore nicotine stains.

"It ain't that hard to figure, if you put your mind to it," Nadine said. "When a young girl ain't got a home, food, any kind of education worth a damn, she's got a choice. Stay homeless, or spread your legs for a man. They start out thinkin' they're gonna turn tricks and get some money. They wind up in the warm cab of a truck, and suddenly a free ride outta wherever they are looks good. When you're young, where you're goin' matters a whole lot less."

Nadine took another drag and tapped ashes into the cut-off bottom of a Howitzer shell her father brought back from World War II. When she didn't speak again, Garrett gave her a gentle nudge. "Thank you for helping, Nadine. Is there any chance you can remember the last man you saw her with?"

"No, I'm sorry. I spoke to her outside the truck stop diner, wasn't anyone with her. When I didn't see her again, I figured she finally found a ride to California. For some reason, they all seem to think that's the Promised Land."

The last bit was delivered with a pointed look at

Garrett.

"Now," she said. "Can we talk about those damn kids I saw drinkin' and drag racin' out on Eisenhower Road?"

***

The Mustang's rear end slid out as Garrett hit the onramp, giving LaSalle a good look at the guardrail. "Hey, man, don't all you West Virginia rednecks drive pickup trucks with four wheel drive?" LaSalle said.

"Mine's in the shop."

Garrett got everything straight again and pointed them toward the truck stop, even though he knew it would be useless. None of those guys would admit to seeing a missing girl.

"Can I ask you something?" LaSalle said, and continued without waiting for a yes. "You seem like you're from here... but you're not *from* here."

"Not much of a question," Garrett said. The rumbling laugh surprised him.

"I guess it isn't. May I ask then, what the fuck you're doing in the backwoods of West Virginia?" LaSalle said.

"Well, I did grow up here. But I was one of the California runaways Nadine talked about. I wanted anything but this place when I was a kid. Got accepted to UCLA, went out there thinking I'd work my way through college. Student loans and the cost of living in California laid that to rest pretty quick."

"And LAPD came callin'?" LaSalle said.

"Sort of. I applied at a job fair, got in, and quit school. I always thought I'd come back and finish."

They watched the snow melt on the windshield

and the mile markers slide by for a while. Maybe they both had a few things they always thought they'd finish.

"My dad was the Chief here. Widower. Mom went years back to emphysema. Dad got killed in a traffic accident last year about this time, and I took some leave to come home for the funeral..." Garrett trailed off. With him and LaSalle both packed in here, the air in the Mustang felt close and humid. He cracked a window and let the frigid air blast him in the face. It eased the tightness in his chest. He hadn't talked about this in... Ever.

"I had a fiancée out there. She was on the Job, too. Right before I left, she went to a Domestic call with her partner. Pretty low key, just a couple arguing. When the guy answered the door, he shot Michelle in the face. Just like that. Then he dropped the gun and surrendered before her partner could even clear leather. Never even explained why. Maybe it was the meth, paranoia, whatever. Didn't even have a fucking record."

LaSalle examined the back of one of his ugly hands. "If I'd been there, I believe the report would have read that he still had the gun in his hand. Probably a good thing I'm not a cop."

"Probably a good thing I never had the chance to make that decision. Anyway, when I got the call about Michelle, I'd just packed my suitcase to come home for Dad's funeral. I kept packing. Packed fourteen boxes and never went back."

***

Burton's Truck Stop had legendary status among truckers who traveled through West Virginia. From another era, the place was tiny compared to modern truck stops on giant lots. Burton's L-shaped gravel lot filled up fast and most truckers would have to drive back to the rest stop to sleep, but they came here anyway.

Burton's featured down-home country food, still cooked by one of the ancient Burton brothers, Garrett forgot which it was, Donny or Bobby. Served on mismatched plates in a narrow dining room with tiles scuffed all the way through in some places by decades of heavy boots.

Proud of their Appalachian history, the Burtons left strings of dried green beans hanging in the kitchen window where everyone could see them, authenticating their Leather Britches and ham as the real deal.

LaSalle wiped his mouth with a paper napkin. "I have eaten a lot of local food in the last two years, but this is a first."

Garrett hadn't eaten this stuff since his grandmother passed. The salty richness of comfort food took him back to her kitchen. "My Granny used to make Leather Britches, too. But she didn't hang her beans to dry, she spread 'em out on a screen in the sun. Pain in the ass, had to bring 'em in every night and take 'em back out every morning till they dried."

A big purple Mack growled into the lot outside. It had a sledgehammer painted on the driver's door, and curly cue letters arching over it. *Hank the Hammer.*

"Now there's a gentleman worth talking to," Garrett said.

He and LaSalle went back out into the blustery cold. The snow flurries had stopped, but the wind still bit like a mean little dog. They hadn't had much luck so far. As Garrett suspected, no drivers wanted to talk about picking up truck stop girls, much less ID a missing girl.

The only two girls working the parking lot today had beaten a quick retreat when they first saw Garrett and

LaSalle. They sat inside and watched the men with hooded eyes.

Hank the Hammer climbed down from his cab. A portly man with a penchant for wallets with big chains, he didn't look happy to see Garrett. "Hey, Chief. Little outta your jurisdiction, ain't ya?"

"Little bit. But this isn't official, Hank. This gentleman's looking for a missing girl."

Hank eyed the flier, then LaSalle. "Gentleman, huh? What's this got to do with me?"

"Do I really need to answer that?" Garrett said.

Sometimes Hank liked to pick up a girl and take her to the motel in town, rather than cram into his sleeper for his fun. He'd been Garrett's first arrest as Chief last year, after he got drunk and kicked a girl out into the snow buck-nekked.

"All we want to know is if you've ever seen her hanging around," LaSalle said. "I'm not the police. I'm just a man looking for a girl whose family misses her."

Mention of a family missing their kid bled the confrontation out of it for Hank. He blinked at the photo, probably seeing her as a young girl at a birthday party for the first time.

"Maybe... Yeah. Long while back, year, year and a half. I remember her. She had this tattoo—" Hank stopped short.

Garrett would have pounced on the guilty hitch, but LaSalle's voice stayed low and reassuring. "I don't care how or why you saw it. But that tattoo is one way I have of knowing if I'm talking to someone who really knew her. It's not on the flier."

"She told me she was eighteen, you know."

"And she would've been, about the time she met you," LaSalle said. Still smooth, but Garrett's practiced eye could see it. The tightening around the eyes, the slight lean in. LaSalle had been looking a long time for this, clearly the first positive thing he'd heard in ages.

"It said, *Daddy's Girl* in flowery letters on her butt cheek," Hank said.

"That's the one. You said over a year ago? Do you remember exactly when?"

"No. I do remember it was the end of summer, still warm, you know? I told her I'd drive her the rest of the way to Texas, if she wanted to go. But she asked me to let her out at the rest stop up on Forty-Five."

"Why would she do that?" LaSalle said.

"Some girls do," Garrett said. "They'll work the guys up there if it's busy, then hitch with one of them back here if they can. New customers are usually through here by then."

"Right," LaSalle said. Flat, no emotion.

Hank the Hammer licked his dry lips. "Look, I just drive cross-country, man. Sometimes I pay a girl for her company. But I don't ever hit on 'em, or dump 'em out on the highway like some do. In fact, I tried to talk her out of the rest stop. That place is just bad luck, if you ask me."

"Why?" Garrett said. "I lived here all my life and I never heard that."

"Girl got cut up somethin' horrible. This woulda been about seven years back or so. I'm sure your daddy heard about it from the State Troopers. I'm surprised he didn't tell ya."

"We didn't talk very often," Garrett said.

"What happened?" LaSalle said. "With the girl?"

"There was an old timer named King who used to come through, play with the girls before he got too old to care. Hauled seafood in from the East Coast. He's the one found her. Florida Girl, they called her. On account of how she had the shape of Florida tattooed on her thigh. Some sick bastard cut her face up so bad, they couldn't put out a picture of her."

Hank shivered, but it had little to do with the fresh snow starting to fall.

"So King found her..." LaSalle goaded him to continue.

"Yeah, anyway, after he ate his dinner, old King lit out up the mountain, but realized he left his wallet back at the truck stop. He slipped into the rest stop to turn around, late at night, the only guy there, ya see? Whoever did it must've seen his headlights coming and skedaddled. Poor girl was still steaming."

LaSalle's passive mien broke. "Did he get a description of a car, a truck, anything?"

"Hold on," Garrett said. "That's seven years ago. I'm sure it has nothing to do with your missing girl."

"Why are you sure?" LaSalle said.

Good question. Garrett thought on it for a bit. "One murdered girl seven years ago doesn't tie into every girl who goes missing in this area. For all we know, some trucker got crazy, cut the girl up, and never came back."

"Don't matter, either way," Hank said. "Old King never saw nothin'. He just started screaming into his CB."

"You suppose he's still around?" LaSalle said.

"Nah, he passed years back. Heard he just went in his sleep in his cab one night."

LaSalle raised an eyebrow at Garrett. "I don't suppose, for argument's sake, you have any records of that case?"

"No, that'd be State Trooper territory."

***

27

"I shouldn't be showing you this stuff," Clancy said.

"I know," Garrett said.

He went to high school with Clancy Parker, had been drinking buddies, even. Once, when Garrett came back from LA for Christmas, Clancy got a little too drunk and sobbed about being jealous of Garrett going to a big place like LAPD when Garrett never even wanted to be a damn cop in the first place. Clancy grew up thirsting for it like a fine wine he couldn't wait to taste on his twenty-first birthday.

Heavier now, jowly and putting a little strain on the buttons of his uniform shirt, Clancy moved his mouse around, sifting through file folders. He glanced over his computer screen at LaSalle but spoke to Garrett. "Not enough you're not even on official duty, but you gotta bring a...civilian in here?"

They sat at a cubicle in the Records Department and Garrett saw some of the strange looks cast toward the hulking black P.I. with the bad knuckles and thick neck.

LaSalle simply smiled back.

"Here she is," Clancy said. He clicked on a slideshow of catalogued crime scene photos. Neither Garrett nor LaSalle spent much time looking at the screen. Not enough to be violated and slashed like she was, but he left her there, legs splayed, showing the world what he did. No modesty in death.

"How much do you know about this one?" Garrett said.

"Not much." Clancy had to clear his throat. Reading official words somehow gave his voice strength. "Bit of a party girl, trace amounts of ketamine and cocaine found in her blood. Victim a known prostitute, but never positively identified. No match on dental records. Genetic material, not her own, recovered from under her fingernails, and a partial tooth impression found on her right knuckles."

"She was a fighter," LaSalle said.

Garrett nodded. "Seems so. 'Known prostitute.' Tells me why I never heard any gossip on this. Wasn't anybody local, so best to just not talk about it. They ever get anything from the scrapings under her nails?"

Clancy scrolled through a few pages. "Skin from a white male, B negative blood."

"All the makings of a generic peckerwood," LaSalle said. "I seen one or two of them around lately."

Clancy escorted them back through the polished tile hallway and rode the elevator down with them. He waited until they got to Garrett's Mustang, his hands tucked into his puffy Statie jacket, looking like a dark green teddy bear.

"Sorry to hear about Tom. I happen to know the investigator's gonna clear you for duty by Monday. But, you know..." Clancy said.

"I didn't hear it from you," Garrett said.

"Exactly."

LaSalle held out a big mitt. "Thanks for your help."

Clancy's hand came out of his pocket a little slow. Could have been the cold. "Anytime."

On the way out of the parking lot, over the rumble of the Mustang, Lassalle said, "I appreciate you doing this. You're probably right. This is just some poor girl who got killed. But I only have one client. I have time to check everything."

"Don't blame you. I like to be thorough myself," Garrett said.

Clancy appeared from between two parked cars,

waving them down. Garrett hit the brakes and the Mustang's fat tires slid on the snow. Clancy's hands slapped the hood when the car finally stopped.

Garrett rolled the window down. "Holy shit, Clance. Are you trying to get run over?"

"Sorry, sorry. I just remembered something. About three years back there was a running joke around the station. Some people put Wanted posters in the locker room. 'Be on the lookout for jungle tribesmen kidnapping white women.'"

"Say what?" LaSalle leaned over the gearshift.

"No, no, seriously. Some girl whacked out on speed said she got dropped off at the rest stop, did a couple of tricks, and went into the ladies room to uh, freshen up." Clancy laid a finger alongside his nose and sniffed.

"When she comes out, she swears up and down some kinda dart hit the tree next to her. Like one of those blowguns the jungle guys used in Indiana Jones, you know?"

Garrett exchanged a look with LaSalle.

"Our guys went out and looked around. No darts in the tree trunks, no jungle tribesmen. But still...weird thing to say, huh?" Clancy said.

"Yeah," Garrett said. "Weird thing."

4

Smiley took his time putting the tranquilizer gun back together. He worked in the kitchen, preferring the bright overhead light now that his eyes were getting worse. On the counter across the room, a clear plastic container writhed with dermestid beetles. He liked to watch them clean the bones. The bone they were currently packed around came from the latest trophy's foot. Soon enough, all her remaining flesh would be beetle shit.

The sweet smell of Neetsfoot Oil on old leather gaskets pleased him. It smelled like order, cleanliness. Respect. Like Papa always said, "A man who cares for his tools is showin' respect to the man who made 'em."

The man who made this old dart rifle in the late '60s probably didn't give half a damn that Smiley still kept the leather gaskets supple and took care to store the rifle properly instead of keeping it in a damn gun rack, so's the barrel didn't warp over time. But it was the principle.

A heavy crystal tumbler of Jim Beam sat at his elbow. No ice. He didn't want the glass sweating a circle on the flawless oak surface of his table. He'd made it from separate oak planks, dovetailed together so tight the table looked like a high-end machine had made it. Most folks would glue the wood, but the painstaking process of cutting and fitting the dovetail grooves appealed to Smiley's meticulous nature. A threadbare towel kept the gun parts from scratching the table as he worked.

The highly shined toe of his cowboy boot tapped the linoleum in time to Hank Williams. Senior. Not his damn rock star kid.

By the time Smiley got the air rifle back together, the needle started the hitching scratch at the end of the album. He had a CD player, of course. He was no backward hillbilly. But he only used it when Misty brought little Angela over. She played her songs from one of those dang puppet shows all the kids loved and just had herself a high old time. The stupid songs didn't really grate on his nerves as much when her laughter rang like a clear crystal bell.

He lined up his silver darts and checked each needle carefully. Years back, he made the mistake of using one with a dull tip. The little whore's leather pants partially stopped the dart and she didn't get a full dose. He'd had to fight her, and wound up leaving her there with her throat cut and her face slashed when someone drove up the hill. Scared the hell out of him. He didn't take another one for almost a year.

Tires crunching the gravel out front gave him a start. Misty was dropping Angela off early. Probably so she could see that idiot Bradley Wentz before she went to work.

With quick steps, Smiley gave his place the once-over. He scooped up the tub of hard working beetles and put it under the sink. Angela knew the cabinet was a "No-No Zone." Everything else in the kitchen looked pretty much the same as the day his momma died. Clean, orderly. Out of step with this century.

He met them on the front porch of the

farmhouse. Misty wore a denim jacket not meant for this cold. The eight-year-old perpetual motion machine named Angela Heideman was stuffed into a pink snowsuit. She leapt out of the truck, blonde locks flying out around the edges of the hood.

"Smiley!" The little girl ran to give him a hug and hit him like a playful dog that doesn't know better. Oofed his air out and everything.

Misty's folks had lived down the road from Smiley since both Smiley and her dad were in diapers. When her parents both took jobs working on a highway project, Smiley babysat Misty when she was just a little girl herself. Now with her dad passed on and her mom crawling farther into a bottle by the month, Smiley had come to be a lifesaver, always available to babysit Angela in a pinch.

Misty handed a bag of clothes to Smiley. "She's been looking forward to this. Something about ice cream sundaes if she answers all her safety questions right?"

Smiley looked a little guilty. "I hope you don't mind the ice cream. Just seemed like a good way to get her to listen. Here, watch."

Smiley spun Angela around to face her mom. He put his hands on her shoulders like a proud teacher. "What do we do if a stranger talks to us?"

"Run away and call the police. One scoop for me," Angela said.

Misty laughed, which she didn't do very much. It made Smiley's heart feel good.

"What do we do if somebody tries to touch somethin' that ain't none of their business?" Smiley said.

"We shoot him in the No-No with Smiley's gun."

"Uh..." Smiley gave Misty a sheepish grin. "No, no. The other one."

"Oh. We run away and tell Chief Evans or one of

33

his officers. Two scoops for me."

Misty laughed again, but her eyes danced toward her pickup. She'd be late for her date. "Thanks so much, Smiley. I'll pick her up by midnight, I promise."

Sometimes Smiley would tell her not to worry about it and pick up Angela in the morning. But not today. He knew where she was going, and Misty couldn't meet his eyes.

"Angela, honey, why don't you go inside and get warm? I need to talk to Smiley for a sec," Misty said.

"Okay. Love you, Mom." A quick squeeze and the pink dynamo charged into the house. Within seconds, yammering animated dragons or some such had commandeered Hank Senior's status as entertainment for the evening.

Misty had money in her hand. Smiley pushed it way, of course.

"I been doin' okay, Smiley. With tips and all," she said.

"Have ya? Bradley helping you out with groceries and such?"

"I know you don't like him, Smiley, but he's a different guy now. He's putting together a business deal in Oklahoma, and if it goes through, we can buy a house out there."

A boy who could barely spell his own name without looking at his ID had a big deal going? Any business he put together would no doubt be outside the law.

"That sounds like a good plan." Smiley smiled and patted her arm. "You have a good shift at work and don't you dare hurry to pick her up. Can't have you slidin' all over the roads."

"Thank you, Smiley." She gave him a chaste kiss

on his leathery cheek and he watched her hurry back to her warm pickup.

His pale blue eyes followed her as she turned around and drove back up the half-mile gravel track to the main road. The chilly wind cut his cheeks and made his eyes water, but he stood like a statue. This kind of discipline made him strong when the Hunter had work to do.

***

Chester LaSalle traveled with a lot of clothes. His grandfather always said a man who wants to be taken seriously dresses seriously. He didn't have to say the part about a black man having trouble getting respect even then.

LaSalle flipped through the shirts on the motel closet rack, checking the creases, noting any fuzz or loose threads. Nothing out of place, of course. This just served as his version of white noise, background music, what have you. The muse came to him best when his conscious thoughts were occupied.

He'd been to a lot of places looking for Britney Santini. Heard a lot of stories about girls disappearing into thin air, sold on the foreign sex market, taken by aliens. The poison dart bullshit had just been an excuse to work a jungle tribe story in there, but the girl murdered at the rest stop had him thinking.

He remembered a case in California where a few girls had been murdered over the course of several years. Turned out to be a Highway Patrol officer who worked a certain stretch of deserted highway. Maybe this Clancy guy wanted to throw them off his own trail with the dart story. LaSalle didn't necessarily believe it, but it sent his mind down certain paths, exploring the possibility of someone who knew the area well taking a girl who no one knew at all.

He stepped over to the suitcase on his bed. He planned on taking a ride to the rest stop tonight and he wasn't about to fall into the clutches of some inbred family in the woods. Maybe he'd seen one too many cable movies in motel rooms, but he wasn't taking any chances.

The suitcase contained four more shirts, folded with cardboard inside them, two extra pairs of shoes, a variety of colored socks, and a Browning Hi Power nine-millimeter pistol. Not the new shit, either, but the original version from Fabrique Nationale in Belgium.

There were newer, better combat guns out there, but the Browning pointed so natural, so smooth, it felt connected to his brain somehow. Balance, baby.

He tucked the gun inside his belt on his right hip without a holster. Mexican Carry. He had a second barrel for the pistol hidden in the trunk of his rental car. The barrel extended about an inch beyond the slide when installed, with threads that accepted the suppressor LaSalle had built himself. But those were the tools of a killer. He didn't need those tonight.

Tonight, he needed the tools of a private investigator. He picked up a few fliers in case there were some truckers up there.

Squeaky brakes outside.

LaSalle killed the lights and pushed the curtain open a millimeter. A police unit at the light up the street. Maybe the chief had his boys watching him? He didn't really seem like that kinda dude. When the patrol car pulled away, LaSalle relaxed and put on his long coat without turning on the lights.

In his rented Volvo, the traction control made the

winding highway up to the rest stop an easy drive. A yellow Mack with no trailer and a Peterbilt hauling lumber were the only two trucks in the parking lot. Both had their heaters running, but no one up front. They were probably sleeping, and this deep in redneck country, no way was he poking his head in somebody's truck window this time of night.

He knew that before he came out. He didn't drive up here to drop off fliers. He stood there in the dark and smelled the pine on the cold mountain air. Deep woods loomed dark and close behind the brick building housing the restrooms. Through the trees, the moonlight glistened on an open field maybe half a mile down the slope.

On that night back then, did the guy who did the cutting run down there? Have something waiting? Four-wheel drive maybe?

The clip-clop of high heels to his left— A skinny girl wobbled out of the ladies room on four inch Walmart specials. She pulled up short for a second when she saw LaSalle. Her eyes darted toward the Mack truck.

"Hello," LaSalle said.

"Um, yeah. I'm kinda already..." Again, she looked at the Mack.

"That's not what I'm about, girl. I'm just looking for someone who went missing."

She took a polite look at a flier, but her eyes skimmed right over the face. Nothing.

"Nope. I never seen her. That's so sad. Sorry, mister." She took another look at the Mack truck. Now LaSalle saw a dim outline, the pale moon of a face behind the window.

"That's okay," he said. "Thanks for taking a look. You, uh, you got somewhere to get warm, right?"

"Oh yeah. I got a road daddy. He's takin' me all

37

the way to Florida."

"Is that right? No money, just a ride?"

"Well, you know, he takes care of me and everything."

"Uh huh."

She shivered so bad her teeth clicked. Her bare legs stuck out of a man's goose-down coat, and LaSalle figured she didn't have much on underneath. He pulled a folded Benjamin from his pocket and extended it between two fingers.

"Take this. And keep it, you hear?"

"Uh. Wow, thanks." She made the money disappear.

"Now get your skinny ass out of the cold."

He turned back toward his car. Time to get his not-so-skinny ass out of the cold.

"Hey, Mister." She stopped halfway back to the truck. "I really am sorry about that poor girl. Have you shown her picture around the truck stop?"

"Yeah. Heard from a trucker who saw her before, but it was over a year ago."

"Oh, too bad." She thought for a second. "Did you see an old guy down there, like a forest ranger or something?"

"A forest ranger? No, I don't remember that."

"He might know her. He eats at the truck stop sometimes and he's always staring at us. Never tries to hook up a party or anything, kind of creepy if you ask me. But if anybody knows who's around, it'll probably be him."

"Thank you, young lady. Where are you from?"

"Lawton, Oklahoma."

"You ever tried to go back home?"

"Wouldn't work out. Too many issues," she said.

"Yeah... I hear you."

Sitting in his warm car, watching her climb back into the truck's cab, LaSalle imagined another cold night, Britney Santini climbing into a truck. Or out of one? And then she vanished like a magician's assistant who never came out of the magic cabinet again.

***

Smiley threw another hunk of wood on the fire. One thing Papa did right was build this big old fireplace. Kept the whole front half of the house warm when a body put in enough work to stoke it right. A scratchy old recording played on his mother's antique reel-to-reel. Supposedly a bootleg of Hank Williams singing in a honky tonk, somewhere. Could've been anybody, sure, but the mournful soul who slurred out the lyrics to "Hey, Good Lookin'" spoke to Smiley's heart.

The fire popped and flared up and Smiley wondered if the thing under the barn appreciated the space heater he left on down there.

He pushed the thought away and set about making Angela's bed. He tucked a down comforter into the couch cushions and threw another one over the top, tucking the edges in to make a nice warm cocoon.

"Smiley, I'm done." Angela came into the room in her pajamas, her long blonde hair hanging wet around her shoulders. "I let the water out and everything."

"Just in time. Your bed's ready. Should we get you a snack before nighty-nite?"

"Nah, I brushed my teeth already and things taste funny after toothpaste is in your mouth," Angela said.

"I'd have to agree with that, darlin'."

"Will you brush the knots out of my hair?"

She handed him a red sparkly brush, the kind that probably came with a matching barrette and a little tube of lip-gloss.

"Yeah, turn around here. If I can curry a horse, I'm sure I can get some tangles out of a girl's hair."

Angela giggled and whinnied like a horse. Smiley laughed out loud. It sounded odd bouncing off the hardwood floors. Not much laughing went on around this place when Angela wasn't here. He brushed the hair away from her neck and froze. He could see down the back of her loose pajama top as far as her delicate shoulder blades. And the long, straight-edged bruise running diagonally between them.

If Angela had been facing him, she would have wondered where Smiley went. A dead mask dropped into place, the warm smile banished like a criminal.

The smell of the barn is hot in his nose, skinny seven-year-old wrists burning where the rope holds him to the whipping post, swish-crack swish-crack of the leather strap.

— Please, Papa, stop. I'll be good.

— Shut up, you son of a whore, you sorry little shit. You shut your mouth and take what's due to you!

Swish-crack swish-crack.

"Smiley?"

He'd stopped brushing. He snapped back to the present and drew the brush through her hair. Gentle, tugging the knots free without pain.

"Yes, darlin'?" he said.

"You had a funny face. You okay?"

"Sweetheart, ol' Smiley's just fine. Right as rain. You sure you don't want a little ice cream before bed? You could rinse the toothpaste outta there with root beer."

She gave him a conspirator's smile that melted his heart.

40

"Okay. Don't tell Momma."

"I won't," Smiley said.

Later, when Angela settled into the deep breathing of sound sleep, Smiley left the baby monitor in the living room and went out to the barn.

Once inside, he locked the doors behind him and walked around the stack of hay bales near the back wall. He pushed away a bale on the floor, deciding he'd better come up with another way to hide the trapdoor soon, before he got too old to move bales on his own.

He found the familiar knot in a floor plank and stuck his index finger in the hole. His fingertip found an eyebolt and pulled it gently. The trap door sighed open on hydraulic hinges he ordered from an online auto parts warehouse. Usually, these went on the fancy trunk lids of upper end cars.

He went down to the latest girl. Angela's bruise burned in his mind like a mental road sign. *Danger Ahead.*

That son of a bitch boyfriend of Misty's. Smiley didn't have to ask. He'd known Misty since she was smaller than Angela is now. Always a gentle, caring girl, Misty would never lay a hand on Angela. Bradley, on the other hand, had all the signs of a classic little shit. Put more money up his nose than he ever put into Misty's pocket for groceries, rent, all the things a man should be taking care of.

Smiley's dentures ground together so hard he feared he'd pop them out of his mouth. He had to release some of this rage or he wouldn't be able to sleep tonight. He'd just lie there with Bradley's long rat face in his mind like the burning bush of old, telling him to do horrible things.

The blackthorn cane felt heavy in his hand, good and smooth. He beat on the girl for five minutes before the tremors got the better of him. Though he took good care of himself, his old heart still fluttered in his chest like a bird with a broken wing.

He sat in the antique dentist's chair he modified to hold his trophies still while they were alive. This trophy lay there on the floor, flat eyes staring at him through dirty strands of hair. The beating had taken the edge off, but it wasn't the same when they were dead.

Nope. Just not the same.

He had to try to maintain discipline, though. The last few years, it seemed his will had become weaker. It grew harder and harder to wait in between. He'd already heard about a colored fella in town asking around, looking for a missing girl. Men had come through before. Private investigators looking for girls no one around here would ever miss. They all left eventually. Smiley could wait this one out, too.

5

Garrett wore a charcoal gray suit to the funeral. The same one he wore to Michelle's funeral, and his Dad's funeral.

Since Tom had served in the Marines before becoming a police officer, an honor guard from the local Reserve station performed the twenty-one-gun salute. Garrett closed his eyes through the rolling crackle of rifle fire. The sound carried across the Artemis cemetery, echoing off headstones of other soldiers and Marines, some with dates all the way back to the 1880s. Country boys had a way of ending up in military graves.

Afterward, the Marine color guard folded the American flag draped over Tom's coffin and brought it to Garrett.

Though he stood with his remaining officers and Shirley, he felt apart from everyone here. Tom's wife, Junie Poston, sat motionless through the whole thing, refusing to look up when Garrett offered her the folded flag at the end. Tom's mother took it, her lips tight, her eyes holding an accusation.

He'd heard the rumors already. Some people were saying he shouldn't have gone out there, shouldn't have been on Robert Lee's property with something so flimsy.

Then the whole thing never would have happened.

The fresh deer carcass investigators found in the barn didn't really seem to matter. Folks around here didn't cotton to law enforcement intruding on someone's private property.

There were some who thought of Garrett as a big-shot LAPD cop, back from Los Angeles looking for action in a small town that had none. His reputation preceded him when he came back for his Dad's funeral. Lamar Evans had bragged to everyone about his son Garrett being on a special robbery team, how his boy "won" five deadly shootouts with dangerous felons.

If only these people understood how much Garrett wanted to leave that behind, how much he dreaded the thought of having to draw down on yet another human being. So he bore the sidelong glances, the stopped conversations when he walked by, and got the hell out of there as soon as the casket sank into the ground.

Without thinking about it, he drove to Tracy's house. Out on the western side of town, close to the highway, the Ellsworth place had once been a small dairy farm. The accidental fifth of five kids, fifteen years younger than her closest sibling, Tracy had been the only one who stayed in Artemis. She'd inherited the place by default.

He didn't bother checking the house. With the light bouncing off the snow like this, Garrett knew where she'd be. He parked between the house and the barn and went on foot.

She stood under a special overhang she installed behind the barn to act as her studio. It kept the snow or rain off her while she worked, but allowed her to see the woods and open fields.

To Garrett, Tracy felt like the only unspoiled thing about this place. After coming back from LA, everything else seemed old. Or small.

He stood there watching her paint. It gave him a calm center, still waters where he could float and do nothing. No worries, no guilt, no feelings of panic. Just Tracy. Painting. With her wild red hair spilling over her jacket, squinting at her canvas and chewing on the end of her brush. All the brushes beside her palette bore tiny tooth marks on the end, like the brushes of an artistic mouse.

She would have heard the Mustang pull in, so she knew he was there. She turned with a smile and came to him smelling of oil pants and turpentine.

"I thought maybe you forgot the way here," Tracy said.

"No, I couldn't do that—" His voice broke and she hugged him. Not like a lover. Like a friend who knew how desperately we all needed to be held now and then.

In fact, they weren't lovers, and never had been. They'd somehow managed the delicate balance that lets a man and woman be friends as long as they had.

(He'd been with one woman since Michelle died and it was so disastrous he hadn't done it since. He cried after. Not silent bitter tears on his pillow, but braying sobs she couldn't ignore.)

"I'm so sorry about Tom," Tracy said. "You guys were just doing your jobs."

She stepped back and waved at her easel. "What do you think?"

The painting featured the snow-laden woods across the field from them. Though it was only some skinny birches, a few pines, and snow, the muted light she chose made the whole thing haunting. Between teaching

45

Art classes at the community college two towns over and selling her paintings online, she managed to make a living at it.

"It's pretty good," he said.

"Pretty good?"

"I mean, it's nothing like the giant penis you painted for Mrs. Simms."

She laughed and punched him in the arm. "That was a turkey with a long neck, damn it. And thank you for comparing my recent work to fourth grade Art class."

Her smile worked like a poultice on his soul, drawing out all the poisonous shit he'd stored up. She invited him to stay for lunch and he helped her pack up her canvas, easel, and paints and put them away in the barn.

"You won't believe what I thought about yesterday," she said over red beans and cornbread in her warm kitchen.

"That time Lenny Brewster snapped your bra and all the toilet paper poked out the front?" Garrett said.

"I try to never think of that, so thank you. No, I saw Greg Sewell down at the grocery store—"

"Oh no."

"Oh sure, you can bring up my bra-stuffing tragedy, an event which scarred me for life, but I can't bring up Greg and Lucy?"

She giggled at the look on his face, her laugh light and quick, flashing blue eyes catching and reflecting her mirth in a mischievous way that made his breath catch.

"Your old man was soooo mad at you," she said.

"Yeah, I don't even think it was him being the police chief, and all that. Later, when everything settled down and we were all alone, he said, 'Son, there's no woman ever worth pickin' a fight over. If she's gonna go sweet on another guy, kickin' his ass won't change that.'"

"Unless you punch him out in Typing class, right?" she said.

"Shut up."

They ate in silence for a while. Sometimes when he came by, they hardly talked at all. He'd watch her paint, or they'd walk around her wooded lot while she took reference photos. It was good between them, and he didn't want to fuck it up. Relationships were tricky enough in a small town without one half of the equation being stuffed full of emotional dynamite. (The volatile half being him, of course.)

She wrangled all the leftovers while he rinsed the dishes and put them in the washer.

"I heard there was some kind of private investigator in town," Tracy said.

"News do travel fast 'round here."

"What else are folks going to talk about? The latest road kill Smiley scraped up?"

"Did anyone describe him to you?" Garrett said.

She gave him a look. "You know they did."

"He seems like a decent guy. Rough around the edges, for sure, but he's been looking for this missing girl for two years. Dedicated to his job. Maybe I'll bring him by for dinner if he sticks around much longer."

"My, my. Wouldn't Nadine and the old gals down at Artemis First Baptist have a time with that? Two single men in the home of that liberal hussy. Just give me a call so I can go to the store first."

"How about if I bring the groceries?" Garrett said.

"Sorry, sweets, but you have the palette of a fifth grader. We'd be knee deep in macaroni and cheese, chicken fingers, and bacon."

"And?"

47

"Let me worry about the menu, Chief. You just bring a decent red."

They bundled up in their coats and she walked him to the Mustang. He hugged her again, still smelling the paint in her hair. She brought out the teenager in him and he almost swapped ends trying to spin the Mustang's wheels for her.

Embarrassing, but he did get the beautiful ring of her laughter to take home. In the coming days, he'd need it.

***

Garrett wore his Chief's uniform to the City Council meeting, even though he felt like a little boy playing dress-up. The closed session had been called by Samuel Redding, the senior member of the three member council. Samuel and Dorothy Martin were both in their seventies, but Samuel had been on the council longer.

They were in the private chambers, with two rows of folding chairs shoe-horned before a long oak table with three microphones and padded swivel chairs behind it. The faux wood paneling on the wall had been installed when bellbottoms were the rage.

The three remaining officers on the Artemis Police Department, Lyle Hampton, Dougie Armstead, and Whit Abercrombie, sat in the front row of the stuffy council chambers, all in formal long-sleeve uniforms. Lyle, the youngest of them, gave Garrett a sorrowful look. What was that for?

He didn't have to wait long to find out. Samuel gaveled the meeting to order, and Fonda Morrison, the only council member south of forty, examined a piece of paper before she spoke.

"Uh, Chief Evans, we have received a statement from the West Virginia State Police that Robert Lee Withers' death has been ruled a Justifiable Homicide. However, before we return you to duty, the Council has a few questions for you in regards to your decision-making process which led to the shooting."

"Okay. Go right ahead," Garrett said. His teeth clinched so tight he heard them grind. These fuckers were going to sit behind a table and question his— He choked that down. Irrational anger. What had the damn shrink in California said about it? Never mind, he'd already missed half of what Dorothy Martin was saying.

"... at best a possible identification of a green pickup and a deer with an arrow wound. What made you think that was enough to go out and confront the man?"

"Past history, I guess," Garrett said.

"Yours or his?" Samuel Redding said.

"What's that supposed to mean?"

"Your father and Smiley were good friends for many years. We know how much poachers upset Smiley; you sure you weren't just going out there on behalf of an old friend?"

"Look, you hired me to be the Chief of Police. I see a deer shot with a bow out of season, hear of an ID on a truck matching a local guy on probation for poaching, in my mind it's worth at least talking to the suspect."

Samuel tented his dry, pale fingers. "Maybe in Los Angeles, Chief. But around these parts, folks feel like you need a lot more than a *maybe* to go on a man's private property. Poaching is a law on the books, that's right. But feedin' your family off the land goes back in these parts long before the law got here."

Garrett had always been one of the smarter kids in his class. Did well on standardized tests in school,

49

which got him accepted to UCLA in the first place. He saw what was coming, so fuck it. He looked Samuel in the eye. "And I'm sure all of this has nothing to do with the fact that your family and the Withers go way back."

Samuel gave him a wintry smile. Dorothy and Fonda looked down at their papers.

"Chief, may I ask you a question, point blank? Are you on psychiatric medication?" Samuel said.

"What? Look, you hired me—"

"We did, Chief. We hired you to fill in after your father passed. There were other applicants, as well."

Garrett flicked his gaze over to Whit Abercrombie, a veteran officer hired not long after Tom Poston. He wore Sergeant's stripes, but didn't get the pay. In Garrett's book, any man who wanted the power over the pay was the wrong guy for the job.

"What does that have to do with your question?" Garrett said.

"Honestly, Chief, we didn't do our usual background on you because you were a hometown boy and we figured we already knew it all. But we have heard you were under the care of a psychiatrist in Los Angeles before you came back. Doesn't matter who told us, the fact remains that we know. And so I have to ask. Are you taking psychiatric medications?"

"Yes."

Everyone just sat quiet for a second. They all looked like they'd been prepared for more of a fight. "Oh," Samuel said. "Well... Sergeant Abercrombie, could you step forward?"

Whit stepped up with the tiniest tug of a grin on his lips. He'd always considered Garrett a smartass kid anyway. And Garrett knew Whit hadn't been happy when the Council went with Lamar Evans's kid out of sympathy.

Samuel looked at Fonda and Dorothy, getting a nod from each. He spoke for them all.

"Chief Evans, it is the decision of this Council to temporarily suspend you as Chief of Police. We are requesting a psychiatric evaluation before you return to duty."

"And if I don't take one?"

"If you don't take one within thirty days, you will be dismissed." Samuel nodded to Whit. "Sergeant Abercrombie, you will serve as Interim Chief until such a time as Garrett Evans is certified as fit for duty, or the city of Artemis officially hires a new Chief."

Already stalking toward the door, Garrett heard Whit clear his throat. "Uh, Garrett? I'll need your sidearm."

Whit's eye twitched just a bit at the smile on Garrett's face when he turned around.

"*Chief* Abercrombie, this gun wasn't issued to me by the Artemis Police Department. In fact, it belonged to my father. If you figure you can take it, you're welcome to it."

The air in the tiny council chamber grew still.

"Well... you can't carry it in city limits," Whit finally said.

"I'll try to bear that in mind."

Garrett gave them his back without another word.

***

He got a few strange looks standing in May's Diner in his uniform pants and tee shirt. He'd stripped off his Chief's shirt and gun belt in the parking lot of City Hall. Even though a brisk wind brought news of more snow, he didn't feel the cold, didn't feel much of anything.

Misty brought his food in a Styrofoam container. "Anything else, Chief?"

He didn't bother correcting her on the title. "Nope. Thanks, Misty. How's Angela?"

She propped up a smile. "She's great. Staying at Smiley's again."

"Old Smiley's a good guy. That girl loves him to pieces," Garrett said. He shoved the change back across the counter. "So. How are *you* doing these days?"

"Oh, you know. Okay, I guess." Her lower lip trembled just a little but she got it under control. "I'm pregnant. Bradley's gonna be a daddy."

"Oh. Uh, congratulations." The polite thing to say, but Garrett knew it couldn't be good news to a woman who could barely afford the child she had.

"Thanks. Bradley's working real hard right now. He's putting together some money for a business deal in Oklahoma. We might move there in the summer," Misty said.

Sure. Any business deal involving Bradley Wentz meant methamphetamines. He wasn't smart enough to do anything else. Hell, he barely had what little brains it took to deal drugs.

"I hope it works out for you guys, Misty. I really do."

He propped up a smile of his own and left. There were days, like today, when Misty's hair looked extra tousled from long hours at work, she reminded him of Michelle in the morning. Hair frazzled from sleep, no makeup.

Tears rolled down his cheeks on the drive home. He repeated his mantra out loud in the empty car, but it didn't do much but make noise.

He ate standing in the kitchen, like his old man after he came home from a late shift. LaSalle's flier looked up at him from the kitchen table. Garrett reevaluated the girl, with the knowledge her family could afford to keep a guy on her case for two years. Her haircut came off a fashion magazine cover, gold chains hung around her neck. He tried to figure what would make this girl run away with some idiot to live on the street.

What would a father who kept a guy like LaSalle on the payroll be like? How many boyfriends wound up being "interviewed" by LaSalle or someone like him? Garrett's own father might have had something, or everything, to do with him leaving for UCLA. Were they kindred souls, he and this girl?

Garrett grabbed his cell and called the number. LaSalle answered on the first ring.

"You feel like having a beer?" Garrett said.

***

Just like high school. Standing under the stars behind the truck stop with a six-pack on the hood of his car. Trucks rumbled through the slush as they left the pumps on their way to destinations local people dreamed about. To the drivers, Artemis represented one tiny dot in the supply line that fed the country.

"Look, man," LaSalle said. "Big city, small town, politics are the same no matter what. I've known a few cops in my day. If they had a bad dude in the neighborhood, they went to see him when shit happened. Most of the time, they're right. I would've done the same thing if I gave a damn about deer poaching."

He took a long pull off his beer. Garrett saw scarred up knuckles and a crooked pinkie finger on the left hand. "Nice one."

LaSalle followed his gaze and held up the little finger. It broke ranks with the others around the second knuckle.

"Yeah. These are what I got instead of family photos," LaSalle said.

"How's that?"

"Kind of like normal people have pictures of birthday cakes and swimming parties from when they were young, I got these. That pinkie finger reminds me of the first time I ever broke somebody's nose. Broke the hell out of my hand, too."

"How old were you?"

"Fourteen. The OG's in the park used to bet on us young dudes in bare-knuckle fights, see? It's how I made my first real money. I had some talent for it, took some boxing lessons to back it up, but I was too much of a hardhead to stick with training. The streets didn't make me work hard like that. It came easy, you know?"

"Sounds like a Lifetime Movie. 'I Was a Teenage Prize Fighter,'" Garrett said.

LaSalle laughed, a deep rumble. "I don't know if I'd call a couple of skinny kids swingin' wild at each other prize fighting."

"Did you always make your money in the ring?"

LaSalle took a long pull. That one needed no answer. After a while, he said. "Younger times, dumber times. Probably redundant to say it that way."

They clinked beer bottles.

"You got somebody waiting back home?" Garrett said.

"Nah. Good woman ain't gonna put up with me."

"Maybe you should stick to bad women."

They clinked bottles to that one, too.

A couple of working girls smoked cigarettes out by the gravel lot where the truckers slept in their cabs. "You could transplant those girls to LA right now. Just leave them right there and kind of shuffle the world past behind them and stop it when you hit Hollywood Boulevard. They wouldn't look any different," Garrett said.

"Tell me something funny about those days," LaSalle said.

"What?"

"Yeah. I never met a cop who didn't have a funny story about some dumbass he met on the job."

Even though he recognized LaSalle's intent, Garrett indulged him. "Okay, a quick one. I was a boot, riding with my FTO. We go to this call about a GTA. Guy's beside himself because somebody stole his '68 Camaro. We roll up, he meets us at the curb, waving his arms like this shit just happened or something."

Garrett pantomimed the guy, getting into it now.

"But come to find out, he can't even tell us when it happened. He saw the damn thing yesterday, and then it was gone, you know? Even as new as I am, I can see he's tweaked out of his mind. I can barely see any fuckin' color in his eyes, his pupils are so big. My FTO says, 'Yeah, that's all fine. We'll take a GTA report. But, uh... is that your meth lab behind you?'"

"No," LaSalle said.

"Oh yeah. Guy'd been up for three days cooking and cooking. Got into such a panic about his Camaro, he totally forgot he left his garage door open with his lab all set up."

Garrett shook his head and took a drink. "If people only knew how much law enforcement depended on dumb shits like that."

"You miss LA?" LaSalle said.

The smile died instantly. "Not for a minute. Not for a second. There are stories like that, you know, they're funny. But there are others. And they're not so funny."

"I hear you," LaSalle said.

Garrett took LaSalle's empty and stuck it back in the cardboard pack. He handed over another and cracked open his second.

"So, what, you give your client a discount rate by the month? The hourly for a guy like you has to be pretty sweet," Garrett said.

"What about me says expensive?"

"Seriously? With those clothes?"

That nailed him. LaSalle laughed and waved him off. "Okay, okay, officer, you got my profile. Look, this is a family favor kind of thing. The girl's grandfather is a friend of mine. I knew Britney personally."

"You mean you know her," Garrett said.

LaSalle took a drink. His eyes went to the two girls across the lot. One of them held an animated conversation with a trucker. They seemed to reach an agreement. The girl hugged her friend goodbye and headed off toward a big Volvo rig.

"For some time now I've considered the fact that I may not be looking for a missing girl, but for the last person to see her alive," LaSalle said.

"What happens if you find out she's dead, but you get a lead on the guy who did it?"

"I believe I'd have to turn such information over to local authorities, wouldn't I? Whoever they may be."

Garrett tipped his beer toward the big man. "Here's hoping they're in Arizona."

LaSalle grinned and returned the mock salute.

"Had any luck interviewing other drivers?"

56

Garrett said.

"Not really. But I met a girl who told me there's a forest ranger, or somebody, who eats here a lot. He might have seen Britney."

"Forest ranger?"

"She wasn't sure. Something about his uniform."

"Hmm. We don't have any rangers stationed close. Maybe she means Smiley. He works for County Animal Control and wears a uniform. I know he likes to eat out here. He loves Burton's old school cooking."

"You suppose I could meet Smiley?"

"Sure. If you don't mind being seen with the disgraced former police chief, I'll introduce you sometime."

6

Artemis, West Virginia - 1961

The *pop-whoosh-whoosh-whoosh-pop* of the old hit-and-miss engine stutters across the still barnyard.

Smiley's skinny legs poke out of his short pants, bare feet caked with mud from helping Papa fix the well pump. At eight years old, folks in Artemis already call him Smiley because of the mask he wears when he goes to town with Papa or Ma. When Ma was alive.

Folks can't see the stripes on Smiley's back.

Papa's nose is starting to rot away. They got new doctors who can close the hole, but a body doesn't ever look right after. Like some geek you'd pay a nickel to see at the circus. Even though Ma is gone, she's reaching back from the grave to punish him. Leastways, that's how Smiley sees it.

"You payin' attention, boy?"

"Yessir."

Papa shows him how to switch the engine over from gasoline to kerosene. Start it with the good stuff, run it on the cheap. Papa sounds like he's talkin' through a duck call.

Ma slipped on the ice last winter and cracked her head on the steps. Right about the same time Papa said he'd caught the devil's fever from her. He's always been quick with his hands or a belt on Smiley, but since last winter it's gotten worse.

Papa holds out a wrench, but Smiley's daydreaming. The

wrench falls into the mud—

Back in the barn again, the smell of hay and dirt hot in his nose.

The rawhide straps hold his bony wrists against the whipping post. Swish-crack of the leather strap that Papa likes to use. By now, Smiley knows screams don't help. There is no mercy for the weak. And so he endures the punishment, only letting out the occasional grunt when one catches him good in the ribs.

At the age of twelve, he'll kill a litter of puppies three farms to the west and Papa will knock his teeth out.

Five years later, the old man will fall out of the hayloft, drunk as a lord and snap his neck clean in two. Most folks won't care about it enough to run a big investigation. Smiley had been the only other person there, and heavens, Ol' Smiley would never do somethin' like that.

***

Faded yellow paint flaked off the antique hit-and-miss engine, but the young picker looked like he'd landed a private viewing of the Mona Lisa.

"This is a beauty," he said. "How much you need for her, sir?"

"I'd like to get around three." Smiley grinned down at Angela in her puffy snow suit. "Sound about right, Angie?"

"Wow, three hundred dollars? That's a lot of money," she said.

Both men laughed. The picker brushed dirt off his knees and looked around the barn. Everything in its place, tools hanging from hooks on the walls, hay bales stacked neatly by the rear wall. He was probably used to junk piles and glorified lean-tos some folks called barns.

"Can I offer you two-fifty?" the young man said.

"You sure can," Smiley said. "But I wouldn't hear ya unless you said two seventy-five."

They shook hands on the deal. Smiley let Angela ride on the Bobcat with him while he loaded the engine into the picker's cargo van. With the engine gone, only one other thing Papa had put in this barn was still there. The stump of the old whipping post. About two feet of it stuck out of the lone square foot of dirt left from the original packed earth floor. The stump looked like a maniac had been at it with an axe.

Smiley and Angela waved goodbye as the young man drove away with his antique treasure. She insisted they wave until the picker's van went out of sight, and even though his shoulder joint developed a burn he knew would keep him awake later, Smiley would pay anything for her smile.

He even jogged alongside her when she wanted to race him back to the front door. Thoughts of another time running through the snow after another girl tried to intrude, but he crushed those predator dreams.

By the time Misty's truck splashed through the slush on the road out front, Smiley had Angela's stuff all packed and ready to go. Instead of Misty's pretty face, Smiley saw Bradley Wentz climb out of the pickup in pants drooping so low most of his boxers were visible.

They went through the minor pleasantries for Angela's sake and Smiley waited by the tailgate while Bradley got her situated in the truck, waited until her door shut.

"Can I talk at ya for a second, Bradley?" Smiley waved him back by the tailgate, out of Angela's sight.

"Sure, Smiley. Hey, Misty said to tell you she really appreciates you taking Angela on short notice. She couldn't turn down that shift. We're putting together some money for a move."

"Yeah, I heard all about it. I actually wanted to talk to you about Angela."

Smiley couldn't miss the giant pupils, the redness around Bradley's nose, the jittery fake smile. Stupid druggie kid. Smiley saw plenty of them during his time as an Army medic. Except they were on heroin in those days.

"I'm just gonna shoot straight, Bradley. I saw a bruise on Angela's back last time she was here. Long, like a belt makes. I'm here to tell you, young man, you shouldn't be whoopin' on a little girl."

Faced with someone who didn't buy his bullshit, Bradley changed in an instant, the placating smile turning into a bully's sneer. He glanced back at the truck to make sure Angela still faced forward, then stepped up close to Smiley.

"Is that right, old man? How we discipline that kid ain't none of your business. She spilled juice in a seven hunnerd dollar laptop. Who's gonna pay for that? Her idiot mother, working at the diner?"

The girl under the barn would have recognized the smile. She would have told Bradley he *never-ever-ever* wanted to see that smile.

"You can give everyone else your shit-eatin' grin, *Smiley*, but I got your number. You're hoping that hot young thing will see how good you treat her daughter, how you help her out with money, and just maybe she'll move out here and take care of your old ass."

Bradley completely missed the change in Smiley. But then, Smiley had been hiding his real face much longer than this kid had.

"I said that wrong, I guess. What I meant to say was *don't* whoop on that young girl no more," Smiley said.

"Or what?" Bradley grabbed Smiley's collar. He

stopped cold when the Smith and Wesson's barrel poked him just above the belt buckle.

"We ought to have more manners, but for some reason, men can't talk to each other these days without pushin' and shovin'. Let's not do that," Smiley said.

"No, sir. You're right," Bradley said. He let go.

"A kid that young doesn't deserve to be beat on for making mistakes. But grownups, well they most likely deserve what they get for theirs. Take her home, Bradley. And treat 'em both right, you hear me?"

If a breeze came up when Death called on you and his hood blew back, surely he'd have pale blue eyes just like Smiley's.

"Yes, sir. I'm sorry, I just—"

"Get on your way."

And he did.

7

The last two pills rattled in the bottle. Garrett washed them down with tap water. At least now that everyone knew, he wouldn't have to drive so far to get his prescription refilled.

He'd known cops who worked on antidepressants for years. No one really asked. Sort of the police department's own version of "Don't Ask, Don't Tell."

He knew damn well it didn't affect his decision-making process, but Whit Abercrombie had been lobbying for Garrett's job from day one. This gave Samuel Redding a good excuse to push Garrett out. In these mountains, sometimes people saw certain laws as flexible. Samuel had told the truth. Plenty of families in Artemis had made their way through a winter by poaching a deer now and then. For those people, Robert Lee Withers and Tom Poston's deaths were unnecessary. And of course, Garrett's fault.

Pretty much everyone in town had loved Chief Lamar Evans, including bartenders and truck stop girls. After the accident, the entire town had been numb with grief. Garrett coming in with all his experience, willing to leave the big West Coast department and fill his Dad's shoes, felt like the perfect choice. A choice based more on heart than anything else.

The smell from the toaster hit Garrett and jogged something hidden in a back corner of his mind and suddenly he stood over a young kid in the parking lot of a McDonald's. The smell of gunpowder hung in the air and the kid coughed a bubble of dark blood. Maybe sixteen, skinny, with gang tattoos. Little bastard took a shot at Garrett and his partner, so they put him down.

Garrett went to the sink and splashed cold water on his face, pretending it helped get rid of the memory. That had been the most justifiable shooting in the world. So why did it still pop up out of the blue like a fucking blood-soaked jack in the box?

He left the toast cooling in the toaster, not hungry anymore. He walked into the living room and started putting all the odds and ends back in The Box.

Last night had been filled with bad decisions. One of them was switching from beer to the distilled stuff on top of the fridge. Rarely a good idea. He wasn't really sure what time he dragged The Box out of the closet, but he could see the drunken progression of his self-flagellation.

First the pictures of him and Michelle with a group of friends at a Halloween party. Frankenstein's monster and Ripley from Aliens. Their first date.

Then came random stupid things. Her old ID card, a goofy photo booth picture of them at her sister's wedding, wrist bands from Disneyland. The damn ring box. They buried her wearing the ring, so why didn't he throw the box away?

He never went to see her at the morgue. Didn't go to the viewing, either, and never walked up to the casket at the service. They'd fixed her face, of course, those masters of artifice at the funeral home. But it still wasn't her.

He'd rather not go through life remembering her the way his mother looked in her casket. Too much makeup, face not looking quite right, stiff hands across her middle.

Nope.

Two last pictures, both taken at work. Her in uniform, him in plain clothes with a ridiculous handlebar mustache.

In the first picture her eyes were dry, the next they shined with tears because he'd just popped the question. Right after she and a squad of uniforms had assisted his robbery team with a warrant service. Okay, not the most romantic setting at first glance, but how many girls could tell their friends their fiancée proposed at the scene of a high risk warrant service?

He gathered up his medals from LAPD, which were scattered around the trashcan in the kitchen. He must have gotten to the point of no return and tried to throw them into the trashcan from the living room. Usually, he could put at least three of them into the can. Last night, he'd missed them all. He stuffed The Box back in the closet, not bothering to have the mental conversation about throwing it out someday.

His appetite came back from the grave and he decided to celebrate with proper biscuits and gravy at May's Diner instead of toast in his lonely kitchen. Throw in some hash browns with a liberal dose of Louisiana Hotsauce and you had the best hangover cure this side of menudo.

The old farts were parked on the bench outside Davis Hardware as usual. Garrett had hoped the cold would drive them inside, but the day had dawned bright and clear, prompting the old farts to come out and sun themselves like lizards. He steeled himself as he parked in front of May's. He tried heading straight inside.

Melvin Davis and Earl Hunsacker glared at him in silence, but Poor Boy Willis wasn't about to leave it alone. "Say there, Quickdraw, I heard you saved Bambi's mother from that desperado Robert Lee Withers."

Any other day, Garrett would have ignored it. Or maybe he would have found a joke to sling back. Today wasn't the day for it.

Garrett stopped cold and fixed them with a gaze none of them had seen from him before. He'd presided over the death of more than one human being in his time, and that can give you a chilling way of looking at the living.

"Any time you old farts wanna peel your asses off that bench, strap on a gun and badge, and give it a shot yourselves, you're welcome to. Until then, you can keep your bullshit opinions about how I do the job to yourselves."

He strode into the diner before they could recover. Later, he'd feel like shit for jumping the old goats, but right now the fire in his gut made him warm. Eunice Smith, great granddaughter of May herself, worked behind the counter.

"Misty take the day off?" Garrett said.

Eunice looked a little sad, and maybe a little embarrassed too. "Between folks eating at the truck stop and the new buffet place, we just don't have the business to keep her going full time. We had to cut her back to weekends for now."

"Sorry to hear that." Garrett placed his order and sat down at the counter. He figured he might as well eat there. If you let white gravy cool down, it turned into a gelatinous cap on the biscuits that never tasted right after being heated in the microwave. He stared at the soda fountain behind the counter while he waited, feeling the eyes on his back, pretending like he didn't give a shit. When his food arrived, the smell actually made his mouth water.

He dug right in, the black-peppery goodness of Eunice's gravy doing more good than a herd of therapists with fistfuls of Xanax.

***

The beans were especially good tonight. Probably the second day since they were made. In Smiley's perfect world, red beans were at least two days old and had slices of red onion on the side. The way Ma used to eat them.

Tucked into a booth by the front window of Burton's Truck Stop diner, Smiley didn't give much cause to be noticed. Off duty, he didn't wear the khaki uniform, but the dark gray Dickies and lighter gray work shirt might as well have been a uniform. Quiet, unassuming, with a big smile for every waitress, Smiley let his eye wander over the girls outside the plate glass window.

Whores. Some city, some country, all poor. And stupid. And filthy.

They wandered around under the bright lights at the gas pumps. He could see garish green eye shadow on one of them. He thought she'd look nice in his trophy room if he kept her face intact.

A trucker called his name and said goodbye on the way out. Smiley grinned so fierce his cheeks burned with it.

Like Papa taught him to read a game trail, Smiley knew the worn path these girls would take. Between here and the rest stop out by the "new" highway, as anyone over forty called it. If a trucker didn't get his spot in Burton's lot, he'd get gas and food, then sleep for a few hours over at the rest stop. Or not sleep for a few hours, depending on how much extra cash he had.

Some nights the rest stop would be packed, and the girls tried to negotiate a ride back down the mile of blacktop between Burton's and there. But some nights there just weren't any trucks headed this way. Those times the girls would walk down the lonely black road, past the woods, back to the truck stop and more customers.

There were many nights of patient waiting, going home with nothing, holding out for the perfect scenario, when the prey walked alone, separated from the rest of the herd. He'd learned long ago to choose ones on the fringe, the ones the other members of the herd didn't care about.

Like any responsible hunter, he tried to limit himself. Lately though, it seemed he couldn't control the Hunter as well. He'd been twenty-four when he took the first. He waited two years until the next. In that time, he learned from his mistakes with the first one. After an exhausting day of replacing blood-soaked floorboards in his barn, he hit on the idea of an underground shelter of some sort, like those damn militia fools over in Braxton County.

A cellar/bunker would also help with the screaming. He'd had to kill the first one way too early. Even though he lived a good mile from the Heideman farm, sounds carry at night.

One of the whores outside struck a deal and climbed into the cab of a truck. She had thick red hair like Ma. The desire to have it bunched in his fist overwhelmed Smiley. He imagined the chicken frying in the kitchen to be the smell of her flesh when his branding iron touched her and he felt himself stir down there.

"Poor young things." Nadine Pearson had snuck

up on him while he mused.

"Oh. Yeah. Runaways, nowhere to go, I guess," Smiley said.

She'd caught him looking and they both knew it. Of course, she only thought she knew why. She judged him from behind those ridiculous damn frames with no lenses. He waved a hand at the empty seat across from him. "Have a seat, Nadine."

"Thank you, Smiley. Maybe next time. I just came out to minister to the girls a bit. You out for a late supper?"

"Yup. I watched little Angela for Misty today and I was too darn tuckered to cook. I think I'm gettin' old." He gave her his biggest smile. The one he used to save for the Sunday School teacher, even after he patted Smiley on his bruised back.

"Oh please, Smiley. If you're getting old, I don't know what that makes me." Nadine gave him the cocked eyebrow that always preceded gossip. "What do you think of this Bradley Wentz boy Misty's taken up with?"

"Not worth much, honestly. But you can't tell young ones anything," Smiley said.

"Sad, but true. And now I hear she's pregnant. You don't watch it, Smiley, you're going to be running a daycare out there."

He smiled because he knew he should show emotion. But inside, a pilot flame *whooshed* into a full-blown fire. Pregnant by that little shit. Which meant they'd probably get married and make Bradley a legal guardian of Angela.

"Smiley?"

He came back to find Nadine giving him an odd look.

"Sorry, what was that?"

69

"You lost your smile for a second there."

"Did I? Just thinkin' about how the poor girl is gonna make ends meet, I suppose."

"I know. There's a lot of that going around," Nadine said.

She looked out the window at a lone girl trolling past the trucks with sleeper cabs. Nadine patted her bible. "Let's just pray all these young girls figure a way out of this."

"Yup," Smiley said. "Let's pray they do."

***

Fascinated by the selection, Garrett thumbed through the shirts hanging in LaSalle's motel closet. "You're worse than a woman with shoes."

LaSalle glanced up from his laptop. "Believe me, you do not want to see my collection of shoes. Now come look at this."

LaSalle spun the laptop around. A map of West Virginia with red dots along Route 45.

"Okay. Lots of cases of missing girls in West Virginia. You pull up a map of the whole United States with red dots for missing girls, it'd look like the country had measles," Garrett said. "Besides, the dates on some of the cases you're using are from before your girl was born, much less went missing."

"Who says she has to be the first?" LaSalle said.

"Wait a minute. The first what? For all you know your girl is in California, shacked up with some guitar-playing surfer."

LaSalle retrieved some papers from a worn briefcase and handed them to Garrett. An arrest report and a booking photo of the girl in LaSalle's flier. Santini,

Britney.

Garrett looked at him over the photo. "Georgia?"

"Closest I ever got to her. Flew in a day after they issued her a summons and let her go. She still has a warrant there."

"So what does this have to do with your map?"

"I talked to a guy in Georgia who remembered her. Said she got herself a road daddy who was headed to West Virginia, but then taking a trip all the way to Cali for some high-pay gig. I found that dude, but he said he left her in West Virginia. Got tired of her fucked up attitude."

"She known for her bad attitude?" Garrett said.

"She's got some Daddy issues."

"Yeah, well, doesn't everybody? Who's to say she didn't find herself another road daddy and head on out?"

"Nobody. But these," LaSalle pointed to the red dots along WV Route 45. "These give me a certain feeling."

"Such as?" Garrett said.

"This part of 45 runs through maybe seven or eight different jurisdictions. Nobody talks to each other, nobody compares notes. Nobody's looking that hard, anyway, right?" Not for a missing hooker. LaSalle didn't say it. He didn't have to.

Garrett pointed at the two cases that were the farthest apart. "So you're saying somebody's been working a twenty-five mile stretch of highway, snatching up girls but never ever leaving a body behind."

"Except one," LaSalle said. "He got interrupted."

"Okay, so one. One in what, about fifty here? Someone killed fifty girls and only one body turns up?"

"I'm not saying *all* of the twenty-five mile stretch of road," LaSalle said. "So it wouldn't be all these missing girls. If you ask for detailed information from the written report, you can find out where the girls were actually last *seen*, including Britney."

He hit a key on the laptop. Out of all the red dots, a small group turned blue. Twenty-eight, in all, spread over forty years. All last seen at Burton's Truck Stop.

"Damn," Garrett said. "Still, this would have to be a family business. A couple of these cases are forty years old."

"The Green River Killer operated from the Eighties into the Nineties," LaSalle said.

"And he littered the place with corpses. When DNA testing technology caught up with him, he got nailed," Garrett said.

LaSalle shrugged. "So he was stupid. But what if he knew about the DNA stuff back then? What if he'd been careful, put the bodies somewhere where nobody could ever find them? He might still be killing people today if he had."

"Maybe," Garrett said. "But a guy like that needs to be anonymous. Get lost in the crowd, you know? Not exactly something you can do out here in the sticks. The closest city a guy like that could hide in is over an hour away. I guess it would throw off suspicion, if he came all the way out here to do his thing."

"He could also be a trucker."

"True," Garrett said.

"Feel like taking a ride out to the truck stop with me? I figure the crowd has turned over by now. New faces to see," LaSalle said.

"I guess so. I'm suspended, though, so I'm only there as an observer. Last thing I need is trouble with the 'new' chief."

8

The big trucker gave LaSalle's ID the once-over. Garrett wouldn't have thought it possible to make LaSalle look small, but this guy went six-six easy, six-eight in the boots he wore against the slush in Burton's gravel parking lot. And he didn't look impressed.

"So? New York private eye. That supposed to mean something to me?" The trucker said.

"If you're not impressed by that, I also have one that says I'm a cab driver." LaSalle grinned, but for some reason Garrett didn't think he was kidding. "I'm not trying to give anyone a hard time, sir. I'm just looking for a girl who was last seen at this—"

"So? What's that got to do with me? And who the hell are you supposed to be?" The last bit directed toward Garrett.

"Me? I'm nobody. I'm with the band," Garrett said.

The guy looked more and more agitated by the second. "Well fuck you, and the band. I stopped here to eat, not to get questioned about some missing truck stop whore. I got two daughters at home, assholes. I don't play that game."

For a split second, he became Robert Lee

swearing at them from the porch right before the shooting started. Garrett choked it down, but he felt the red rising behind his eyes.

LaSalle produced his flier. "All I'm doing is asking everyone who comes through here if they've seen her. That's it. It doesn't make you a bad guy if you just saw her."

"Buddy, I've seen 'em all, from one end of this country to the other. Stupid little whores who want to get a look inside your cab, steal you blind if you let 'em. They all look alike to me. You know how that is, right?"

LaSalle's Zen master calm never broke. "That I do."

The big trucker sneered and turned to go back inside and Garrett knew it would go bad from there. Too late to stop. The red tide had risen and the little voice of reason his therapist taught him to consult had been told to shut the fuck up. He knew the words came out of his own mouth, but it sounded like someone talking underwater.

"What if that was your daughter? Would you want some asshole to call her a stupid whore?" Garrett said.

"The fuck did you say?"

There was the expected quick turn to face them, big strides coming back, arms cocked to give Garrett a hard shove. The trucker was a big man, but not a fighter.

Everything blinked red. The big man oofed out a blast of air and doubled over before Garrett even realized he'd hit him in the solar plexus. It felt good to hit him.

His first year on the streets in LA, Garrett learned not to break his knuckles on someone's head. He hit the trucker hard across the face with two elbow strikes. Robert Lee's face flashed over the trucker's and Garrett hit him again. And again.

Hands like industrial vises grabbed Garrett's upper arms and stopped him cold. He came back to reality and found himself staring into LaSalle's dark eyes. "Easy, easy. It's over, he's done. Go wait in the car, my man. I have a feeling we should go elsewhere."

"You mean we better get out of here before someone calls the cops," Garrett said. For some reason that made him giggle. Maybe he *should* go sit in the car. Get his shit together. Because right now, his shit was anything but together. He headed back toward the Mustang.

LaSalle helped the big trucker to his feet. "There you go. Just take it easy for a second and make sure you can stand up. Sorry about that, my friend has been going through some personal issues lately. You know about that, right?"

Eyes still rolling a bit, the trucker nodded. LaSalle let him go and he staggered toward the diner. That's when LaSalle noticed the two other truckers. Mouths open, standing stock-still.

LaSalle waved the flier at them. "Could I talk to you gentlemen about a missing girl?"

"Yes, sir."

"Absolutely."

***

Temperatures had dipped again, making the Mustang lots of fun around icy corners. The gray afternoon sky dropped lazy tufts of snow like tiny paratroopers attacking the roads. LaSalle gripped the console as Garrett tapped the gas and steered into a slide. His confident grin looked a little shaky, but he got the car back under control.

No one had thought to confiscate the County radio in the former Chief's personal car, and Garrett was making full use of it. He and LaSalle were headed out a lonely two-lane blacktop. They'd heard the dispatcher send Smiley out to handle a deer hit by a truck and Garrett figured it would be a good spot to talk to Smiley without attracting prying eyes in town.

"Hey, sorry about back there," Garrett said.

"The fucked-up driving, or beating that guy's ass?" LaSalle said.

"The driving is not my fault. It's icy and I'm in a Five-Oh. Cut me some slack. But yeah, about the other thing."

"You figure to see trouble?"

"Oh, probably. Just a misdemeanor, though, so it won't be too bad," Garrett said.

LaSalle's deep baritone laugh actually made Garrett smile.

"Look at you," LaSalle said. "Five minutes off the job and you're workin' the system like a career criminal."

"That's only half a joke. I've got a little money put away, but I may just have to resort to a life of crime before long. I've got two years of questionable grades in college and I'm an ex-cop on psych meds. Maybe I can get hired as a door-greeter somewhere."

"You know anything about cooking meth? It's a growing industry," LaSalle said.

"The only chemistry I know I learned from Bill Nye the Science Guy. I'd burn the place to the ground." A flurry of snow hit the windshield and Garrett turned up the heater. LaSalle opened his coat.

"You tryin' to raise exotic snakes in here?" LaSalle said.

"Sorry. I hate the cold." Garrett snapped the

heater back down a notch.

"I don't understand you, my man. It seems like not one thing about this place appeals to you, yet you willingly came back."

"If I knew the answer to that, I'd probably know the answer to why I just went ape-shit on a marginal asshole. And for the record, there is at least one thing here that appeals to me."

Up ahead, a big farm truck had pulled off to the right. Garrett saw the County Animal Control pickup behind it. "There they are."

Garrett parked far enough behind Smiley's County pickup to let him to winch up a dead deer if need be. LaSalle saw Smiley through the windshield, the white hair under the hunting cap. "Little old to be manhandling dead deer, isn't he? What's the retirement age around here, seventy-five?" LaSalle said.

"Small towns have a way of holding onto their old people. All the young ones are anywhere but here, if they can be. You tend to see folks with gray hair in charge of things most of the time."

Garrett got out and zipped his coat to his chin. He and LaSalle walked up just as Smiley put a tiny rimfire shell into his bolt-action .22 rifle. He still gave Garrett a big smile.

"Garrett, how the hell are ya?" Smiley said.

"Fair to middlin', Smiley. I promised my friend I'd introduce you sometime, and I heard this call go out. Hope you don't mind."

A slight falter in the smile when he saw LaSalle? Smiley held the rifle in his left hand and stuck out his right.

"Jebediah Carmichael. Folks call me Smiley."

"Chester LaSalle. Good to meet you." LaSalle shook the hand and turned an eye on the deer. "What

77

happened?"

"This old girl decided to run out of the trees just as these fellas come along. Bang." A farmer and his teenage son stood near their truck. The front left fender was dented to hell.

"You fellas might want to step back and plug your ears," Smiley said. He squatted down next to the deer. Obviously mortally wounded and in pain, the doe tried to move broken legs and snorted blood out of her nostrils.

"Easy old girl," Smiley whispered. "It's all over now."

He put the rifle's barrel behind the doe's ear. A flat *bang* and the deer went still. Smiley stood and nodded at the farmer. "Darryl, it would take me a coon's age to load this thing up and dispose of it properly. I don't suppose you'd have any use for venison?"

The farmer grinned. "We could probably take care of that for ya, Smiley."

Garrett and LaSalle followed Smiley back to his truck and waited while he put the rifle away. "I'm not really supposed to do that, but I'm just gettin' too old to drag all these deer back to the County lot," Smiley said.

Smiley offered a hand to Garrett once the rifle was secured. "Garrett, I ain't had a chance to tell you how sorry I am. I feel like everything that happened is my fault."

"No, it isn't," Garrett said. He gripped Smiley's hand, remembering the first time they shook. Garrett was probably five years old and his dad was teaching him how men greet each other. "It's my judgment they questioned, not yours. Something about the Law of the Hills outweighing the actual law."

"It's a tough damn thing to get away from, I'll give ya that. Old ways die hard." Smiley shifted his gaze to

LaSalle. "What can I do for you, Mr. LaSalle?"

LaSalle took a flier from his coat. "I've been hired to find this young woman. She went missing about two years back. Some folks said you eat at the truck stop quite a bit, so I thought you might have seen her at some point. She, uh, she ran with those girls who work the truckers."

Smiley accepted the flier. A flicker of recognition? Garrett couldn't be sure.

"Poor girl," Smiley said. "Doesn't look more than fifteen or sixteen. You know, maybe. It's hard to say. There's been so darn many girls come through there over the years."

"Anybody else you think might have seen her?" Garrett said.

"Maybe a few of the boys who work for the County. Can I keep this? I'll show it around and see what people say," Smiley said.

"Please do," LaSalle said. "I'll give you my card so you have my number."

Smiley put the card in his wallet and the flier on the front seat of his truck. From his angle, Garrett saw Smiley carefully smooth out the crease down the flier's middle where it had been folded in LaSalle's pocket.

"Have you talked to Nadine?" Smiley said. "She sees darn near everything goes on around this town."

"We did. She remembers the girl, but didn't know much more about her," Garrett said.

Smiley shook his head. For once, he wasn't smiling. "Damn shame. What kinda world makes a girl have to sell her body to get by?"

"We're all trying to figure that one out," Garrett said. They shook hands all around and Garrett and LaSalle got back in the Mustang. Before they could leave, Smiley's county pickup swung around the farm truck, skidding a bit in the new snow.

Then it straightened up and took off like a shot.

"Looks like he's in a hurry," LaSalle said.

Garrett chuckled. "It's almost five o'clock and he's a county employee. Probably in a hurry to turn his truck in on time."

***

Smiley forced himself not to look at it. Not until he got downstairs and secured the door to his special room. The physical arousal started before he even scanned the photos pinned to a corkboard on one wall. She wouldn't be in the fading Polaroids. Those were old ones.

She'd be in the glossies from his printer. Misty showed him how to use one of those new digital cameras and set up his printer for him. She said the new inks didn't fade for decades.

There. Halfway down, between a chubby brunette from Riverside, California and a red-head who didn't have ID.

She looked so different. In the colored fella's flier, she was bright and lovely and had a defiant air about her. In Smiley's picture, she was small and scared, her breasts caked with dried brown blood from some preliminary cuts.

He smoothed the flier on his workbench with trembling hands. Pale blue eyes drank in every detail. She still had the eyebrow piercings when she met the Hunter, which gave the picture an immediacy that set his heart racing. He tried to resist, to deny himself. But it was just a game. He knew what he'd do.

He pinned the flier to the center of the corkboard and stripped off his clothes. He donned the rubber apron, smelling the moldy copper of dried blood.

His fingertip tingled as he brushed it against the power button on the flat little DVD player Misty and Angela gave him for Christmas. All his recordings resided in a leather-bound steam chest from another age. Some were just audiocassette tapes. Those were from his early ones, the ones he only saw in his fading memories.

The newer ones, like the girl from the flier, he had on video.

9

Garrett spent the morning pacing, pacing, his mind going everywhere and nowhere at the same time. He tried to think of the last time he'd been this bad, unable to sleep, unable to focus on a single goal and map out a plan. A plan for the day, much less for the rest of his life.

When he quit LA, he quit therapy. The tools were still there, you know, in his head. He'd spent enough time with enough shrinks to know all the catchy mental triggers he was supposed to use. Knowing it and doing it always seemed to be polar opposites. Kind of like knowing you shouldn't smoke because it turns your lungs into blackened cancerous chunks, and doing it anyway because your body runs the show and it wants that cool nicotine rush.

If he hadn't hit the guy in the parking lot, he would have tossed and turned all night, imagining it, going through varying levels of damage in his head, ending with the guy pulling a knife or something and Garrett putting a bullet in his head. As it turned out, hitting him didn't make things come up roses.

He wandered into the kitchen. LaSalle's flier hung on his refrigerator under a magnet from Davis Hardware. *American Tools for American Homes!*

Alongside the flier, he'd stuck a printout of LaSalle's map with all the red and blue dots.

LaSalle's case, if you could call it a case, helped Garrett focus. Looking at the girl's picture settled his mind, made his thoughts move into more constructive areas.

The longer he looked at the map, the more he thought the big man might have something. A trucker could get away with coming through here from time to time, strangling an anonymous truck stop girl in his cab, or whatever means he used. If Garrett was going with this theory, then he had to admit the guy used a knife at least once.

Where the hell were all the bodies? If these girls weren't just runaways no one could find— and there were thousands out there— where could you put twenty-eight people without a hunter, hiker, or a motorist who pulled over to piss stumbling across at least one bone?

The knock on the door triggered a flash of anger. What the fuck? He was trying to figure something out here.

Opening the door didn't do much to douse the fire.

Whit Abercrombie stood on his front step, grinning like an idiot. He had Lyle Hampton and Dougie Armstead with him. In other words, the entire Artemis Police Department.

Clancy Parker stood to one side in full State Police uniform, looking embarrassed.

"Hey, Clance," Garrett said. "What's got you running with this rabble?"

"Hello, Garrett. I'm sorry to say I'm here on official business. You know the deal. If I come into your town, I ask you to go along as a courtesy."

Garrett pushed open the screen, causing Whit to have to step back into the yard. Garrett looked Whit in the eye.

"And it takes three of you to show courtesy? You expecting trouble, Whit?"

"From you? Not likely." Whit put on the macho act, but it didn't work well when everyone there already knew Garrett. If it came down to a shootout, they probably hadn't brought enough people.

Clancy stepped in. "Now, Garrett, this has nothing to do with what's going on in town. It's, just... a trucker out at Burton's filed a report, says you beat him up. Even has a few witnesses. That's State jurisdiction, so it falls to me, unfortunately."

"You here to arrest me?"

"Nope. Just here to get your side of it. It's a misdemeanor at this point, so this report will just be filed with the DA. You won't go to jail today, but you will have to go to court. But you know that."

"Yup."

They all stood there breathing white plumes in the cold.

"Anything else?" Garrett said.

"I would like to hear your side," Clancy said.

"Guy came at me and I put him down. You must not know me very well if you think I'm stupid enough to elaborate. Now, anything else?"

"Yeah, I got something else," Whit said. "Folks told me you been goin' around with that PI from New York, asking questions about missing girls and such. You need to remember you're not law enforcement anymore, Garrett."

"And you need to crack open a law book and tell me what's illegal about handing out fliers and asking if people have seen a missing girl. If you can't tell me, then you can get fucked." Man, he was really using his words to hurt instead of heal today. His therapist would be disappointed.

A deep red crept up Whit's neck and into his jowls. "You want to watch your mouth."

"Or what?" Garrett said. "Even in the backwater, it's called Freedom of Speech. If you're going to use your position to screw with me, Whit, you better make damn sure you know the law. Because I do."

Whit's jaw clenched and unclenched. Whatever he was holding in, it didn't seem like something he wanted to say in front of a State Trooper. He ignored Garrett and spoke directly to Clancy. "We done here? He obviously doesn't want to talk."

"Yeah," Clancy said. "Thanks for the company, Whit."

Without so much as another glance at Garrett, Whit stalked back to his car, his boys in tow. Clancy stayed back, waited until they left.

"I don't know what's up with you lately, man, but I hope things get better for you," Clancy said.

He held out a hand and Garrett took it.

"It can only go up from here, Clance."

***

"How do you make the woods look so lonely?" LaSalle said.

Tracy said, "I just paint the woods. You're the one who decides whether they look lonely or not."

Garrett sipped some sweet tea and watched LaSalle move around Tracy's tidy living room. She had five paintings on her walls, all personal favorites of hers.

LaSalle stopped in front of one featuring a dilapidated barn with a shagbark hickory growing up through the roof. "What's this?"

"That one's really from memory. My mom took me berry picking one summer and we came upon this barn in the middle of nowhere, with a tree growing through it. Even as young as I was, it gave me the feeling nothing we do is permanent. It all gets washed away by time."

"Is the barn still there?" LaSalle said.

"No, it fell down years ago. The tree's still there with all the rubble piled around it."

"Here's to the tree." Garrett held up his tea.

While they worked their way through some amazing roasted pork and red potatoes, Tracy and Garrett took turns telling LaSalle embarrassing stories about each other as kids. LaSalle laughed in all the right places, and they didn't delve into anything beyond Junior High where the stories were still innocent. It made Garrett feel warm.

But it was cold outside and there were other things happening in the world.

"A few years after I left, there was a murder out at the rest stop. You ever hear about that?" Garrett said.

"Of course," Tracy said. "Some crazy trucker cut up one of those girls from the truck stop. Horrible."

"What makes you say it was a trucker?" LaSalle said.

"Nadine told me stories. Some of the things these guys do to the girls..."

"Any guys in particular like to get rough?" LaSalle said.

"Oh, I wouldn't know. She never goes into too much detail. We're usually at church when we do our gossiping, after all," Tracy said. She started clearing dishes and both men jumped up to help. "You know who you guys should talk to? Smiley," she said.

"Popular man," LaSalle said. "We got that recommendation already. He doesn't remember our girl, but he's gonna show the flier around to the other county guys."

"That's what I love about Smiley. He's always helping people out when he can. He looks after Misty Heideman's little girl like she was his own grandchild," Tracy said. "I guess it's kind of natural, since he treated Misty like a daughter when she was young."

Garrett handed over the last of the dishes and Tracy put them in the washer. She snapped him with a towel and he flicked dishwater at her. He caught LaSalle smiling at their interaction.

Later, Garrett watched LaSalle try to gingerly place the painting of the barn and tree in the Mustang's cramped trunk. Garrett couldn't believe Tracy agreed to sell it, but LaSalle convinced her there was a place in his apartment back home desperately in need of the piece.

Tracy pulled her sweater tight against the evening cold and Garrett felt a deep need to put protective arms around her. Instead, he bumped her shoulder with his, like a kid would do. "Thanks for having us over. I have a feeling it's been a while since he had a home-cooked meal."

"It's not every night a girl gets to entertain a PI from New York and a police chief who's a wanted man," Tracy said.

"Ex police chief. And I'm marginally wanted at best."

She zipped his jacket up the rest of the way and patted it like his mother used to. "You're wanted. And you're loved. I think you need to hear it from time to time. Are you still taking your meds? You can't do cold turkey on those."

"I know, I know. Yeah, I am. But..."

"But?"

"I did just kick the shit out of some guy who had no idea why," Garrett said.

"How's the depression?"

"It's at least staying outside the door now."

"I thought maybe I'd see you sooner. After the Council meeting," Tracy said.

He shrugged. "Meh. I would've only moped around."

"That's okay. I'm thinking of entering a Dali phase and I need some droopy faces around here to model." She gave him a hug and he had to hold his breath. She'd put on some perfume tonight and it made him want to bury his face in her hair and stand there until the cold drove them inside to the bedroom.

The Mustang's trunk lid thumped closed and Garrett pulled away from the hug. Not in time to avoid LaSalle's grin.

***

LaSalle picked Garrett up at his place the next morning. Something about his sporty rental Volvo being safer in the snow. On the drive to Nadine's, LaSalle made a point of pushing the cool little traction control button and smiling at Garrett.

"Yeah, yeah, anyone can let the computer do the driving. Anything new from the fliers?" Garrett said.

"Nope. But most of the time it's boots on the ground that gets me there. Talking to people. And dumb luck."

"Sounds like police work."

"When are you gonna get back to it?" LaSalle said. He turned a corner and a man in a snowsuit shoveling his driveway stopped to stare at the black man in a Volvo. Garrett smiled and waved. The man went back to shoveling.

"Not sure I want to. I should have an attorney by now and be suing the shit out of the city for firing me over a justified shooting," Garrett said.

"And why aren't you?"

Garrett focused on the scenery, tried to put it into words. The fields sliding past his gaze were fallow farms and empty woods now, choked with weeds. As a kid, this place been uncharted lands to be explored, huge dark forests filled with orcs, battlefields of World War Two with machine gun bullets zipping past the barbed wire.

"I thought I was coming back to a different place. Something I remembered as pure and simple. All neighborly country folk who seemed to have Mayberry RFD problems when my old man was Chief."

"People are people, man, no matter where they live. You get more than two of 'em together and somebody will start talking about chopping the third one out," LaSalle said.

"I guess the fantasy was I'd find a time capsule of a place where that wasn't true. And what the fuck do I find instead?" Garrett said.

LaSalle chuckled. "Normal people."

"I hate normal people."

"Then what are you gonna do?"

"Hadn't really thought about it yet. I'm good at that. Not thinking about things. I can stare at a wall like you wouldn't believe."

"I appreciate you giving me valuable time you normally devote to not thinking."

"This," Garrett said. "This I've been thinking about. I've got new questions for Nadine."

They had to wait until Nadine settled them in with coffee in yellowed, chipped China. She lit her cigarette and a cloud rose past the Savior on the wall. Her voice had a little extra rasp. She'd probably been smoking too much lately.

"Yeah, I knew the poor girl they called Florida. In a manner of speaking, anyway. She never did tell me her name. Thought I was some kind of social worker. If she was afraid of that, then she was probably under eighteen."

Nadine pointed her cigarette straight up and watched the tendril of smoke rise.

"But you can't think about that," she said. "You got to think of them like this smoke. Real enough while it's in front of you. If you try to take hold of it, why it just disappears."

One wrinkled hand wafted the column of smoke away.

"So you can never get involved, never care too much, just try to talk to them as best you can. Mostly they roll their eyes and get in the next truck. Sometimes I don't know why I go out there. And then I think of my Lord and Savior stopping those self-righteous bastards from stoning that prostitute and it gives me strength to go on."

They all looked up at the Savior. A little dust and some nicotine stains, but still a figure of hope.

"Do you remember if Florida had a regular guy? A road daddy, I think some of the girls call it," Garrett said.

"None I saw. I can usually spot those. They keep the girls close, or make them go right back to the cab. Can't have some guy offering money to screw up their deal, you know?"

"You've been ministering to the girls as long as I can remember, Nadine. Do you think you'd know a regular trucker who came by out there?" Garrett said.

"Oh sweetie, I've seen so many of those guys come through Burton's over the years. They've learned to avoid me, because I used to strike up a conversation and get to know personal things about them. Then when I saw them picking up a girl, I'd yell over, 'Hey, Bob, is your little girl in school today?'"

LaSalle and Garrett both chuckled.

"I know this is kind of hard to say, but if I gave you a list, do you think you'd remember any of the missing girls by name?" LaSalle said.

Nadine considered them, crammed together on the love seat. Garrett had seen the look before during countless interrogations. She wanted to tell them something.

"Come on," she said.

They followed her down a dim hallway with stacks of neatly bundled newspapers lining one side. Garrett saw 1966 on one front page. LaSalle had to angle his body to get past most of it.

She led them into a room dominated by a rollup desk that probably weighed at least a ton. On the desk sat a bright red laptop. Nadine plopped into a leather chair and fired up the computer. In a few seconds, they saw a folder filled with little thumbnails of young women.

"What's all this?" LaSalle said.

"Sometimes they'll let me take a picture. I used to use a Polaroid, but I got a digital camera off Amazon a couple years back."

"I thought you didn't keep track of them. Smoke disappearing," Garrett said.

"You wanna be a smartass, or you wanna see some

pictures?"

Nadine clicked and a slideshow started. Various pictures of girls out at Burton's, or at the rest stop. The hair colors changed, the clothes and background changed with the seasons, but all of them had the same tightness around the eyes, fear, borderline despair no one that young should know.

"I have first names on some, full names on others. Hard to know if they told me the truth, so who knows if you'll match any," Nadine said.

"Do you remember any girls just up and disappearing, anything unusual about the way someone left?" Garrett said.

"Maybe one a few years back who I thought might be on the verge of going home. I always offer to buy them a one-way Greyhound ticket, and I've bought exactly three in over thirty years. This girl never turned up to go through with it. But you can't be sure. She could just be flat on her back somewhere outside Omaha, still feeding the drug monkey, or those daddy issues, or whatever made her do it."

"Any more like her recently?" LaSalle said.

"Not anyone I knew well. There is one the other girls were talking about, though." Nadine stopped the slideshow and scrolled through some photos in the latest folder.

"There she is. Taylor, she said her name was." Nadine enlarged the photo and Garrett saw a heartbreakingly young girl in a puffy blue Gore Tex coat. Damn thing made her look like a bright blue teddy bear.

"One of the girls told me Taylor skipped out on paying her back for a night in the motel. Seemed unusual. She was well-liked by the other girls. Genuine and scared, not like a con artist out to take people for something, so they're worried about her."

"How long ago?" Garrett said.

"Hard to tell. First time somebody noticed she wasn't around seemed like maybe four or five days back."

"Ma'am, could I take a screenshot of that photo?" LaSalle said.

"Don't be silly. I'll email it to you."

10

The forlorn picture lay on the desk between Garrett and Trooper Clancy Parker. It wasn't much to look at. The image of a girl in a puffy blue jacket with the name "Taylor" scrawled across the top in Garrett's chicken scratch.

"I don't really know what to do with this, Garrett. I can't file a Missing Person because Nadine overheard a couple of hookers griping about a friend who skipped town," Clancy said.

"Just put out a Suspicious Circs bulletin with a description of the truck she was last seen in. Who knows, maybe one of your guys pulled over a trucker yesterday and saw her in the cab. Problem solved," Garrett said.

"What problem?" Clancy scanned the State Police briefing room. His shift had just gone out, so the place was empty. "I'm gonna tell you something, because you been a friend since grade school. People are talking. Saying you quit LAPD because you had shell-shock, or whatever, and they never should have hired you to be the Chief."

"And that has what to do with this missing girl?" Garrett said.

"That's just it. Nobody says she's missing. Except you. And maybe that New York P.I. character. What's his name?"

"LaSalle," Garrett said.

"Yeah, him. For some reason, you're fixated on helping the guy with his case. I understand wanting to help, but now you're grasping at shit that isn't there. These girls come and go all the time. We have no way of knowing whether or not one of them is really, truly missing."

"No, we don't, do we?" Garrett said. He stared at the wanted posters on the wall behind Clancy's head, something stirring in the back of his brain. "No one really wants them. No one looks very hard."

"You know better than that, Garrett. We can't do a sweep search for every Missing Person report we get. Hell, it'd be a full time business all by itself," Clancy said.

"If you were a smart guy, it would be easy to count on that. If you take people on the margins, nobody gripes too much," Garrett said.

"Take people? Are you listening to yourself? First you tell me a bible-thumping busybody heard about a girl skipping town and you figure it's a Missing report, and now we're suddenly talking about kidnapping?" Clancy said.

"If somebody is taking girls out there, we wouldn't be talking about just kidnapping. But you're right. Let's stick to the basics. How about a Suspicious Circs bulletin?"

Clancy leaned across the table and spoke slowly, as if he'd thus far been using vocabulary too complicated for Garrett. "There are no suspicious circumstances involved in a hooker skipping town. I'm not putting my career on the line because we used to get drunk together in high school."

"I understand," Garrett said. He wanted to grab Clancy by his jug ears and slam his forehead into the desk.

Instead, he shook his hand and left. He felt the looks from the other Troopers when he drove out of the State Police barracks parking lot.

***

Runoff from the melting snow banks beside the highway made the little creek behind the rest stop burble pleasantly. LaSalle took off his jacket and sat on a rock about three feet from the water. So much for him and Garrett splitting up and conquering the world. He hoped Garrett had better luck with his buddy in the State Police.

LaSalle had struck out with the flier, with only one trucker saying Britney looked somewhat familiar. He even tried the picture of the girl Nadine had called "Taylor." One guy had seen her in the truck stop, but never talked to her. A big nothing.

So what the hell was he doing in the woods, then? He should've been on his way back to the motel. Something... something called to him about this place.

The girl the State Troopers called "Florida" had been murdered at this rest stop. LaSalle couldn't shake the sick feeling there was a bloody tendril in all this connecting Florida to Britney. The locals assumed the killer was a trucker and left it at that since Florida was a transient prostitute. Any more investigating would have to be done by him. And Garrett, of course. LaSalle felt a twinge of guilt about involving the former Chief. The dude had enough problems, and he seemed like a good man. He'd be sorely disappointed when he finally found out what LaSalle was really here to do.

LaSalle donned his jacket again and made his way through an evergreen thicket, until the rest stop was off to his right about fifty yards. He could see a few cars and two eighteen-wheelers, a young couple at a cement picnic table, and a trucker hitching up his pants as he left the bathroom. Between the distance and the light scrub brush in the tree line, they couldn't see LaSalle watching them.

This would make a really good ambush spot. And he should know.

He made his living by tracking people down. He was very good at it. Of course, most of the time when he found them they went missing all over again. The investigative principle was still the same, though. He had an innate talent for finding people from the tiny clues they left behind in their travels, not all of them physical. It frustrated him that he hadn't been able to get closer to Britney in all this time. It also saddened him, because he knew the biggest reason people always slipped up, always left a way for him to find them.

They were alive.

When you're alive, you need food, drink, and some form of human company sooner or later. These things make you interact with the checkout girl at the grocery store, your neighbors down the street, the mailman. Someone has always seen you, because you're alive.

It's when you're dead that you drop off the radar.

LaSalle forced those thoughts away and started through the trees again, meaning to loop around back to his car. Instead, he ran across a game trail partially covered with a light dusting of snow. From his background in the city, some might be surprised he even knew what a game trail was. He'd been on more than one trip to track some cat hiding out in the boonies, so he had become a somewhat decent woodsman out of necessity.

He followed the trail until it dipped away from the highway and angled down a slope. At the bottom of the slope lay the snowy open field LaSalle saw the last time he was here. Even though the slope wasn't terrible, if a man got interrupted mid-murder and ran this way in the dark, he'd have a hell of a time. Unless he knew the area very, very well.

The woods got thicker before they opened into the field. As good a place as any to hide a body. LaSalle had hidden bodies in places like this before. And if he found someone who had in fact hurt Britney Santini, he'd need to hide another one.

He headed back to the rest stop rather than go down the slope, unwilling to risk it in three hundred dollar shoes designed to clip-clop down city sidewalks.

LaSalle observed how the rest stop appeared through the trees when someone came from the woods. The game trail kept him hidden until he was within fifty feet of the brick bathrooms. He stood there, perfectly still, dappled in sunlight and shadow like he wore the camouflage of the gods. The light hit the trail from the side, casting shadows across the ground and his eye picked out a straight shadow not made by the natural world.

He knelt and saw a depression in the earth, a couple of inches across, made by something straight. The mark ran into the snow and disappeared.

LaSalle brushed snow away from the line, all around the trail. He discovered the line had a twin a couple of feet away. Two straight lines together. Skis? Nah, skis weren't this skinny.

He reversed course and now that he was looking for them, he found the tracks leading past the rest stop parking lot, out toward the road. Faint, hard to really tell how old. They stopped about three feet away from a giant snow bank created when the plows cleared the highway.

Mostly dirty snow, the bank was surrounded by

various footprints. LaSalle spotted two small, dingy snowmen where people at the rest stop obviously let their kids blow off some steam before getting back on the highway.

Near the spot where the tracks ended, the snow bank had a U-shaped chunk taken out of it. Odd. Could someone have been dragged from the parking lot, through the bank, and onto whatever left those tracks?

Again, he stood still and looked around. His process worked best if he didn't let his brain get in the way. The new snow had melted enough for something beneath it to catch the sunlight and glimmer.

LaSalle bent down and picked it up. A charm bracelet of some kind, with only four charms. Silver teddy bear, cheap red plastic heart, Eiffel Tower, and the letter T.

He looked at the picture Garrett printed out. Nadine had captured the girl in a waist-up candid. Closer to a mug shot than an Annie Liebovitz portrait, but you could see the girl's hands. Hard to tell what, if anything, was around her wrist. He'd have to pull it up on the computer and zoom in.

He searched the immediate area for another hour, but found nothing else. He decided he'd come back in some decent hiking shoes, maybe with Garrett. And maybe not. He didn't want Garrett there if he found something definite.

LaSalle wasn't being paid to send anyone to prison.

***

The gravel of Smiley's driveway crunched and popped under the Mustang's fat tires. After being shut down at the State Police barracks, Garrett felt like talking to a friendly face. With Tracy teaching, he figured he might as well show the newest picture to Smiley.

He shut off the rumbling car and got out to stretch his back. The Carmichael place still looked good. Little two-bedroom farmhouse with a tidy yard and a well-kept barn out back. Even at his age, Smiley kept the place tight as a drum. Before Garrett could mount the front step, the barn door swung open. Smiley came hustling out with a manic grin plastered on his face.

"Hey, Garrett. I thought I heard your monster of a car out here."

Garrett went to meet him and shook hands. "Sorry about just dropping in. I've been helping LaSalle with his Missing Person case and I wanted to run another picture by you. I called the County Dispatcher, but they said you took the day off."

"Yup. Misty had somethin' come up, and she needs me to look after Angela. And don't apologize, you're not botherin' me one bit. Anything I can do to help."

The barn door stood open a bit, showing Garrett a wedge of clean wood floor and a scythe hanging on one wall. Smiley stepped between him and the open door.

"Did you say you had a picture?"

"Yeah, hang on." Garrett took the picture of Taylor out of his coat and handed it over.

Smiley's eyes roved over the girl's face and body. "She doesn't look familiar, but then I don't get a very good look at most of them. Can I keep this one and show it around, too?"

"Sorry." Garrett took the picture back. "This is my only copy right now. I'll make another one and get it to you."

"Sounds good. How are you and Tracy gettin' on?" Smiley said.

"What? We're not— I mean, I've known her a long time."

"I know, I know. But I hear things from time to time. I think you two would make a great couple," Smiley said.

"Oh. I don't know, Smiley."

"Not today. Or maybe even tomorrow. It takes a heart as long as it takes to heal. Tracy seems like a good person to be around while you're healin'," Smiley said.

"She is that." Garrett looked around for anything else to talk about. "The place sure looks nice. You really kept her up."

"I guess I can't help it. It's the way my daddy raised me."

Garrett took in the front of the barn. Weathered and beaten, but it got a new coat of paint every five years. The raspy growl of a busted muffler interrupted. They watched Misty's tired pickup drive up the gravel road and pull in behind the Mustang. A little blonde dynamo in a pink snowsuit leaped out and ran over to hug Smiley.

"Hey, Smiley," Angela said. She turned and waved to Garrett. "Hey, Chief Evans."

"Uh," Garrett said.

By now Misty had caught up and she gave Garrett an embarrassed look. "Angie, sweetheart..."

"Best darn police chief this sorry town ever had." Smiley clapped Garrett on the shoulder. He winked at Angela. "Wanna hear a story about him when he was your age?"

"Sure," Angela said.

"When Garrett wasn't much older than you, his daddy and I took him on his first fishin' trip in a boat. The water got a little rough on the lake and Garrett made yeck over the side."

Misty and Angela both said, "Eeeww."

Smiley and Garrett laughed.

"Before ya know it," Smiley said, "them fish decided somebody put out a buffet for 'em. They all swam up and we caught our limit in no time flat."

Angela made a face. "I wouldn't want to eat those fish."

"Me, neither," Garrett said. He turned to Misty. "You working tonight? Good to see you getting some more hours. They told me you'd been cut back to weekends."

"Oh." Uncomfortable pause. Hand to face gesture. Garrett knew she was about to lie to him. "Yeah, they squeeze me in when they can."

Misty touched Angela's red nose. "I should get this little booger factory out of the cold."

"Ew again," Angela said.

Smiley laughed and dug out his house key. He handed it to Angela and said, "The fire should be about perfect by now."

"Race you!" Angela took off for the front door. Misty gave them an apologetic shrug and sprinted after her. "Angela Wisteria Heideman, you get back here!"

Garrett shook hands with Smiley and locked eyes with him. "The way I remember the story, we didn't catch any fish, and the old man called me a fucking idiot for puking in the water and scaring them away."

"Hmm. Maybe I'm just getting' too old to remember things right," Smiley said.

"Maybe. You know what I remember? On the way home, when we stopped for gas and Dad went inside to piss, you told me not worry about it, that you got airsick in the Army and threw up all over the inside of a helicopter."

"Ah, I was just tellin' stories."

"Uh huh. Maybe one designed to make a boy feel a little better?"

Smiley put a hand on Garrett's shoulder and pinned him with those blue eyes. "Your father was a good man. We all got our faults, the places where we fall down. He loved you a lot, and he was proud of you. Boy, you shoulda heard him brag on you when you got assigned to that robbery team."

An emotional surge he wasn't prepared for washed through Garrett. He blinked back tears and choked out a goodbye to Smiley. He saw him in the Mustang's rearview, still smiling and waving. If the world had a few more like Smiley, it might just be a better place.

11

Angela lay on a blanket in front of the roaring fire. She'd reached the age where she took her time and colored in the lines to make a pretty picture. It looked like some kind of gnome with a curly-cue on top of his head. She'd colored his eyes bright blue.

Smiley peeked in on her from the kitchen. The fire glowed off her burnished gold hair—

Ma's hands shake as they hand over a wad of bills to Papa. Her lips are bright red, her eyelids blue. Tarted up, Gramma Gigi would say. The fire roars hot and bright, snapping and snarling, dazzling Smiley's eyes as he peeks from the kitchen.

You know what to do, Papa says.

But I gave you the money. You— You wanted— Now!

Ma kneels, hands behind her head, on the hardwood floor in front of the snapping and snarling fire. Papa's belt hisses against his loops as he draws it like a sword. Smiley turns away before the first lash strikes her skin.

When Papa accuses her of sucking cocks for money, Smiley hides under his bed—

But he doesn't hide anymore. No, sir.

Smiley released a shuddering breath and strode

into the living room. Angela grinned and showed him her picture. "Look, Smiley."

"That is the prettiest... uh, little fella I have ever seen."

"His name is Phred with a P-H. He's part of the Gogo Monkeys."

"You know what, I think I got a Gogo Monkey right here in my house."

Angela giggled and capered about like a monkey, accompanied by some kind of spider monkey screech. Not that Smiley ever heard a spider monkey screech. But it had to be close.

He laughed and laughed until her pajama bottoms came loose and fell down around her ankles. He spun around immediately, his back to her. He heard her giggle while she got them back up.

"You can turn around," she said.

When he did, his smile had fled. "Angie, honey, come here for a second."

He led her to the couch. "Now, I want you to know I would never ask you to do this, and if anybody else ever does, why you run and tell the police like we talked about, okay?"

"What is it?" Angela said, her eyes wide.

"I thought I saw somethin' on the back of your leg, love. I'd like to look again, but that means you have to take your pants down. If you don't want to, you don't have to."

She did look nervous. "I'm not supposed to talk about it."

Normally, he would never deceive her, never do anything but shoot straight with this kid. This time he played on the simple value system of a child.

"Who's known you longer, me or Bradley?"

"You."

"Who does your momma trust to take care of you, even if Bradley's home?"

"You."

"Okay, then. You and me are friends. That means I would never tell your secrets."

"Okay," Angela said.

She turned, hesitant, but undid her drawstring. She slid her pants down and his heart broke. "Put 'em up again, sweetie. I'm sorry. We won't tell anybody you showed me."

Angela faced him again and reached out to touch his cheek.

"Why are you crying, Smiley?"

"What happened?" Smiley said. Control. He had to keep control here.

"I got a whoopin'. I'm not supposed to go in the old barn out back anymore."

"Why not?"

"Because Bradley's got a art project going out there. It's like a bunch of glass bowls and stuff. I'm not allowed to say anything, because he doesn't want people to steal his idea. I don't know what kind of art it is, though," Angela said.

"Me neither," Smiley said. He had a sneaking suspicion the only art Bradley Wentz ever created was the patterns he made in his diapers.

Smiley waited until Angela fell asleep.

He paced the floor before he went out, the guilt gnawing at him, pushing him into a panicky, tight feeling in his chest. He'd never, ever done anything to Angela. Tonight he gave her something to make sure she slept soundly and now he felt a tiny bit of slime had worked its way into their relationship. Before Bradley came along, this never would have happened. Misty was a good mother, but she was weak. She'd chosen a con man and drug dealer over the bruises on her daughter's legs.

He went to the barn and fired up his snowmobile. He wouldn't have the sled behind him tonight, so he'd be light on the snow. Through years of trial and error, he'd engineered his own extended muffler system to quiet his little hunting machine. He didn't need performance exhaust. He needed stealth.

He took Papa's best filet knife with him. The mean blade, the cutter of fingers, unforgiving of any mistakes.

It didn't take long to get to the Heideman place as the crow flies. He made sure to approach down a narrow draw running between his property and theirs, further masking his engine's sound. Even though his bones bitched him good for coming out into this cold, he stopped and walked the last quarter mile.

The house stood dark, black windows on the front seeming to follow him like the eyes of a watchdog. The house knew the Hunter was in the woods. The person in the barn didn't.

Smiley crept up slow and quiet, careful to avoid narrow blades of light shining through the warped planks of Heideman's barn. Damn shame. The grandfather had been one hell of a farmer and a fair carpenter. He would've shat his overalls to see this barn now.

A sharp chemical smell burned his nose, made his eyes water. He forced himself to peer through the crack in the door.

Bradley stood in front of a large beaker bubbling away over a burner like they used to have in Science class. His head bobbed up and down in time to some crashing metal shit blaring from speakers buzzing like they'd blown ages ago.

Smiley took in the modest meth lab. In his mind, in stark relief, he saw himself stride right in, cut Bradley's throat, watch his heart splash the walls with bright jets of red, like his girls sometimes did. Then he'd set fire to the place.

His gaze found a table in the corner and his eyes welled up for the second time that night. *Papa would've called him soft for crying.*

Misty sat there, bundled up in her dad's hunting jacket, weighing and packaging little clear baggies of white powder. Smiley stood there watching until his knee joints took command of the whole operation. They told him a story about a night of pain ahead as he stiff-legged his way back to the snowmobile.

By the time he got back to his own barn and put the machine away, every step induced a groan. This would be the last year he could take a girl during the winter. He couldn't handle sitting in the cold anymore, waiting, like a patient trapdoor spider, night after night. He stopped on the front porch, knees throbbing, and looked back toward the barn, his special room. The drive to fill the room was a different kind of ache, and no pill he took so far had stopped it.

He went inside to wash down some painkillers with two fingers of Jack and sit in front of the fire until his knees would let him sleep.

***

Garrett dozed in front of the television, Kimmel barely halfway through his monologue. He stuck to beer, and had eight dead soldiers lined up on the coffee table. On a dishtowel, of course. Even now, he couldn't bring himself to commit the heresy of glass on the bare table. His dad may have paid the bills, but all shiny surfaces in this house belonged to Mom. He woke himself with a snort and stared at his empty beer bottles with bleary eyes. He tried to figure out how the bottles made a knocking noise on the table.

About the third time, his sloshing brain said, *Someone's at the door.*

Shirley Rankin, the dispatch supervisor, stood on his front step. She ran a critical eye over his disheveled clothes and the stubble on his face. He felt like his mother had caught him drinking. He noticed her hair was a mess and she wore a simple housecoat over sweats. She'd left her place in a hurry. She got straight to it, as Shirley always did.

"Garrett, I want you to know I don't hold you responsible for Tom's death."

"Thank you, Shirley, but you didn't have to come over at this hour to—"

She stopped him by holding up an honest-to-goodness brown paper grocery bag. Those were practically as illegal as moonshine these days. For reasons known only to him, Lamar Evans used to keep his working case files in paper bags instead of file folders. Dad's blocky print marked the front of the bag— *Ortega, Danielle.*

"What is this, Shirley?" Garrett really wanted to be sober right now.

"It's something your daddy left behind. Some of his personal things are in there, one of his cigars, a tee shirt, and a personal file he was working on. Nothing in here belongs to the department," Shirley said.

"But how did you— I'm so sorry, please come in."

"No, I better not. It took me half the night to

109

work up the nerve to drive over here."

"Were you and Dad..."

"Only after your mother passed. I'm not that sort of woman. We kept it quiet, as quiet as you can in a small town. You know, he couldn't have people think he gave me preference at work and all that," Shirley said.

"Right, of course. That sounds like him."

"I'm sorry I kept it so long. He had it all bundled up to take to work with him the next morning. He was just going to run down to May's and pick us up some dinner..." Her chin quivered and her face folded in around her frown.

"I know, Shirley. I know."

She leaned against him, and he held her and weathered her sobs. He still had the paper bag in one hand and he could smell the wet cardboard odor of it. Once she got herself composed, Shirley let go, looking embarrassed. She covered it by waving at the paper bag.

"When I heard you and that fella from New York were looking for a missing girl, I knew I had to give this file to you. It's something he worked on in his spare time. He took a Missing Person report about ten years back. One of the truck stop girls had taken a room in the motel with her friend, and the friend claimed she just up and vanished into thin air. Really stuck with him. Nothing ever came of it, but he took to watching that TV show about people who disappear. I'd see him check the bulletins every morning when he came in. If he saw one, he'd jot it down. To tell you the truth, I didn't think it was healthy."

"I don't get it. Why would a Missing Person report stick with him so bad?" Garrett said.

"I asked him. He said he could never really put it into words. He said her friend *believed* she disappeared, you know? He looked into her eyes and knew she was telling him the truth."

"Truth about what, she didn't come back? I've heard of girls skipping out on bills and leaving the other girls stuck."

"There's a copy of the report in the bag. I've read it, of course. She said her friend left with a trucker she had partied with before, headed for the rest stop. He wanted her to stay the night. When she didn't come back the next morning, the friend called in," Shirley said.

"Did Dad find the trucker?"

"He put out a BOLO and a trooper got the guy, right at the state line. The driver said they argued over her wanting more money to stay the night and she got out, said she was walking back to the truck stop. The last he saw of her, she was walking down the blacktop into the dark. Like so many have before her," Shirley said.

"Did they do a polygraph, all that?"

"For what?"

"To corroborate the guy's story," Garrett said.

"You've been in this business since you were a youngster. How much effort do you think they put into corroborating a john's story about a hooker who stiffed her friend for half the motel room? These girls come and go like the wind," Shirley said.

"Smoke," Garrett said.

"Whichever you like."

"He never talked to me about any of this," Garrett said.

"You two never talked about much of anything. I think he always regretted that." She gave him an impulsive kiss on the cheek. "I loved your father very much, Garrett."

"Yeah. Lots of folks did," he said.

After she drove away, Garrett carried the bag

inside and emptied its contents onto the kitchen table. The cigar and tee shirt combined to give him memories of being young, hugging a furry-chested laughing giant clad in a white tee shirt and uniform pants, the sweetness of cigar tobacco mixed with Aqua Velva.

When Mom died, the laughing giant shuttered up and never came out again.

More of Dad's blocky print, this time on the lines of a Xeroxed police report. Ortega, Danielle. Five-four, black over brown. Nineteen. A single photo. Candid, snapped in a hotel room somewhere. Garrett thought he recognized the orange walls from the La Quinta over in Wheeling. Odd, though. She wasn't posing like she would for a friend. Her hair tousled on a pillow, she gazed at the camera the way a woman looks at a lover in the morning.

A paperclip attached the report to the front of a large manila envelope, the kind secured by a little white string running around two posts. Garrett unwound it and let the contents slide out. A folded map, a list of female names with dates beside them starting in the year 1984, and one old Polaroid photo.

The yellowing Polaroid had the halo of a fading memory that would probably be gone in another year or so. Garrett turned it all around, trying to puzzle out what it was. A picture of the ground with an impression of two straight lines diagonally across the frame.

He flipped the picture over and saw his father's handwriting again. *Travois?*

Garrett shrugged and unfolded the map. His dad had pretty much done the same thing LaSalle did, but without a computer. He had little X's instead of dots, but there were two dozen marks on the map, with six on the rest stop up on 45. Not as comprehensive as LaSalle's list, but arriving at the same conclusion.

Lines in blue ink partitioned off the land mapped below the highway, dividing it up into some dozen or so family farms. All the family names appeared in his father's scrawl. He saw Heideman circled with *Jeremy?* written next to it.

Jeremy Heideman, Misty's uncle, started stealing tractors at fourteen. He got into heavier things, like heroin, by the time he hit eighteen, and was later accused of having sex with a thirteen-year-old girl at a crack house in Georgia.

There were lines drawn on the map in blue ink, looked like possible routes from the Heideman farm up to the woods at the rear of the rest stop. Not a bad theory, maybe. But Jeremy had been in prison for five years now on a cocaine trafficking bit. He wouldn't have had anything to do with LaSalle's girl, or this latest one, Taylor. If that was really her name.

Garrett listened to his mother's old clock tick in the living room. The map of missing girls lay on the same table where he'd gagged on runny egg yolks the first time he tried "over easy" like Dad always had. The old man laughed and laughed, Mom's eyes crinkled at the corners with her easy smile, and she was ready with a plate of scrambled because she knew.

He'd always seen his father as a stoic cop who bore everything with a steely-eyed mountain man resolve. To know the job drove the old man to a certain level of obsession could have been something they shared, something to talk about. Could have been.

Garrett looked at the faded Polaroid again. Travois?

12

The bull circled the matador, hooves scraping the earth raw, blood and mucus dripping from the black muzzle. His regal head drooped low, his *morrillo*, the massive neck mound, already weakened by the spear of the picador. Blood pattered onto the warm dirt from the wounds where the gaily-decorated *banderillas* hung from his flesh.

Smiley's shining eyes drank in the last part, the preparation for the killing thrust, the *estocada*. The dance of the cape, the edge of danger, the matador allowing death to brush his body as it passes. The Hunter toys with the girls this way, even pulls a red cloth over their pitiful faces when he's feeling merciful. Which is rare.

Smiley's one real indulgence, the massive big-screen TV bolted to the living room wall made the bloody bullfights feel so immediate, so hot and coppery when the blood ran. The Internet wasn't good for much, in Smiley's opinion, but he had found these bullfighting DVD's on a site hawking bloodsport videos. People fighting, animals fighting, and in the case of the bullfights, human against beast. Not unlike the internal battle waged inside Smiley every day.

A sexual release paled in comparison to the twitching pleasure inside Smiley when the matador slid his shining blade into the hump of muscles on the beast's neck. The crowd roared and Smiley bared his teeth as the bull collapsed in the ring.

After they dragged the bull from the ring, Smiley retrieved his own sword from the kitchen. About two feet long, thin and sharp. He'd forged it himself from a billet of stainless steel and sharpened it with loving care.

His practice dummy knelt the way he liked them to be when he chose to perform the final strike down past the clavicle. The subclavian stab, they called it in the Army.

He had to use his practice pieces sparingly. He could only sew up punctures so often before the skins started to degrade. This skin was stretched over a cloth under-form packed with buckwheat hulls. It gave him the best tactile sensation when the blade punched through the tanned hide.

The Hunter stood tall and proud over her, like the matador. He whirled a bolt of red silk, just brushing her face with it. The faces never looked the same once he pulled them off the skull, but her hair moved like the green limbs of a willow in the breeze.

He rose up on his toes, ignoring the crackling from his ankles and came down on her with a thrust he knew as well as his own heartbeat. The blade pierced the perfect spot and punched into the body until his fist met the cold skin over her collarbone. Or where her collarbone would've been.

Smiley backed away, his breathing ragged and short, not just from exertion. It had actually been quite a while since he dealt the final blow in this particular way.

Maybe he'd put Bradley Wentz in this position

115

before he opened his no-good heart.

***

LaSalle sipped his coffee and watched the snow whipping past his window. The temperature dropped again last night and a thick white blanket had erased the world outside. He knew the tracks in the dirt behind the rest stop would be gone, but he didn't need them.

He took the time to finish his coffee. Not nasty truck stop shit. He brought his own French press and electric boiler with him when he traveled. In LaSalle's world, man's ability to make a decent cup of coffee is what separated him from the animals.

He fired up his laptop and tried to zoom in on the picture of Taylor one more time. No use. Nadine's camera hadn't been set on the highest resolution, so every time he tried to blow up the area on the girl's wrist the image became so pixelated he couldn't see shit.

Something shiny there. No way to tell if it was a charm bracelet. He doubted even Garrett would consider it good evidence.

His cell phone bleated and he snatched it up. "LaSalle."

A man's voice with a bit of Maine drawl to it. "Yeah, uh... I pulled into Burton's here in Artemis and I saw a flier."

LaSalle sat up and grabbed a pen.

"Can I have your name, sir?"

"Look, I didn't do anything, I just saw this girl, okay?"

"Absolutely. I am not a law enforcement officer, sir. I'm a private investigator trying to find a lost girl," LaSalle said.

"Okay... It's Boyd Cummings."

"Mr. Cummings, would it be okay if I drove out to Burton's and met with you?"

"Just you, no cops, right?"

"Yes, sir. Believe me, I prefer it that way."

LaSalle had trouble keeping his foot out of the Volvo's carburetor on the way out there. The only thing holding him in check was the new snow dusting all the roads, making it a wheel-gripping drive, even with traction control. His mother would have surely thanked the Good Lord when he pulled into the truck stop's gravel lot in one piece.

Boyd Cummings looked pretty much like he sounded on the phone. Craggy New England face under a broad-billed cap, maybe fifty years old. LaSalle could imagine him leaning on a split-rail fence saying "A-yup" to something his neighbor said.

After a quick handshake, they went inside the truck stop's diner to escape the bitter chill. Once they settled into a booth in back, Cummings took LaSalle's flier from his pocket.

"This was around a year back, but yeah, I definitely remember her. Great girl when she was happy, but when she wasn't..."

"Britney was known to have an attitude from time to time," LaSalle said.

The trucker snorted. "Attitude? She threatened to jump out of the darn cab because I didn't want to stop for ice cream. Ice cream!"

To LaSalle that was no surprise. He even knew her favorite flavor. He pushed it out of his mind for now. "So how did you part company?"

Cummings looked embarrassed. "I'm not an asshole. If I pick up a girl out here, I treat her right, ya know? We ate and drove up to the rest stop because the lot was too full to sleep here."

"Were there other trucks at the rest stop?"

"There was a car, somebody taking a nap, probably. But that was it."

"You remember what the car looked like?" LaSalle said.

"No, I'm sorry. Just a dark colored car, that's all I remember. Anyway, we got in an argument up there. She wanted to go back to the truck stop because she forgot to buy...well, more rubbers. I told her I wasn't turning my damn rig around and going back for that. She started in on me, about how I was just an asshole like any other trucker and she could find those guys dime a dozen out here. I told her, fine, go ahead, get the hell outta my truck then."

"Did she?"

"Yeah. Middle of the night, too," Cummings said. Then he added, "But it was summer, see? I knew she'd be okay, not like now."

"Of course. What happened then?" LaSalle said.

"I was pissed off, so I figured I'd just get outta here. Drive a few more hours up the line and sleep at the next truck stop I came to. But...I started feeling guilty. I turned around about three exits west of here and came back. By the time I got back, she was gone. I drove down, looking for her along the way, didn't see her. Didn't see her at Burton's, either. Hell, I just figured she'd already picked herself up another john."

"Was the car still there?"

"Yeah, but I didn't check inside or anything. You know...there was something a little weird," Cummings said.

"About the car?"

"No. When I first went back to the rest stop, and didn't see her around, I checked the bathrooms. As I was getting back into my truck, I heard a small engine. Like a snowmobile running all out, but real quiet like. Must have been far away, I guess."

"You're sure?" LaSalle said.

"I'm from Maine, buddy. I know a snow machine when I hear one. But it was like one in the morning, you know? And whoever it was had it flat out, sounded like it. Got quieter, so it must have been going away from the rest stop."

LaSalle thought of his impromptu hike through the woods. "Let me ask you something, since you're the expert. How do people move something large if they're on a snowmobile?"

"Easy. Just buy yourself a sled, or make one."

"Is it hard to move a sled without it being attached to the machine?"

"Not if it's snowy. Hell, not even if it's warm and the load is light," Cummings said.

LaSalle gazed at the snow falling outside, disengaging from the here and now, from conscious thought. Trucks leaving the pumps put temporary tracks through the whiteness, down to the cold gray concrete. Soon enough, white flurries blew into the tracks, at first leaving a ghost of them, then making them disappear completely. In his mind's eye, LaSalle wove through the trees, white snow crunching under his feet, breathing hard because he's pulling a load, the sled behind him leaving behind those straight tracks, flurries coming in like conspirators and making his path invisible again.

Except where the snow was too thin. There he left his marks in the dirt.

"I got a schedule I'm supposed to be on. I'm really

sorry." The Yankee was yammering about something. Oh yeah, they were just talking, weren't they?

"Of course. I understand completely. Thank you so much for your honesty. It really helped," LaSalle said.

"I hope so. I feel bad she's missing. I hope you find her soon."

LaSalle offered him a sad smile as they shook hands.

***

This time he wore better shoes. LaSalle followed the slope down from the rest stop, along the game trail, through the heavily wooded area below the highway. Rabbit tracks marred the fresh snow, but nothing else. Odd thing about rabbit tracks, their front feet make the mark behind, with their longer back feet hitting the snow ahead. If you didn't know what you were looking at, you'd be hard pressed to know if the animal was coming or going.

At first, LaSalle had to push through brush and tree branches arched over the trail. Then it opened up in an almost unnatural way. Like it was groomed.

He went slow, examining everything around him. Bushes seemed a bit too rounded on the side facing the trail, not wild enough. Small trees with branches angled up instead of arcing over the trail. Something weird about one of the trees made LaSalle stop and give it a closer look. He ran a finger over one branch and found a manmade bump on the bark. *Rusted wire* buried in the wood where the branch turned away from the trail. Someone had directed this branch as carefully as a bonsai master forms his miniature creations.

Now he saw the hand of a man everywhere. All

the signs were old. More rusted wire, deadfalls obviously hacked apart with an axe and moved off the trail years ago, and right there, at the bottom of the slope, on the edge of the open snowy field, a lump of bramble and tree branches almost natural in the way they fell together. Almost.

Like the rabbit tracks, the hunting blind was deceiving. It looked like a wild growth covered with snow. Once LaSalle pushed aside some bramble, he saw a nice space inside. He didn't know jack-shit about snowmobiles, but they couldn't be much bigger than a jet ski, and you could definitely park a jet ski in there.

He stepped in, the low ceiling making him stoop, and examined the workmanship. Dim light and a bit of snow filtered through the carefully woven branches tied into tall bushes, creating a narrow natural parking garage of sorts.

LaSalle's white breath hung in the still air like he'd expelled a ghost. Strange tracks marked the ground in the hide. He knew snowmobiles were driven by something like tank treads. Wide tracks with vertical lines across them. These particular ones had what looked like three open crescent shapes grouped together in the middle of the tracks. Hard to tell how old, but some looked fairly fresh. He pushed aside the bramble again and went outside.

The empty white fields seemed to mock him. *Now what?*

A hunting blind with snowmobile tracks inside. A bracelet found by the highway. Track marks on a game trail. A jumble of nothings he wanted to force into something concrete.

It frustrated him to be this close again, speaking to people who'd laid eyes on Britney, but unable to jump the gap like he had so many times before. Make the next connection leading him to the person he really wanted.

Snowflakes blew into his face and he stood like a little kid, tongue out, face turned to the sky as the white bits drifted down, looping on the wind. It reminded him of a snowy night in Jersey, when he had a man on his knees behind a construction site on New Year's Eve. He'd had no mercy then, and he wouldn't now, if he found a killer of women.

13

"Whit would lose his mind if he knew I was talking to you."

Lyle Hampton sat in his police unit behind the abandoned Buster Brown shoe store on the south side of town. Garrett sat in the Mustang, parked door to door with Lyle.

"Wouldn't be a tragedy. Whit doesn't have much mind to lose," Garrett said.

Lyle couldn't help but grin. He looked at the report again, and then at the map Garrett gave him. "Your dad took the report about a year before I started here, looks like. I never heard him talk about it. Kinda weird he spent this much time on it and nobody knew. No offense."

"No, no, of course not. It was weird, trust me. I never knew him to get this involved in anything. You remember any Missing cases before I got here? I don't remember us taking even one report last year," Garrett said.

"Nope. I've never taken one. Wouldn't even know how to put it in the system." Lyle snapped his fingers. "You know, when I was on training, me and Whit took a courtesy report for the Staties one morning. Roads were icy up over the pass and they had a triple fatal that morning. They couldn't spare anyone to go to the rest stop and the victim needed to get on the road or he'd miss his delivery time."

"What kinda report?" Garrett said.

"Theft. Some trucker did a deal with one of the girls up there and he claims when he woke up in the morning, she was gone and so was his wallet."

"Not unusual, unfortunately. Sad thing is, I don't really blame the girls. The chumps who pick them up should know better. Any ID on the girl?" Garrett said.

"That's just it. He knew exactly which girl. She kinda stood out, had a whacky hairdo, all dyed green. We went down there, but no one had seen her since the night before. That was as far as we took it. Whit figured she caught another ride out of the rest stop and moved on up the road. Makes sense to me, if she did steal a wallet."

"Yeah, it does." Garrett hated to admit it. He wanted to find Whit at fault somehow.

"Same summer, we all went fishing on Big Top Lake. Me, Whit, your dad, and Smiley," Lyle said. "Whit joked about how the green-haired girl could be in the lake underneath us right then and we'd never know. Man, how Smiley laughed, fit to be tied. He said how he'd seen so many come and go through that place, we had no idea. He bet us five bucks that girl was somewhere warm and safe and having the time of her life."

"Most likely," Garrett said.

Shirley's voice sounded tinny over Lyle's radio.

"Dispatch to Car Two."

"Hey, you got a promotion," Garrett said.

Embarrassed, Lyle keyed the mike. "Go for Two."

"Chief Abercrombie needs you to do that Code Forty-Two."

Garrett looked confused. "Got a new radio code?"

"Sort of. Whit wants me to swing by May's and pick up his chicken fried steak." Lyle put his unit in gear, but kept his foot on the brake. "For the record, Garrett, I think you were a great chief. I never had the kind of training you brought here. You made me a better cop."

He drove off before Garrett could respond.

Memories of his father, Shirley crying on his shoulder, he felt nothing. But something like that had him blinking back tears? Holy shit, he was a wreck.

Garrett took a circuitous route back to his place. He drove past muted forms smothered by snow. Trees he climbed as a kid, dead lawns he earned money cutting during the summers, coming home with the green blood of the grass splashed across his shins, shoes, and socks.

His dad always made him save the money and put it in a college fund account, allowing Garrett only a few dollars to spend on "junk" like cassette tapes of his favorite band, or Valentine candy for whatever girl he was sweet on at the time. Garrett paid a total of three thousand and forty-five dollars into his pipe dream called a college fund. Would three grand even cover books?

Why the hell would the old man get so involved in this missing girl? Sure, he'd always been kind to the girls out there. He never treated them like garbage the way a lot of cops would. Hell, he even put a couple up in the motel on the harshest winter nights, which led to the only big fight he'd ever heard his mom and dad have.

Surely, he wasn't— no. Garrett couldn't even imagine the old man taking one of these girls somewhere and— no. Ugh.

The first week here, he had crammed all the boxes of personal stuff from Dad's office in the garage and hadn't bothered to open them. Hadn't wanted to. Until now.

It took eight beers and three hours of digging to make it through old file cabinets, a trunk kept on plywood across the garage beams, and the moldering manila envelopes in his dad's gun safe. He found two things for all his troubles.

A black and white photo of Lamar Evans and Jebediah "Smiley" Carmichael in Army uniforms. They were both corporals and they had their arms around two young Filipina women.

Scratched in white letters along the bottom: Subic Bay

Garrett spied the second thing while sitting on the floor of his father's bedroom, finishing off the eighth beer. (He still slept in the guest room, though he lived here a year now.)

The gun safe stood empty and cold, all the guns and personal paperwork scattered on the bed behind Garrett. He tipped his beer up and when he brought it back down, his gaze landed on the floor of the safe. One corner looked odd. Too high.

After some judicious prying with his dad's old skinning knife, he got the false floor lifted enough to look beneath. He found an old packet of photographs from one of those places you mailed your film to for developing back in Dad's day.

Garrett sat at the kitchen table, drinking sweet black coffee for some time before he could bring himself to open the packet. Lamar Evans had always been a man who kept private business to himself. As affable as he'd been when Mom was alive, he'd never been one to chatter about things going on in his life. It broke Mom's heart to a certain degree when Garrett inherited his father's solitary nature. It took three years, but Michelle worked some of it out of him. Mom would have loved her.

"Shut up," Garrett said in the empty kitchen. He picked up the packet. Whatever it was, the old man was dead and buried and no one could change it.

The top picture rocked Garrett back in his chair. He finished his coffee with just that picture lying in front of him. She stared up at him the whole time. Ortega, Danielle.

In front of the orange walls from the La Quinta over in Wheeling. Her hair tousled on a pillow, she gazed at the camera the way a woman looks at a lover in the morning. Not sure he wanted to go on, but knowing he absolutely had to, Garrett spread the other pictures on the table, one by one.

Ortega, Danielle in a red blouse, black skirt, and boots. Just the skirt and bra, less and less clothing from there. Different underwear, the light slanting through the gap in the curtain at a sharper angle. Even with the implications of the pictures of the girl, the hotel room, all of it, still the last picture was the one he had the most trouble looking at.

Clearly caught unaware by the girl, his dad had his pants halfway up. He'd seen her getting ready to take the picture, and he was laughing so hard his eyes were crinkled shut.

Laughing.

That night, Garrett dreamed of his first partner. The guy who giggled uncontrollably every time he saw a dead body.

***

Tracy Ellsworth, the girl Garrett was sweet on, walked out of church in a blue dress almost exactly like Ma's church dress. Her red hair flowed behind her and

127

Smiley caught the smell of perfume and paint thinner as she passed.

He wondered what she would sound like if he poured paint thinner in her eyes.

A little girl's giggles pulled him away from the Hunter's thoughts.

Angela ran around and around in circles, laughing and grabbing Misty's hand every time she came by. Not the best behavior at church, but service had ended and everyone was filing out, so most of the stodgy old folks smiled at the rambunctious girl.

Pastor Dean shook Smiley's hand and checked out his shiny boots. "You have got to teach me your secret, Smiley. Those boots looked that good when I was in Junior High."

"It takes patience and work, Pastor. Just like the good Lord done with his disciples, and hopefully he's doin' with me," Smiley said. He gave Pastor Dean the really big smile he practiced in the mirror every day.

Nadine Pearson came over in her best black dress. Nadine had always been a bit of a busybody in Smiley's book. He wondered what it would feel like to strangle her.

"Howdy, boys," she said. "Pastor Dean, what a wonderful sermon. I do love when you preach on our Savior's forgiving heart."

Even a humble preacher loves praise now and then. Pastor Dean grinned. "I'm glad you liked it, Nadine. I hope it spoke to your heart like it spoke to mine when I wrote it."

Someone called Pastor Dean to meet a visiting friend, leaving Smiley and Nadine alone.

"Haven't seen you out at Burton's lately," Nadine said.

"I've been watchin' Angela quite a bit." *It makes my*

palms itch to go there.

"I almost got one of the girls to go to church with me today, but she backed out when some of the others made fun of her," Nadine said.

Thank the good Lord. "Too bad. Woulda done her some good," Smiley said.

He wouldn't have been able to stand the smell of her if she stood next to Nadine right now. Worse and worse. His ability to control the urges, his desire to act on them. It seemed like it ran through his head non-stop these days. Was he getting too old to control the Hunter?

Angela crashed the conversation in her usual style.

"Hey, Smiley! Watch this." She did her best cartwheel, showing off her gymnastic skills, and a set of mermaid princess panties.

"Angela Wisteria Heideman!" Misty hustled over and grabbed Angela by the arm. "We're still in church, young lady."

"Aw, she's just lettin' off some steam," Smiley said. "Folks around here don't get to see real-live Oh-lympic gymnasts too often." But he knew Misty was more worried about people seeing the fading yellow bruise.

Angela giggled and hugged Smiley. "I love you, Smiley."

Misty and Nadine exchanged the "aww" look.

Smiley smiled for Angela. Not a mirror smile, or a church smile, or a grocery store smile, but something real that leapt out of a place he usually kept well guarded. He tousled her already gymnastically ruined hairdo. "Old Smiley loves you too, sweetie. Don't you ever forget it."

He saw Misty waiting. She wanted to ask, but not on top of something like that. He did the asking for her. "You need me to watch Nadia Comeneci here tonight?"

"That would be great, Smiley. Eunice is giving me

a full shift tonight and we really need the money," Misty said.

"What do you say, Angela? You up for ice cream sundaes for dinner?" Smiley said.

"Yes!"

Misty arched an eyebrow. "You two are trouble when you're together."

Smiley held up his hands. "Okay, okay. We'll wait till after dinner."

"What are you all having?" Nadine said.

"Dinosaur steaks and onions," Angela said.

"Wow. I never heard of those," Nadine said.

Liver and onions, Smiley mouthed over Angela's head.

"Oh," Nadine said. "I do love those dinosaur steaks."

"Angela, did you know to this day, Nadine makes the best cherry pies in West Virginia?" Smiley said.

"Really?" Angela said.

"It's a certified fact. Writ in the Federal lawbooks," Smiley said.

Nadine looked embarrassed. "I'm not certain one ribbon at a County Fair amounts to all that. Now, if you folks don't mind, I need to go to the parking lot and smoke a 'dinosaur bone'."

Nadine strode away, digging a pack of cigarettes from her purse.

"A what?" Angela said.

"Nevermind," Smiley and Misty said over one another. They shared a grin and Smiley felt warm. Not as warm as blood made him feel, but that would follow.

***

The Mustang rumbled in Garrett's earmuffs, low and steady like a thunderstorm on the other side of the mountain. He sat inside with the heater running, snowflakes dancing across the windshield, dying on the warm glass before they got halfway.

He'd parked right on the concrete behind the firing line, since no one else was stupid enough to be here on a day like this. Although the Artemis Pistol Club owned the range, it sat on county property. He wouldn't accidentally run into anyone from town out here, which suited Garrett right down to his bones.

Last night had been a bad one. The dream started with sweat rolling down the trench of his spine beneath his Kevlar. A hundred degrees in early May, standing in front of a rundown craftsman house with peeling green paint and wet mossy stains four inches up the wall from the damp flower beds. A couple arguing inside from the sounds of it. Confusion. He couldn't place the neighborhood. He never worked this beat.

A black and white rolled up and Michelle and her partner got out, and Garrett knew where he was. He'd never been there, but he knew. The house. Where it happened.

He stood there mute, his dream-mouth full of cotton, unable to speak to her.

"Hey," she said, waggling her fingers as she went past with her partner. The partner checked his cell phone for a message and Garrett tried to scream at him to pay attention.

It quickly became a dream he knew was a dream and he screamed at himself to wake up, his words jumbled and tumbled and then the door opened and the gun barrel came out, obscenely long and impossibly big and the boom made Garrett's heart stop.

He opened the Mustang's door and stepped into the frigid air in one fluid motion. He flexed his knees and moved forward in a semi-crouch toward a row of bowling pins on a sawhorse. The Colt came up smooth and natural, he'd always had a knack for the gun.

Bang-bang. Bang-bang. Bang-bang. He shot on the move, double-tapping as he went, bowling pins splintering, flying under the impact of the 230 grain .45 caliber bullets.

The slide locked back, Garrett ejected the empty mag, slapped a new one in, and thumbed the slide release. He stood still, hot gun in his hand, snowflakes hitting his face like little molecules of winter. The first time his old man let him shoot a semi-auto had been at this very range. He bought Garrett a little Marlin .22 rifle and Smiley carved these amazing wooden rabbit silhouettes for Garrett to shoot.

They all came to the range and Garrett abided by every safety protocol, drank in every lesson. Soon, he was knocking down wooden rabbits one after the other. Then he got a crazy notion in his head and cut loose with all the ammo he had left in the Marlin's magazine in a *pow-pow-pow-pow* rapid-fire string, tearing the hell out of one of Smiley's bunnies.

His dad snatched the hot rifle from him and called him an idiot who didn't deserve to have a gun. Smiley had, of course, given them a big smile full of dentures and crinkled lines around his eyes. "Aw, he's just havin' a little fun, Lamar. No harm done, don't ya think?"

Garrett's dad relented, but still sulked on the tailgate of the pickup, drinking beer while Smiley reset the rabbit targets until they were wood chips and Garrett was out of ammo.

Dad certainly hadn't sulked that night at the La

Quinta. Or maybe it had been many nights. No way of knowing, really. He laughed it up and had a good time with his hooker. Who knows, maybe he fantasized about saving her. And what, live happily ever after in Artemis, West Virginia with a twenty-year-old prostitute? Go to bake sales with *Ortega, Danielle* and buy pies from the Methodist Ladies Club and invite them over to have tea with his runaway hooker?

The front sight on the Colt found the sawhorse's crossbeam and Garrett thundered away with the entire magazine, rapid-fire, shattering wood and old memories. While he waited for his heartbeat to stop rushing in his eardrums, he picked up his spent brass and put it in a fifty-five gallon drum the club kept under a lean-to behind the firing line.

By the time he cleaned up his mess, he had to admit two things. One: He hated the cold much more than he ever admitted. Two: For all his faults, his old man didn't do things like compile a list and put a map together because his heart went pitter-patter. Something about the girl's disappearance sparked a fire in Lamar Evans, the old country cop.

And as much as Garrett hated to admit it, that alone made it worth looking into.

***

Nadine put on her WVU sweat pants, glad to be out of that damnable girdle, and sat in her plush leather office chair, the one indulgence she'd allowed herself in an otherwise parsimonious life.

She sipped a glass of wine and scrolled through the pictures on her laptop. *Like smoke*, she'd said. Bravado for Garrett Evans and the big black fella. In truth, it wrung her heart to see them pass through, those lost girls, those wandering souls. They made her alternately happy and sad she never married and bore children of her own. If she'd had a daughter, she'd be a grown woman now, having long ago gotten past the age of the girls in these photos.

Nadine hoped she would have given her a fighting chance to not wind up in the back of some smelly truck cab. Or worse.

She landed back on the photo of the girl she told Garrett about. Taylor. Where was she right now? Halfway to California? Florida? New York? Alone and scared. Nadine closed her laptop. She'd be up all night if she let her brain spin and spin like this. She had to do something with her hands, something to keep her occupied.

She stalked the old house in her slippers and sweats, the floorboards creaking out memories of tiptoeing down this very hall when she was twelve and it was midnight and there was cold fried chicken in the ice box—

That was it. Cooking.

She hadn't baked in ages. She'd surprise Smiley and Angela with a cherry pie tonight.

In the kitchen, she ripped a scrap off an old brown grocery bag and found the nub of a pencil in her junk drawer. The first thing on her shopping list was lard. Because that's how you make a proper pie crust, thank you.

Thoughts of missing girls fled, and soon Nadine was puttering toward Delroy's Grocery in her dinged up Lincoln. She made a mental note to brush the top with butter right at the end.

This was going to be a great pie.

14

Smiley had the *mean* blade tucked under his coat, which made the metal warm as flesh.

A new blanket of sparkling white covered the fields and trees around the Heideman farm. Snowflakes swirled in the breeze like fluttering white moths, occasionally highlighted by the industrial lights bleeding through the cracks in the barn doors.

Smiley left his snowmobile where the fence broke years ago and no man worth a damn had been around to fix it. He hefted his air rifle and went to the barn on foot, sticking to the thinnest spots in the snow. Easier for the new snow to fill in shallow prints than deep ones.

His hips muttered their distaste for the cold, the complaints registering as sharp zings up and down his legs. Age had crept up on him like a sly pickpocket and made off with the Hunter's feeling of invincibility. Smiley gritted his teeth against the joint pain. Getting the bulge on an idiot like Bradley Wentz took brains, not brawn.

He wore a small backpack to hold the other things he would need after he used the air rifle. He was disappointed he wouldn't have time to punish Bradley properly. To hold the child-beating son of a bitch accountable for his transgressions.

Angela's welts and bruises flashed in his mind like violent neon, all deep purple and ugly yellow-green. He felt like a shit-heel because he'd given her another sedative in her chocolate milk. The blame didn't really lie with him, though.

He wasn't Smiley tonight. Tonight he was the Hunter. The patient one who waited and watched and thought and planned. Unfortunately, the Hunter would have to leave this particular trophy behind. Then again, Bradley wasn't much of a trophy, alive or dead.

Smiley peered through a gap in the weathered boards of the barn doors. Bradley stood in front of a digital scale, weighing out some kind of red powder. He had a large flask over an open flame, with fluid boiling inside the thick glass.

A gentle test of the door. Loose, with a two-by-four across the latches on the inside. Smiley breathed in the sharp cold air and prepared himself for action.

Calmly, he stuck the rifle barrel through the gap between the doors and raised the two-by-four until it cleared the latches. He anticipated the clatter of the board when it dropped and was already using the rifle to swing the door open.

Bradley heard the commotion and spun around.

Smiley fired the air rifle and the dart hit the younger man in the gut.

"Ow! Smiley, what the hell?" Bradley appeared to suddenly realize what the dart was. He yanked it out and threw it across the barn. He hurled an empty chemical flask by the neck like one of those German potato-masher grenades. It shattered against the wall by Smiley's head and pelted his face with glass shards. Bradley followed the beaker, charging across the barn. Smiley dropped the empty air rifle and reached for the knife in his jacket.

136

Too slow. Bradley covered the distance and hit Smiley with a looping right to the face, knocking him flat on his back. Bradley was on him instantly, choking Smiley with his own bunched collar. "You old asshole, are you crazy? I will fucking beat you to death for that shit." Bradley emphasized his words by shaking Smiley on the syllables.

In the next second the ketamine started to hit Bradley. The dart stayed in long enough to give him a good dose. He shook his head like a dog with a burr in its ear.

Still rattled by Bradley's punch and fighting for air, Smiley's right hand closed on the haft of the filet knife under his jacket. His thumb popped the snap holding the knife in the sheath.

Drooping a little, Bradley hit Smiley with a weakened slap. "You hear me, old man? You are fucking done here. You stay away from my family, you piece of—"

Bradley cut off short when the blade punched through his raggedy sweatshirt. Slim, sharp, and long, the steel entered under the sternum and angled upward.

Smiley had practiced this stroke as often as he practiced the subclavian stab. A variation on the bullfighter's *estocada*. The final stroke straight into the bull's heart.

Sitting astride Smiley, Bradley stared down at him, confused. "S-Smiley? Did you..."

His methamphetamine-accelerated heart thrashed against the mean blade, slicing itself to pieces, spewing blood into the chest cavity instead of pumping it to the oxygen-deprived brain. Bradley slumped to the side and Smiley pushed him the rest of the way off.

It took ten minutes of sitting with his head

between his knees gulping deep breaths before Smiley could stand again. Wouldn't that have made for a great headline? *Over-the-Hill Killer Arrested While Catching Breath.*

He glared at Bradley, inches from his dead eyes. He felt cheated of his clean kill. In his younger days, he would've handled Bradley like a heavyweight taking a bantam.

Now he had blood all over him and Bradley had a hole in his heart. Smiley had to hope for a combination of luck and small town justice. Hopefully, the fire would burn the body too badly for an autopsy. If not, he counted on folks around here not looking too hard into the death of a meth cook whose lab went up.

Smiley spent a couple of panicked minutes searching the barn floor, but he found the dart Bradley pulled out of his belly. It rolled under a table holding scales and boxes of plastic baggies. He tucked the dart away in his coat and got down to the grim details.

He dragged Bradley by the ankles and left him near a table full of beakers and jugs of chemicals. Good thing Bradley was a skin-and-bones tweaker. If he'd been built like a linebacker, Smiley would have had to leave him where he died.

Once he had Bradley in position, things went quickly. A little grain alcohol from his backpack would start things off. Smiley was no chemist, but even if they did run tests on what was left, he didn't think this would seem out of place in a meth lab. He splashed the alcohol over a table filled with chemicals and a plastic tub marked *Red Phosphorous.*

One last look around. He had his knife back in the sheath, his pack on his back, the dart in his pocket. Nothing left behind.

He used a cheap plastic lighter to start the show

and got the hell out of the barn. His old knees complained about how quickly he moved back to his snow machine, but the flames had already climbed into the loft, making the barn look like a macabre lighthouse sending a warning no ship would ever see.

Running the snowmobile flat out, he made it halfway back to his place before the barn went up completely. His whole body trembled with the need to see, so stopped to look back. Seen from the frigid field, the blaze created a warm glow, friendly and inviting. Up close it would roar and snap like a giant's hearth, the fire destroying flesh, wood... and evidence.

Smiley got back on the throttle and raced home through the woods.

Leaving the hot engine running, he pushed the barn doors open in a frenzy, the coppery smell driving him mad. He turned back to his snow machine and stopped moving like the puppeteer cut his strings. His mind slipped into neutral and so many years of his life in this town spun out like fragile webs with tonight's decision at the center.

Nadine Pearson stood in his driveway holding a cherry pie. And Bradley Wentz's blood marked the front of his clothes like a flashing advertisement for *Murder*.

***

The sunrise had warmed the day enough for her to work in oils. Garrett watched Tracy paint until the sun climbed to a position that made the oak tree's shadow in the snowy clearing "too short to be interesting anymore."

He helped her pack the easel and the worn leather case housing her paints and brushes. The pink spots on her cheeks and the wisps of hair curled around her delicate ears distracted him. Her flushed skin reminded him of snowball fights when they were kids. It also made him think of her as a grown woman and the same flush across her neck and chest. Guilt fought with desire.

The silence was comfortable for them, and they started the walk back to her house without saying anything. He figured she was still thinking it all over.

He'd spilled his guts about his dad and the prostitute on the hike out— *wouldn't the old man be mortified*— and then stood and shivered while Tracy painted and thought on it.

They followed their own tracks all the way back to her place before she spoke. "So," she said. "Aside from the girl being a prostitute, let's ask what was wrong with your dad seeing her. Your mom passed years before, and he wasn't seeing anyone else I ever heard of."

"Did you know about him and Shirley?" Garrett said.

"Nope. I'll say this for your Pop; he had a poker face built to clean out Vegas. I saw him and Shirley around each other at church, and it was all Chief and Dispatch Supervisor, no sign of hanky or panky."

"And in your opinion, it was okay that my dad had some young chick in a cheap motel room?" Garrett said.

"First off, I believe the La Quinta qualifies as a hotel, and it's not that cheap. And second— Really? *Chick*?" Tracy said.

"Excuse me, Gloria Vanderbilt."

"Steinem."

"Whatever. We suspended the hooker bit to see what else might be wrong with it, but it's still there," Garrett said.

Tracy stopped outside her front door and looked into his eyes. "Okay, I'm going to ask you something and

I want you to answer yes or no. Just that. As quickly as you can, first thing that pops into your head. Got it?" Tracy said.

"Do your worst, Dr. Freud," Garrett said.

"Are you implying that I'm fascinated by penises?"

"Gross. Ask your question."

She took a deep breath. She actually looked nervous. "Is the fact your dad apparently cared so much about her the real thing that's upsetting you?"

Garrett waited too long. "No."

Tracy simply arched an eyebrow at him and went into the house. He followed, and when they were in the kitchen he took out the only picture he'd brought and threw it on the table. The picture the girl obviously took when his old man's guard was down.

"He's laughing," Garrett said.

"I see. Are you mad because he didn't show that side to you after you mom was gone?"

"Hell, I don't know. If I could just call the problem like that, I'd probably make millions on a self-help book," Garrett said.

"For the moment, why don't you concentrate on why you found all this to begin with? He was looking for her, and looking for patterns, right? You think he was onto something? Did he find something he didn't like?" Tracy said.

"The patterns are there. But it's all still a whole lot of conjecture right now," Garrett said.

"Maybe Whit would be willing to do some poking around out of respect for your dad's memory. You could leave out certain stuff."

"*Please*. Whit Abercrombie would be hard pressed to spit on me if I was on fire. And I probably gave him a reason to feel that way. Besides, he's knee deep in shit with the Bradley Wentz thing."

Garrett almost grinned at the thought of Whit Abercrombie heading an investigation like the one at the Heideman's farm. He kept a straight face by remembering the charred thing they found in the burned-out barn.

Tracy seemed to be reading his mind this morning. "Do you think Misty was involved in the lab? Honestly."

"I have a hard time believing she didn't at least know. Her mom, too, most likely. But that kind of money is hard to turn down. She's had her hours cut at work, shortcut looks good to her," Garrett said.

His pocket chirped and he pulled out his phone with an apologetic shrug. It was LaSalle.

***

She had a cherry pie in her hands and she was walking toward him. "Goodness, Smiley, I was getting worried. I knocked and knocked."

And her eyes opened wide.

"Oh my God, Smiley what happened? You got blood all over you."

Nadine sounded like she was at the bottom of a rain barrel, all hollow and echo-ey.

He stood there for what felt like a long winter's night, his breath hot on the air, snowflakes big as quarters flying between them, his brain going round and round with all the possible outcomes of the burning barn and Nadine seeing him like this.

None of them added up to anything good for him. The Hunter.

Which was unfortunate for Nadine.

The mean blade flashed out and she dropped the pie in the snow.

142

It went easy for her; he's a merciful matador.

Surprise. Her eyes were wide with it. Oh, how he shivered to stare into bottomless black pupils as their owner bled out her last seconds of life. But he couldn't really savor it. He had other work to do.

His insides warm with the memory, Smiley touched the tacky blood in the trunk of Nadine's Lincoln. Putting her in there to move her into the barn worked out perfect. There'd be blood in the trunk when they found the car later.

The screw-up at the Heideman barn with Bradley had turned into something useful. With his bloody shirt, Smiley wiped just a touch of Bradley's blood inside the trunk and a drop or two on the steering wheel. Nothing else. He'd read books about people getting caught because they left what the police called "an orgy of evidence" when they tried to throw people off.

Smiley's eyelids drooped and he felt more exhausted than he ever had. Even back in boot camp. He left Nadine in the side chamber down below for the time being. He'd have to figure out something else later. She didn't deserve to be in the trophy room with his prize beauties.

He'd already put his bloody clothes in his special room and showered while Angela slumbered on the couch. By the time Misty picked her up, the blonde terror was a little more subdued than usual, but none the worse for wear.

Smiley closed the Lincoln's trunk and dragged the tarp into place over the car. He left the barn to keep its tarp-covered secret and latched the door tight. He would call out sick and collapse onto his bed for a few hours. Then he'd deal with this mess.

He was halfway across the barnyard when he

heard Papa's voice.

Idiot!

He spun around, saw nothing but the dead water pump and the snow-covered hump of the well cover.

Worthless fuck-up!

"Shut up," Smiley said.

They'll find out. You screwed the pooch, boy.

"Shut up, shut up, shut up." Smiley stopped and smelled the bloody tip of his finger. The Hunter came to the front of his mind.

"I ain't afraid of you. And I ain't stupid."

He waited, but heard no reply aside from the wind blowing through the elders on the sunny side of the house.

"No, sir," Smiley said. "I ain't afraid of you."

His words were strong, but he felt weak inside. Wrung out. What would he do when his palsied hands couldn't work the dart gun, his legs couldn't pull the sled with its cargo down to the snowmobile?

The urges would most likely drive him insane then.

15

The tarnished silver charm bracelet dangled from Garrett's fingers. "I mean, I get the coincidence. Girl tells Nadine her name is Taylor; you find a bracelet with a T. But there have been a dozen girls up there in the last—"

"Now you're trying to talk me out of it? Even after the stuff from your Pops?" LaSalle said. He finished tying his hiking boots and locked his car. There were two big rigs at the far end of the rest stop, but LaSalle's Volvo was the only car in the lot.

"I'm asking the questions any cop would ask. Will ask." Garrett leaned against LaSalle's fender, twisting the bracelet this way and that so the charms rattled against each other. "So I guess we're not looking for a trucker who takes an occasional hooker. We might as well be honest about it."

"Seems that way," LaSalle said.

Garrett glanced at the trucks in the lot. "He'd have to have a route through here for years and years, which would narrow down the list of suspects. But he'd also kill the girls in his truck, you'd think. Even if he had a dump spot nobody could ever find. You and my dad both found tracks out here right after we think a girl went missing. If the tracks are really involved, why would a trucker go to all the trouble of hauling a sled or whatever around with him?"

"You know what that would mean," LaSalle said.

"Yeah. Somebody local. I don't like it, but I've thought about it," Garrett said.

"Any names?"

"You ask me about illegal liquor, I got two dozen names; ask me about weed, I got two hundred. Ask me about kidnapping or homicide suspects, I'd tell you to drive back to LA, because that doesn't happen here," Garrett said.

"Doesn't it?" LaSalle said.

"Show me your winter hideaway," Garrett said.

LaSalle led the way, stopping along the game trail where he found the parallel track marks. They made their way down through the frosty woods to the field's edge.

Garrett admired the workmanship of the blind. "Took some time. And some knowledge. Whoever wove these branches in did a beautiful job. I bet you can't even see this thing in the summer when the creeping vines come in." He looked at the strange crescent-shaped marks in the snow machine tracks LaSalle found.

"Yeah, that's called a Hacksaw Trail Track. They're made for high performance in backcountry areas," Garrett said.

LaSalle glanced back up at the rest stop, checked his watch. "Okay, figure you could move someone on a sled or travois, as your dad called it, in maybe twenty minutes. Hook up to your snowmobile down here. Then what?"

"Run to your spot," Garrett said. He scanned the open fields south toward more heavy woods. Another half mile beyond and they'd be off public land and back in the city limits. He took a deep breath through his nose, the

146

cold air burning on the way in—

And he's running down an alley in South Central at three a.m. in January and even in LA it's forty degrees and the guy he's chasing trips over a trashcan and his gun skitters across the concrete and Garrett screams at him not to touch it but he does anyway and—

Garrett blew a long column of white frost and noticed LaSalle studiously looking elsewhere. He wondered how long he'd been away.

Nevermind.

"If someone's killing these girls, then he has the world's best hiding place for bodies," Garrett said.

"Public land would be risky."

"Yeah. Hunters wind up stumbling over murder victims all the time. He could put them in a lake, but even if he only took three or four of the girls we have listed, that's a lot of bodies not to have one float somewhere," Garrett said.

He pointed at the heaviest woods to the south. "The other side of those woods would be Artemis city limits. There are a lot of farms along the border, so lots of private property."

"You know how it's split up?"

"Dad had some of it mapped out, but not all. If you go west after the woods, you'll hit the Barclays, Childers, the Heideman place, and then Smiley's. There's more public land on the other side, and then Burton's Truck Stop. We could go to City Hall and ask to see the property lines, but someone would probably call Whit on the sly."

"Yeah, so? You think if he doesn't hear your name again he might send you a Christmas card?" LaSalle said.

"Good point."

They marched single-file back up to the rest stop.

Treading in the tracks of LaSalle's size fifteens reminded Garrett of following his old man around the lake on a fishing trip, his little wader boots splunching into the deeper prints left by Dad's.

Why the hell was Dad so convinced the girl vanished instead of just leaving with another trucker? Was she supposed to stay here? Did he expect to see her again? Shit, was he in love with her?

LaSalle drove them to City Hall and Garrett actually got the printed property maps with no hassle whatsoever. He still saw Sue Ingles on the phone, whispering away while sneaking glances at Garrett and LaSalle.

On the way back to Garrett's, they drove by Nadine's house. Garrett saw a stooped old lady wearing a winter coat over a robe standing on Nadine's lawn, staring at the house.

"That's weird. Would you mind pulling over for a second?" Garrett said.

"Sure, what's up?" LaSalle pulled over in front of Nadine's.

"Gimme a minute here, maybe nothing."

Garrett got out and saw the old woman's face relax when she saw him. "Mrs. Shotwell, what on earth are you doing out here in this cold?"

She grabbed Garrett's arm with clawed fingers. "Chief, I'm worried about Nadine. I can't find her anywhere. I called her to go to Bingo down at the Elks this afternoon, but she didn't answer. We have each other's keys in case of emergency, so I walked across the street and let myself in, you know, in case she'd fallen or something."

"Of course," Garrett said.

"But she wasn't in there. It felt... cold and lonely in there."

Doesn't it always? Garrett thought.

"Did you check her garage for her car?"

"Oh." Mrs. Shotwell looked confused. "I guess I forgot about that. You don't suppose she went without me, do you?"

Garrett trekked through the snow to the side of Nadine's garage. The old detached style from another age, with windows on both sides. He peeked in a window and saw a Schwinn bicycle made just after World War II rusting away in there. Its flat tires looked like they'd taken root in the concrete.

But no crappy Lincoln. Only a big oil spot a few feet away from the front wall.

He came back to Mrs. Shotwell. "She's probably out at Burton's ministering to the girls. You know Nadine. I'm sure she'll be back soon."

Mrs. Shotwell didn't look to be buying today. "You come see what's in her kitchen and tell me something's not wrong."

Nadine's open front door suddenly filled Garrett with dread. Or he might have been on the edge of a panic attack. He needed to get his scrip refilled.

"Please, Chief."

"Technically, Mrs. Shotwell, I'm not the Chief anymore. You should probably call Shirley down in Dispatch."

"And what, have them send out that fool Whit Abercrombie?" She put a hand on his arm again. Thin skin, blue veins, and bones. Like Mom's hand in the hospital.

"There may be some folks around here who like Robert Lee's family more than the truth. But to my mind, you were the smartest darn Chief of Police we ever had. Your daddy included. No offense, but I taught him in

149

Sunday school, God rest his soul."

Garrett grinned. "I guess I could walk into the kitchen, if you came with me."

"Thank you." She shuffled off and Garrett gave LaSalle the "one second" sign before he followed her. The house was creepy enough when Nadine was in it, but empty, it felt like being in a haunted house at the carnival, waiting for someone to jump out at you. Four generations of Pearsons had taken a whack at building additions to the joint and sometimes hallways came to an abrupt end and you had to turn around and come back.

Unless you had a guide like Mrs. Shotwell. She stood to one side, her coat grasped shut in modesty, while Garrett looked around the spacious kitchen. He saw a pie in a strange looking tin atop the stove.

"What kind of pan is that?"

"It's called a Holzit pie tin, made for cooking berry pies. The little well around the edge catches anything that bubbles over. They don't make those anymore, you know. My granddaughter sold two of mine on the eBay for thirty-five dollars each. Can you imagine? I bought them for a dollar apiece."

Garrett gave her a guilty glance and ran his finger through the filling in the little trough. He tasted it. "We definitely have a cherry pie. What's wrong with that?"

Mrs. Shotwell looked at him like she regretted the thing she said about his intelligence. "Look at the can of lard there. It's brand new, and with that much missing there's no way she made just one pie."

"How do you know it's brand new?"

One bony finger tapped a torn piece of brown paper.

Lard. The first ingredient on a shopping list.

Written across the top of the list in a flowing

feminine hand and underlined twice: *Cherry Surprise.*

"That pie is ice cold. Nadine would not have left it out all night uncovered. And I don't see another pie in the refrigerator or anywhere else," Mrs. Shotwell said.

It dawned on Garrett. Maybe he could live up to her expectations after all. "She took a pie to someone. Last night."

***

Smiley took Nadine apart like a prize hog. He used his sharp, heavy knife at the joints, the hacksaw on the stubborn parts.

This he did in the side room. The special room wasn't for wrinkled old bags like Nadine. He carried the parts down a narrow passage lit with small electric bulbs powered by car batteries. Thick timbers supported the dirt walls and ceiling running under his barn. Over the years, his meticulous nature made him add sheetrock to all the walls to make it seem more homey.

He took a left and came to a pit with a trapdoor over it. He tossed Nadine's pieces in there with the last girl's feet and insides. He picked up the bag of lime beside the pit and shook in a goodly amount. The smell made him wrinkle his nose. It would get worse before it got better. He closed the trap door and made sure the rubber seal was tight all the way around.

The underground hide needed air shafts, and although they came up in hidden areas of the barn, the last thing he needed right now was for Misty and Angela to smell something weird coming from the barn.

He stood in the dim light and looked at the last intersection of his tunnel system. He decided he wouldn't go to them tonight. To punish himself for lousing up

Bradley's killing. If he hadn't been covered in blood, he wouldn't have had to kill Nadine.

The Hunter wanted to see his trophies, though. Deserved to see them.

Smiley went down the last short hall to his trophy room. Camouflage netting draped the sheetrock walls in there like ancient tapestries. He turned off the main lights and flipped a separate switch. Ten red bulbs in dangling fixtures bathed the trophy room in murder light.

The only personal thing Papa ever shared with him was his love of taxidermy. He taught Smiley, and even seemed proud of him for a while. Then for some reason he stopped buying the supplies and beat the living shit out of Smiley for asking about it.

Later, Smiley would understand. It was jealousy.

Papa knew the mechanics of taking care of a hide, or a bird's feathers. He knew how to create the body form to hold those hides. The thing he lacked was an artistic flair for it.

Papa couldn't capture the animal at its brightest, most brilliant state. That state of adrenalized flight before the hunter's shotgun booms, the wary stance of the Whitetail as it picks up the hunter's scent.

Smiley did have a flair for it. Practically a dadgummed artist at it. Everyone who ever asked him to mount an animal said as much. His trophies were vibrant and beautiful.

They all knelt with their backs to Smiley, their various wounds marking their identities to him better than their faces ever could. Some were missing hands, some feet.

Since building this room, he'd mounted seven he was satisfied with. Only the most beautiful made the cut. The last girl's skin was still in process, but she'd make number eight. Her body form was almost finished and it pissed him off that he'd have to deal with other things over the next few days instead of working on his latest piece.

He ran his fingers through the green hair of the one closest to him. He'd had thoughts of changing the color to something more pleasing, but he couldn't bring himself to alter the way she'd been the most lovely, when she was strapped into the antique dentist's chair.

He kept a straight-back chair from Ma's dining set against the front wall of the trophy room. He sat there now, like a king receiving his subjects. They still knelt with their backs to him, as it should be.

He turned out the lights and sat in the dark with his trophies. The Hunter was behind them and they couldn't see him, as always.

16

"I want to know what the hell you thought you were doing posing as a police officer and entering the home of a citizen of this town," Whit Abercrombie said. His cheeks had high red splotches and a dribble of juice from his dip stained the corner of his mouth.

Garrett considered Whit like he had a second head. "I made sure to remind Mrs. Shotwell I wasn't the Chief anymore. But more importantly...*that's* what you're taking away from this? I come to you with information about a series of missing girls and now you have someone in town missing, and all you can worry about is your damn job title."

They sat in Garrett's old office. His dad's old office. The disco-era furniture had vanished, which wasn't necessarily a bad thing. It had been replaced with some split-rail log cabin shit that made Garrett wonder if Whit had a coonskin cap in his desk drawer.

Whit leaned back in his chair and shook his head. "You have gone off the deep end, son. A series of missing girls? People go missing all the time, and over the years it'll add up to a lot of folks. And I don't believe you of all people can't understand a hooker leaving town without saying goodbye doesn't amount to some conspiracy to kidnap women."

"What about Nadine?"

"I'm sure she'll turn up. She's been known to drive clear into the next county, handing out bibles and offerin' up Greyhound tickets all the way," Whit said. "You were in there. See any signs of foul play?"

"No."

"Door was locked when Mrs. Shotwell came over?" Whit said.

"Yes."

"I know I'm not a big city LAPD cop, but an old lady tellin' me a pie is cold doesn't add up to a mystery," Whit said. He worked his dip to the other side of his lip. He was one of those guys who'd been dipping so long he swallowed the juice with no problem.

Garrett's stomach lurched thinking about it. "I really wish you'd get off the 'big-city' thing, Whit. All I did was put a training program in place when I took over. I wasn't calling anyone stupid, I was trying to keep you guys alive out there."

"Worked out pretty good for ol' Tom Poston."

In Los Angeles, Garrett had gotten into Brazilian Jiu-Jitsu pretty heavy for a few years. He had a flash of catching Whit in an arm lock and popping his elbow. Instead, he stood to leave. "Okay, Whit. You stay here and keep your head in the sand. It's something you're good at."

Whit launched himself around the desk and got in Garrett's face.

"Let me tell you something, smartass. You and your darkie friend will stand the fuck down inside my city limits, you got that? You are not a police officer anymore, and I don't give a damn about his New York ID. You wanna talk to whores at the truck stop, you go right ahead.

But you keep your shit out of this town."

"Am I talking to the Chief of Police, or a grown man who just got in my face?" Garrett said. The words came out nice and even, without emotion. A bad sign Whit didn't read correctly.

"Oh, you're talkin' to a man in your face, son," Whit said.

"Good."

Garrett grabbed Whit by one sleeve and the lapel of his stupid Chief's uniform and shifted the heavier man's balance onto his left foot. Garrett spun him toward the desk and stepped on the toe of Whit's shoe at the same time. Whit landed on his ass and the wad of dip popped out of his mouth, winding up on his lap.

Garrett was standing over him too quick for any response.

"Don't ever threaten me, Whit. And this is the last time I'll tell you I don't need a badge or investigator's license to look for a missing girl."

"Get out of here, you son of a bitch. Right now." Whit got to his feet and Garrett stood there long enough to let him know. Then he walked out.

He picked up LaSalle in the lobby without a word. Garrett took big strides and shoved open the front doors. Once outside, he said, "Shit!"

"How'd it go?" LaSalle said. With that grin.

"Great," Garrett said. "We talked, we sprayed the walls with testosterone, I got us banned for life."

"Banned? From what?"

"Everything, I think."

***

Back at the motel, Garrett parted ways

with LaSalle. He had something personal he had to do and he wanted to go alone. LaSalle understood. Garrett stopped at the store and bought a card. He took out cash with his purchase. He sat in the Mustang with the heater cranked up while he signed the card, stuffed the money inside, and sealed the envelope.

He drove out to the Heideman place, not knowing what he'd say there.

Angela stayed inside, but he saw her pale face hovering behind the kitchen window like an interested ghost. Misty came out on the front porch to talk to him, which meant her mother was already drunk, maybe even passed out in the living room.

"I, uh, wanted to give you my condolences," Garrett said. He handed her the card. "You can open it later."

She felt the weight of it. "You don't have to do that, Chief— Uh, Mister Evans."

"Garrett, Misty. It's just Garrett. I'm not doing anything, okay? I get it. I've seen people struggle, and it's not always with money. At least with that, I can help a little."

Misty's face developed seam lines and sort of fell apart. She didn't even have the energy to sob, she just leaned against Garrett's chest and cried in silence. He put an awkward arm around her. She'd had a crush on him when she was in seventh grade and he was a mighty Senior. They swung apart for a decade or so, but neither broke the pull of Artemis, and like two breakaway meteors, they slammed together again over the charred hulk of a barn and a nasty death.

"Everybody thinks I'm trash," Misty said, her voice muffled against his coat.

"No. You made a bad choice in men. Nobody's

going to hold it against you."

Misty wiped her eyes and stared at the ruined barn. "They won't even tell me when they'll release his body."

"I might be able to find out for you. No promises, but it shouldn't be too hard. Why don't you go inside where it's warm and give me a few minutes?"

"Okay. Thank you so much. Garrett."

She went back inside and Garrett fired up the Mustang. He sat in his warm cave and dialed the number for the County Coroner. "Coroner's office." A detached female voice, hollow like she was in a tiled room.

"Uh, yes, this is Chief...Abercrombie over in Artemis. Do ya'll have any idea when the body from the barn fire will be released to his loved ones?"

"You mean the meth lab fire? It'll be a few more days, Chief. The autopsy hasn't been completed yet. I mean, we just got the blood tox report back this morning. I know it's hard for them, but they'll have to wait."

"Sure, sure. They understand the process. Like you say, it's a hard thing," Garrett said.

"I'll tell you, it's no wonder the dummy blew up his lab. These guys don't know when to separate partying from their work."

Garrett said, "I don't think I've ever seen a meth cook who could stay out of the product while they cook."

"Oh, sure. But this guy was partying hard, Special K."

"Special K?" Garrett said.

"Ketamine, but some users call it Special K," the woman said.

Garrett turned off the car and sat in silence.

"Yeah, yeah, I know what you mean. How much was in his system?"

"Enough to make him screw up his mixture, that's

for damn sure. Sorry, Chief, but I have a lot of paperwork to finish. We'll call you with the autopsy results."

"Thanks. Bye." Garrett disconnected. He got out and went back to Misty's door. Fresh tears were in her eyes when she answered.

"Sorry, but the coroner says it'll be a few more days. They still have to do an autopsy."

"Okay. Thanks for asking," Misty said.

"Sorry I couldn't do more. Can I ask you a personal question about Bradley? I don't want to, you know, make this any harder."

"No, it's okay."

"I know he did speed, obviously. But did he party with other stuff, heroin, coke, ketamine?"

"Keta-what? And no, he never did heroin or coke. Not that I know of."

Angela ran up behind Misty. "Hi, Chief Evans. See my new dolly? Her name is Anastasia and Aunt Carol got her for me, on account of something bad happened to Bradley and she wanted me to feel better."

"She didn't tell you that," Misty said.

"I know. But I'm smart," Angela said.

Misty and Garrett smiled at each other.

"Smarter than me, for sure," Garrett said.

"It's time for Anastasia's nap now, so she has to say goodnight," Angela said. She stood there, waiting...

"Oh. Goodnight, Anastasia," Misty said.

"Yeah, of course, goodnight," Garrett said.

Angela disappeared with her doll, leaving Misty and Garrett alone on the porch.

"She loves putting those dolls to bed. You should see the fancy little doll crib Smiley made for her," Misty said.

"He really loves that girl. He used to babysit you,

159

too, didn't he?" Garrett said.

"Yeah. I remember being scared the first time my mom dropped me off, but he turned out to be like a grandfather to me. He taught me how to tie my shoes, can you believe it?"

"I can. He taught me how to tie a fishing fly," Garrett said.

"He's really amazing. I told him he should open an online store or something. The little crib is made from young spruce branches he wove together in this beautiful pattern. He could sell those by the dozen."

Garrett tasted metal in the cold air. "Woven branches?"

"Yeah. You got a second? I'll show it to you."

***

Smiley pulled Nadine's car off a wide spot in the road. He'd only gone about a half mile behind the Heideman property line. He would have taken the car farther, but his knees were not in the mood for a longer walk back.

He got out and listened to the night. Probably looked like a damn fool standing out here wearing a shower cap and dishwashing gloves. But the Hunter doesn't care what the animal thinks about his camouflage. He only cares that it hides him.

He pocketed the rubber gloves and cap and put on his beanie and fleece-lined gloves. He started the long hike back home, leaving the car open to the elements. Like someone ditched it in a hurry. He knew enough about modern forensics to feel good about the amount of Bradley's blood in the car. The rest he would leave up to dumbass Whit Abercrombie. Even he could put together a puzzle if you showed him how all the pieces went together.

He cut across the back of the Heideman place. From this distance, the lights in the windows looked like fireflies had landed on frozen blades of grass. Knowing Angela wouldn't have to worry about that piece of shit laying a strap to her gave Smiley a glow in his stomach.

The temperature was dropping by the minute. Forecast said there would be new snow tonight, and most of tomorrow. By the time anyone found Nadine's car, it would be a little island of evidence in an otherwise pristine world.

***

Garrett stared at the blinking cursor in the search box.

He'd begged off dinner with LaSalle so he could stay home and think. Not only about LaSalle's case, but about a lot of things.

He had the old picture of his dad and Smiley on the kitchen table next to his laptop. Grinning like kings with their two hookers. Over the last couple of hours, he'd scavenged a dozen other pictures from albums in his dad's closet, as well as the family album his mother kept in a cabinet.

In one photo, Lamar Evans and Smiley Carmichael knelt next to an eight-point buck. Smiley's rifle lay across its antlers. Early '60s, both with crewcuts.

In the next, Tuffy Baylor, the old Chief of Police, pinned a badge to his dad's uniform as Smiley and Mom looked on. Smiley beamed the biggest damn smile in the world.

There were others, from their younger days, along

with Mom when they were in high school together. The one that stood out the most was from the '70s, given the sideburns his dad sported. His patrol car was cocked across a street diagonally, blocking traffic. A large black bear lay at his feet. Standing near the bear's head was Jebediah "Smiley" Carmichael. The bear had a silver dart in its hide and Smiley held an air rifle in his right hand.

Garrett tapped the laptop keys and "ketamine" appeared in the Google box.

He found numerous links to the dangers of using ketamine recreationally, including warning young girls that it can leave you completely vulnerable and unable to call for help.

Garrett had exactly zero ketamine busts in his police career. Not a big problem in LA, the Kingdom of Crack.

Party drugs weren't really what he was looking for. He didn't think someone gave Florida girl and Bradley a spiked drink at a party. He amended his search to "ketamine on animals."

He had plenty of links to choose from. He hit "images" and saw dozens of thumbnails of downed animals with various teams of humans around them. Some of the people held air rifles.

17

Mrs. Shotwell seemed surprised to see Garrett at her front door. He had a container of coffee and sweet rolls from May's Diner.

"Morning, Mrs. Shotwell. Would you mind if I talked to you for a few minutes?"

While she fussed about in the kitchen, making sure he understood it was *highly* unusual for a guest to bring all the makings for a social call, Garrett strolled around her living room.

At either end of a plastic-covered couch probably sealed when the Beatles were cool, she had two amazing reverse-painted glass lamps, each featuring a tulip field in a country she'd never visited. The antique pickers who came through small places like Artemis would fight each other gladiator style for these two pieces, probably made before even Mrs. Shotwell was born.

Pictures of Master Sergeant Raymond Shotwell held the place of honor on the mantle, his Air Force cap set at a rakish angle. He lived through Korea and Viet Nam, and died three years ago in his sleep about twenty steps away from where Garrett stood.

"Please, have a seat." Mrs. Shotwell came back in with the rolls on a proper tray and the coffee in cups.

Garrett added a splash of cream and some sugar to his. Mrs. Shotwell appeared haggard and her hand shook when she tried to use the cream. Garrett gently took it and helped her get the mix right.

"I don't know what to do with myself," she said. "I just know something terrible has become of Nadine. If they haven't found her by now."

"You don't know that. The State Troopers find drivers who've been stranded in their cars for days. She probably skidded off the road somewhere. They're out looking today, I know. I heard the chatter on my scanner," Garrett said.

"Only the good Lord knows where she is."

The good Lord and at least one other person, Garrett thought but didn't say.

"You came to ask me something?" She took a bite of sweet roll and nodded approval.

"Before my dad passed, he spent some time looking into the disappearances of a few girls. Girls who worked at the truck stop," Garrett said.

"You mean the whores," she said around the sweet roll.

Garrett's eyebrows must have twitched upward, giving him away.

"Oh, I don't mean to be an old bitty. I know Nadine likes to minister to them, but the plain truth is those women are whores who choose to sell themselves."

"I dealt with my share of them in California. Over time I found out most of them were scared and desperate, or hooked on some crap that controlled them in a way you'd have to see to believe," Garrett said.

"I suppose. I know your daddy also felt sorry for them. He didn't brook any trouble, but he didn't go out of his way to run 'em out of town, either."

"That's kind of what I wanted to ask you about. This is a little embarrassing. You were around here when guys like my dad and Smiley were young. Did they ever, you know, with the truck stop girls?"

Mrs. Shotwell surprised him by cackling so hard she nearly spit out her teeth.

"Your daddy and Smiley? Oh, my stars. Neither one of those boys could speak to a girl. Rachel Milner kissed your dad on the cheek when they were in my Sunday School class. He ran out the door so fast he banged his head on a corner and saw birdies for a week."

Garrett grinned, thinking of the self-confident giant as a shy little boy.

"Far as I know, neither of them dated anyone until your dad finally worked up the nerve to ask your momma to the Prom."

"They've been friends a long time, Dad and Smiley," Garrett said.

Mrs. Shotwell sipped her coffee. "May's Diner sure makes a good cup. Yup, your daddy and Smiley were always joined at the hip. I think it hurt Smiley's feelings some when old Tuffy Baylor chose your dad but not him."

"Smiley wanted to be a cop?" Garrett said.

"Oh, yes. As bad as your daddy wanted it, and then some. But you know, Tuffy could never let it pass that Smiley went into the Army to avoid some trouble."

"Seriously? Smiley Carmichael?" Garrett had never heard so much as a whisper about it.

Mrs. Shotwell side-eyed a praying Jesus on her wall. A twin to Nadine's, minus nicotine stains, and Garrett suspected they bought them at the same flea market. "I suppose the good Lord will forgive me. If it's the truth, it ain't gossip."

She leaned across the coffee table anyway, like she

was whispering across the back fence to her neighbor. "A young girl, I won't say her name, said she saw Smiley peeking in her window one night. He was about to turn eighteen and she was thirteen. And he, uh, well, I don't want to say. He was busy with himself."

"You're kidding me," Garrett said.

"No, sir. His pa fell out of the hayloft and broke his worthless neck earlier that year, and Smiley had been workin' like a madman to keep the note current on their place. Some say it was the strain of it all made him act that-a-way," Mrs. Shotwell said.

"What did Smiley do for work in those days?" Garrett said.

"Anything you could name. Build fences, carpentry, clean out animal pens. He even made a bit of money from mounting animals for some local hunters. Yes, sir. That Smiley was a hard worker. A hard worker."

Garrett knew sometimes in country logic, being a hard worker outweighed an awful lot of personal shortcomings.

"His mom passed when he was young, too. That had to be hard. And to lose her like that. I can't imagine my mom falling and cracking her head open right in front of me," Garrett said.

Mrs. Shotwell said, "It was probably a mercy compared to what he might have watched her go through." She seemed surprised she even said it. She stood and busied herself cleaning up.

"Wait, what does that mean?" Garrett said.

She stopped with her back to him. "Sometimes I get lonely for company and I talk too much. Old wounds are best left alone once they've scabbed over."

"Mrs. Shotwell, you've known me for a long time. Am I one to run around town talking?" Garrett said.

She whispered it so quiet he had to learn forward. "She had the syphilis."

"What? How did she—Was his old man running around with the truck stop girls back then? And they could cure it by that time, so she should've been okay," Garrett said.

"They couldn't go to the doctor. At least, that's the way they saw it," Mrs. Shotwell said.

"Why?"

"Not many as know this, but... Smiley's pa was strapped for cash in those days. It was public record they'd lose the place before long. And then, they started to pay down the overdue note. Slowly but surely, until they'd caught up," she said.

"How did they get the extra money? That wasn't even a working farm anymore."

She stayed quiet so long, he didn't think she was going to tell him. She even appeared to consult the Savior on the wall again.

"You can't repeat this, Garrett Evans."

"I wouldn't."

"It wasn't Smiley's pa at the truck stop. It was his ma. He had her selling her tail to pay down the note and it come back on both of 'em. She brought it home to him. By the time he finally decided his pride was gonna kill him and seen a doctor, she was dead, and that foul disease had eaten away his nose."

She shuffled into the kitchen and Garrett carried the tray in behind her. He wrapped the leftover rolls in foil and put them in her refrigerator over her protests. His phone rang and he started to let it go to voicemail, but when he saw the number, he picked it up.

"Shirley?"

Her voice was hushed. "I'm calling you on my

personal cell, so I can't talk long. Lyle just called in on the radio. He found Nadine's car on an access road out behind the Heideman place. Garrett...there's blood in the trunk."

***

Smiley rolled up on the gaggle of Artemis officers with what he hoped was an uncertain look on his face. He didn't really practice those in the mirror.

They stood at the rear of Nadine's car, looking in the open trunk. Whit Abercrombie, Lyle Hampton, and Dougie Armstead. In his stupid uniform, Whit looked like a Boy Scout who forgot all his knots. With the open snow-covered fields, the lines of barbed wire fence on both sides, and the lone car they surrounded, they looked to Smiley like one of Tracy's paintings. Except he had created this particular work of art.

Shutting down the County pickup, Smiley got out and approached Nadine's car.

"Howdy, Whit. Don't mean to intrude, but I couldn't help but hear on my scanner. Thought you might need a tracker to check the fields for ya," Smiley said.

"It's okay, Smiley. I'd sure appreciate the help. Boy, that's a nice shiner," Whit said.

"Yup. Fell down my front steps like a dad-gum five-year-old."

Whit turned back to the trunk. He looked a little green.

"It sounded bad on the radio. Is it Nadine?" Smiley said. The sorrowful face, that one he had practiced before. Living to his age in a small town, you had to expect to attend a certain number of funerals.

"It doesn't look good. Awful lot of blood in the trunk. Have a look," Whit said.

The youngest cop, Lyle something-or-other, looked at Whit like he just invited Smiley to kick him in the balls. Smiley ignored it and approached Nadine's trunk. The coppery smell of congealed blood made his fingertips tingle. It felt like seeing it all for the first time again, here in front of these idiots.

"Yes, sir. That's an awful lot of blood. Poor old Nadine," Smiley said.

And there were the red empty eyeglass frames. Smiley hated to leave those behind, but he wanted Whit's dumb ass to jump to all the right conclusions. Smiley straightened like something had just occurred to him. "You don't suppose... Nah, I'm sorry, you fellas do the police work. I don't mean to put my redneck opinions in there."

"What are you thinkin'?" Whit said.

"I loved Nadine dearly, but you know what a busybody she was. What if she run across whoever killed ol' Bradley and torched the Heideman's barn?"

"How did you know that?" Lyle said.

The more someone annoyed Smiley, the more he usually smiled at them. Given the circumstances, he gave Lyle his second-best sorrowful frown.

"Misty gave me the sad news. She told me they got the autopsy results last night. The Coroner says there's a hole in Bradley's heart?" Smiley said.

"Yup. It's a damn mess, the whole thing," Whit said.

"You ask me, a perfect heart shot sounds like a professional. Some drug enforcer, ya know? Maybe Bradley was sellin' his wares in the wrong person's market stall," Smiley said.

Whit paced toward the front of Nadine's car, thinking and nodding his head. Smiley saw the exact moment when the idea became Whit's own. Dumb people in power are like that.

"I think you're right. State Troopers have been getting a lot of meth traffic through the major highways. We got a bulletin said Mexican cartels were runnin' dope all the way out here, cooking speed in fifty-five gallon drums on the back lots of people's farms," Whit said.

Whit leaned into Nadine's car and peered around like an officious owl.

Exactly as Smiley left it, with the driver's door open. Snow had blown onto half of the front seat, but he could still see the towel Nadine had folded on her passenger seat to hold the pie. Tiny electric fingers worked through Smiley's scalp when he saw the round depression the pie pan left in the towel.

Later, he'd stroke that very pie tin and remember his perfect thrust.

***

By the time Garrett arrived at the access road, the Sheriff's Department had units blocking it off. Whit requested help processing the scene. Two deputies Garrett didn't recognize manned the checkpoint. He parked in front of one of their cars, his face awash with red and blue lights.

Both deputies approached him when he stepped out.

"Hey fellas, can you tell me if they found Nadine Pearson?"

"You're going to have to leave, sir," the senior deputy said. A little gray at the temples, a little sag in the belly. Garrett figured he had about twenty years on.

"Sure, sure, no problem. It's just that I live in town

170

and I've known Nadine for a really long time."

"Look, I'll level with you. The Artemis PD Chief told my sergeant if a guy driving a fancy blue Mustang tries to get in, we're supposed to arrest him," the deputy said.

"Oh. So why tell me?" Garrett said.

"Lyle Hampton went to high school with my nephew. He told me you're the Chief who moved back from Los Angeles. Lamar Evans's son."

"I am."

"Let's call it professional courtesy, then. But you'll have to leave. Sorry."

"No worries. I don't want you guys to catch grief," Garrett said. He went back to his car.

"And no," the deputy said, "they didn't find her. Just her car. But it doesn't look good."

"Thanks, man. I really appreciate it," Garrett said. He revved the Mustang and backed away. His jaw clenched and his teeth ground like tectonic plates. Two years ago, he broke a molar during one of these sessions.

"Calm and focused," he lied.

He drove out past the Heideman place. Shirley told him about Bradley's autopsy. So at least one murder, and possibly two. There'd be nothing left for evidence in the burned out barn. The State HazMat team had responded when it was discovered to be a lab fire. They cleaned the place out, but good.

Even so, he found the Mustang's nose pointing down the gravel road to Misty's house. He didn't see her pickup out front, but he didn't really want to talk to anybody. He parked, got out, and stood there next to his car.

What next? And hurry it up, because it's freaking cold.

Garrett wandered around the barn site, kicking the

odd piece of charred wood. He should have rousted Bradley, should have ridden him harder when he was Chief. Garrett knew the kid was dirty, it wouldn't have taken much work to prove it. He let him slide because of Misty.

Maybe if he had busted Bradley, the Heidemans' barn would still be up and Bradley would still be alive. In jail, but alive.

"Neither the barn nor the man is a loss."

Garrett spun toward the slurred voice. Misty's mother, Emma Heideman, stood on the back porch. Despite the cold, she wore a slip showing her hairy legs. She fought to light a cigarette. There was no wind, she just couldn't get her hand and her wobbling body in synch with each other. The lighter's flame kept weaving a figure eight in front of the cigarette.

Garrett stepped over and took the lighter. He lit the cigarette for her, but had to follow it around as she continued to sway. She'd once been a bright young kid who won the Spelling Bee at Artemis Elementary. It had been a long, hard road from there.

"Still, sorry it had to happen," Garrett said.

She pouted her lower lip and blew a plume of smoke straight up past her oily bangs. "Why do you keep coming back here? Three times now since Bradley started the lab."

"Uh, no, Ma'am. I came out after, you know, to offer Misty my condolences. I came out here today. I can't really say why, exactly. A lot of things have gone wrong lately, and I was feeling like this was one I could have prevented," Garrett said.

"Yeah, if you busted him the other night, instead of just peepin' in the barn, we'd still have a shitty barn out there and Misty would still have a fucking halfwit as the father of her new baby. So all in all, I'm glad you waited."

"What? I never came out here at night."

She cackled and blew smoke at him. "Bullshit."

Red behind his eyes. Garrett had the cigarette crushed in his hand, his palm burning. She stood there with a cartoon O for a mouth.

"I want you to listen to me very carefully," Garrett said. He leaned in close and her nervous eyelids twitched. "I didn't come to your property any night at all. But I want you to think about it and tell me exactly what you saw the night someone peeped in your barn. Do you understand me, Mrs. Heideman?"

"Y-yes. Fine. It was... a man. I know that."

Garrett stood up tall and backed off the porch a little bit. "You think he was taller or shorter than me?"

"I don't know. About the same I guess."

"What made you so sure it was me?"

"I just figured it was, since you're the Chief of Police. Who else would be spyin' on Bradley when he's cookin'?"

"Yeah, I really think they need to put out some kind of community bulletin on the whole Chief thing. Why do you say you're sure it was a man?" Garrett said.

"Walked like a man, you know? Don't no woman walk that way."

"Did you see a hair color?"

"No, I couldn't see much but the shape of him, it was kinda late," she said. She gave him a sad shrug.

"And you were a little drunk?"

"Maybe a little."

"Did you see a car, or hear one?" Garrett said.

"Nope. He left over the knoll there." She pointed to the mouth of a draw leading down to public land.

"Thanks, Mrs. Heideman. Why don't you get

inside now?"

She seemed to just notice her shivers. "Oh yeah."

Garrett watched her list to the right and make a slow turn for the door. She shuffled inside, and he turned back to the place she'd pointed out.

Cursing every inch of the trek, Garrett waded through ankle and shin deep snow to reach the mouth of the draw. It had been snowing off and on for days, so he knew he wouldn't see tracks. He followed the draw as it angled downward away from the Heideman place. Toward the bottom, his feet felt like someone stuffed two frozen steaks in his boots.

He stopped. He didn't know what he was doing out here, wandering. New snow, no tracks. Go home, Garrett.

A chattering gray squirrel jumped from limb to limb, making its way through the dormant woods to the left. The squirrel skittered down a hoary oak trunk and ran across a seasonal creek bed. Springtime runoff would fill this to a respectable two-foot depth. Right now, it was nothing but water-polished rocks poking out of the snow like the scales on some old dragon's back.

Garrett caught sight of mud on top off one of the smaller rocks. He hopped from one exposed stone to the other until he reached it. It had been flipped over at some point. Deep scoring on the other side said something metal did it. Garrett tried to gauge the direction of travel, but couldn't really get a read in the fresh snow.

He saw a natural path up from the creek bed, through a small stand of birches. Following the path, examining the trees and exposed rocks as he went, he came to a low deadfall where a single tree trunk blocked the path. No bigger around than Garrett's thigh and partially buried in the snow. Easy enough to drive over.

He knelt down and brushed snow off the tree.

Crescent-shaped rips in the bark and down deep into the wood. Someone drove over it in a snowmobile. Garrett took out his phone and snapped a few photos.

The frozen steaks that had replaced his feet were in need of defrosting and Garrett had a lot to think about. He trudged back to the Mustang, trying to figure how a bunch of missing girls tied into a burned down meth lab.

***

The flat crack of the .22 echoed through the snowy woods. Smiley breathed in the smell of the gunpowder as he listened to the excited chatter on the County radio. The County Coroner rolled out a forensic team and the whole area had been shut down not long after Smiley left.

Smiley went to the back of his pickup. There were a dozen cages stacked in there from this week's round of feral cat traps. He opened one and a dirty orange cat hissed at him and sprang out. It ran about fifty yards away and went to ground under a bush. Smiley could barely see the orange head in the shadows.

Normally, he'd take most of the cats back to the County shelter to be either adopted out or euthanized. But so much nervous energy crackled through him he was surprised he didn't hum like a high tension power line. None of these would make it back to the shelter today, and still his palms would itch and his scalp would tingle and he would search for something gruesome to do with his hands.

He hadn't felt this unbridled excitement since the long ago failure at the rest stop. The one he had to leave. Florida, they called her. She fought too hard, and the *estocada* thrust had done her, but he vented his rage on her face when he knew the headlights wouldn't go away.

He could see why some Hunters left their prey to be found, or even taunted the idiots on the police department. There was a divine thrill in knowing someone was examining your handiwork, shaking their head, horrified by your art and yet totally clueless they stand in the presence of the artist.

He'd always controlled the need to show the world, choked it down. He buried his beauties below, until he built the trophy room. Then he kept them for himself, as much as he was tempted to share them.

The Hunter rampant in his heart, he leaned across the hood of the truck and sighted in on his orange target.

His prediction had been right. It took every one of the cats to even mildly sate his thirst. He didn't have to be at his place until six, but he left early. He wanted to be sure Angela had nice clean comforters to sleep on tonight.

He left the cat bodies for the coyotes.

***

Misty fussed over the bruise on Smiley's cheek when she brought Angela. A few folks at work had commented as well, but everyone kind of backed off when he said he slipped on the porch like Momma and nearly cracked his own skull.

"Oh my gosh, Smiley, you have got to remember to salt those stairs," Misty said.

"Believe me, I'll remember now."

Angela perched on the couch, looking glum.

"What's the matter, Princess? You okay?" Smiley said.

"I'm just sad for Mommy. She's been crying."

"Oh, baby," Misty said. She sat with Angela and hugged her. "Mommy's gonna be okay."

"But you said the topsy made you cry."

"The what?" Smiley said.

"The autopsy results. I guess little ears hear more than we think," Misty said.

Angela pushed her ears out with her fingers so they looked like monkey ears. This got a ghost of a grin from Misty. Angela held up her doll and said, "Poor Smiley. You want Anastasia to kiss your bad bruise?"

He smiled and winked at Angela. "It's okay. It's gonna get better, you wait and see."

The rumble of an engine outside made his heart race.

***

Garrett parked beside Misty's pickup and shut down the Mustang. He picked up a large manila envelope and saw Smiley's front door open. The smile was bigger than ever.

"Howdy, Garrett. What brings you out?"

"I wanted to talk to you real quick. Wow, nice shiner," Garrett said.

"Yup. Earned it the hard way, not knowing how to walk up a set of icy steps."

Angela and Misty came to the door and waved. Garrett exchanged hellos and pulled Smiley aside. "I'm sorry, I didn't expect you to have company. Remember when I showed you the last picture, but I didn't have a copy for you?" Garrett said.

"Yeah?" Smiley said.

Did his eyes bounce down to the manila envelope?

"I brought one with me, but..." Garrett glanced

back at Angela, waiting in the doorway.

"Misty, why don't ya'll wait inside? Garrett has grownup stuff to talk about," Smiley said.

Misty corralled Angela and they closed the door. Garrett made a show of messing with the flap to open the envelope. He couldn't decide if he was talking himself into it, or if Smiley actually looked anxious. He slid an eight-by-ten glossy of Nadine's lost girl Taylor out of the envelope. He folded the envelope to put it away, but never took his eyes off Smiley's face.

The clear blue eyes went down and back up, down and back up.

"Nope. Doesn't ring a bell, but in the winter, they all look like a puff of hair and a big coat," Smiley said.

"Do me a favor and show it around, will you?"

"Is this an official police investigation?"

"Oh, no. You know that, Smiley. I'm just a private citizen. In a way, it's kind of freeing, you know? You don't have to follow all those silly rules," Garrett said.

Smiley gave him an odd look. "If you say so. I don't mind helpin' out. If you get any information, keep me in the loop."

"Sure thing. I'd appreciate the help. Hell, if I was still the Chief, I'd deputize you."

Smiley beamed at him. "Boy, that'd be the day."

"Say," Garrett said, hoping his acting skills were up to par. "Do you still have that old hit and miss engine of your daddy's? I saw one on eBay go for a pretty penny."

"Nope. Sold it to a young picker not long ago. Sold everything, in fact. Nothin' left in the barn but dust and old cow farts," Smiley said.

Damn. "Too bad. I sure would've liked to see it again. Those things are like a lost piece of the good old days."

"You got that right," Smiley said.

Garrett hadn't really put together a Plan B on how to get a look inside Smiley's barn. No way he would've bet on Smiley to selling the antique engine. Ah well, he'd had to bullshit his way into more than one dope house when he worked Narcotics. He decided to wing it.

"Hey, while I'm here, Tracy has been on a barn kick lately. She's painting different construction styles and has me taking pictures for her whenever I can. Would you mind?"

"You wanna take a picture of my barn? Sure, I suppose."

"Would it be okay to take some of the hay loft and all that?"

"Like, inside?" Smiley said. His smile twitched a little at the corners. "Sure, why not?"

Garrett took out his phone and followed Smiley out to the barn. He felt like time crawled while he took the obligatory shots of the outside. He couldn't wait to get inside.

Smiley cracked the door open and disappeared into the gullet of the shadowy barn.

Garrett eased in after him, letting his eyes adjust. Even in the dead chill, he felt sweat slide down his spine, and his hand desperately wanted to be curled around a pistol, not a phone.

He found Smiley standing in the middle of the mostly empty barn.

"What do you think?" Smiley said.

"Like everything else you own, Smiley, it's in great shape."

Off to one side, there were three large humps under separate tarps. Between the tarp and the floor, Garrett could see the wheels of an ATV and the treads of a snow machine. He spied the crescents down the middle. A Hacksaw Trail Tread.

The third covered thing was a sled of some kind, with wide rails peeking from under the tarp. Rails that would leave parallel straight-line tracks if you pulled it across dirt.

Smiley made no move to show him and Garrett couldn't think of a way to ask. The barn felt stuffy all of a sudden and Garrett's heart picked up speed.

Nope. Everything under control. Focus.

Garrett snapped a few pictures. An old-school wood plank floor. Some sections looked newer than others. Near the back, a big stack of hay bales. Some old tools hung on hooks here and there. And in a far corner, the hacked apart stump of an old whipping post.

Garrett had been in here as a kid when his dad and Smiley worked on his dad's bass boat. His dad explained what a whipping post was back then, and it had always stuck with Garrett.

"You mind if I go up in the loft?"

"Make yourself at home," Smiley said.

Garrett climbed up a ladder made of two-by-fours. The hayloft had no hay. The only thing up here was a dusty stuffed cat with green glass eyes. The gray and white fur looked a little mangy in a few patches. Creepy. He took a picture of it.

"What on earth is a stuffed cat doing up here, Smiley?"

"Oh, I forgot about the darn thing. I musta made it when I was eighteen, nineteen. I guess I left him up there to keep guard."

Garrett leaned carefully over the edge. From up here, he saw a dark spot on the floor behind Smiley, a little less than a foot in diameter. He aimed the phone. "Smile for Tracy."

Smiley gave him a good one.

Climbing down from the loft, Garrett saw an old trashcan, the metal kind. All sorts of odds and ends filled it nearly to the top. Bicycle parts, bits of taxidermy forms, old tin cans with flawless labels antique collectors would swoon over. And stuck down the side, jammed under a sprocket, was the only clean thing in the can.

A pie tin. Smashed by something heavy, but he could still see the little rim it had.

Everything felt hot and loose in Garrett's stomach. Unbidden, his brain produced an image of Smiley teaching him how to gut a fish. He poked around inside the can. "Pickers would lose their minds over some of the stuff in here."

"No," Smiley said. He moved a step toward Garrett, but stopped himself. "Uh, all that stuff kinda reminds me of either Ma cookin' or Papa workin' on an old bike. I'd like to keep it."

"I don't blame you. There's some stuff you don't see anymore. What do they call those pie tins with the lip thing?"

Smiley didn't even look in the can. "I'm not sure. I was never a good cook, so I didn't pay much mind to it. 'Sides, Daddy squashed that one with his truck."

He gestured toward the door. "I hate to be a pill, but I should get Misty on the road. I got old Donnie Burton to give her some shifts now and again waiting tables at the truck stop."

"That's really nice of you. She needs it right now," Garrett said.

"I do what I can," Smiley said.

They shook hands and went back out into the main yard. "I'll let you run. I do appreciate the pictures.

Tracy will love these," Garrett said.

"I hope so. I'd be proud to have my barn in one of her paintings."

Garrett drove away slow, the low-slung Mustang not liking the bumps. At the main road, he glanced in the rearview mirror.

Smiley's lone figure was still standing there, watching.

18

"You seem preoccupied," LaSalle said.

He and Garrett sat at Garrett's kitchen table. Sweet tea in takeout cups and the remains of burgers from the diner stood like islands among pictures of missing girls and scattered copies of Missing Person reports. Garrett's face had gone slack, his mind in "cop mode."

"Hmm? Just thinking. Only three of these girls have even been confirmed as missing by family members. The others could still be out there for all anyone knows," Garrett said.

"Makes 'em perfect, doesn't it? No one to make too much of a fuss over them disappearing," LaSalle said.

"No one local, anyway. These girls are from all over the place." Garrett pushed papers around until he found the incident report for the Florida girl. "So why mess up her face? He had to know nobody around here would recognize her, and he left her teeth, so they might have hit with dental records. He had no way of knowing they wouldn't get a match."

"Anger, man. He was either mad at being interrupted, or for all we know that's what he does to all of 'em," LaSalle said.

Garrett tossed the report on the table and opened

the fridge. He grabbed two beers and gave one to LaSalle. "We're assuming a lot. One murder has us thinking about a serial killer."

"Why do you keep going back and forth on this? You know the pattern is there. Tell me you wouldn't take this case to your supervisor in LA and ask for manpower to look into it."

"Yeah, maybe. In LA," Garrett said.

"That's it, isn't it? You still can't convince yourself someone around here would kidnap and kill these girls. Look, you know these people because you grew up here. But you don't know them as well as you think you do."

"Don't I?" Garrett said.

"When I was nineteen, I helped Moms move to a new apartment. I found a box of pictures during the move and one of 'em was an old mug shot. Of my mom. The most church-goin' woman I ever knew. I asked her about it and she told me right after graduating school, she spent a year in jail for stabbing another girl in an argument. I was blown away."

"She never told you about it?" Garrett said.

"As I got older, I thought about it. I think she locked it away, you know. Put it aside and never talked about it, so it became part of someone else's life. Not the person she was now. Point is, you can't know what people did before you came around. Unless they tell you. And most people don't tell you," LaSalle said.

Among all the reports and pictures on the table, Danielle Ortega stared up at Garrett from a long-ago hotel room. He hadn't told LaSalle all the personal details of the case. No reason to. But the big guy was right. You had no way of knowing what people were like before you were born. Or after you left home.

He decided he wouldn't share his feelings about

Smiley yet. He really didn't have anything beyond a snowmobile tread probably half the people in the state owned, and an antique pie tin. LaSalle wouldn't care how thin it was, he'd insist on checking out Smiley's place. If anyone saw them, Whit Abercrombie would be up their asses in a heartbeat and Smiley would find out for sure. If he *was* taking girls, he'd have plenty of warning someone knew. There might be evidence at his place and there might not. If there was, Smiley could take his time destroying it because Whit would never search the place on Garrett's say-so.

No, Garrett figured he would wait until he had something solid enough to bring in real cops. Like Clancy. Or someone else.

"What do you think about Nadine going smoke on us? She doesn't seem to fit into the picture," LaSalle said.

"That one bothers me," Garrett said. "I think she's accidental. I just don't know how."

LaSalle drained his beer and dropped his empty bottle in the recycling container. "I've been thinking about setting up in the woods and watching the rest area. Might not be a bad thing to photograph all the cars that stop by. Maybe we start showing some pictures of our own to the girls?" LaSalle said.

"Somebody might get suspicious if they see your car there all day."

"I'll park at the truck stop and walk up. Do my big ass some good." LaSalle started straightening all the papers to put them away. "You got something in mind?"

It felt like the big man wanted some time to himself, which suited Garrett. "I want to find out more about the Nadine thing. Just for personal reasons."

"I feel you. It's still your town, Chief Evans."

LaSalle smiled and Garrett couldn't help but grin back.

"Let's not get carried away. I'll dig around on the history of everyone who owns property along the highway there. Probably be better if someone local did it," Garrett said.

"Agreed. I got my share of old white people stink-eye this week. I don't need anymore."

***

Standing outside the impound yard fence, his idea didn't seem so good anymore. Garrett wasn't just going against Whit Abercrombie here. Nadine's car had seals on the door from the County Sheriff's office. It was a full-fledged homicide investigation and he could get locked down for screwing with evidence.

This impound yard was nothing like LAPD's. LA had high fences topped by razor wire and a full time guard. Here, it was a six-foot chain link fence with two strands of barbed wire protecting a small lot with weeds growing up through the gravel.

Garrett flipped his coat over the top of the barbed wire. Might as well get this over with, otherwise he'd have another sleepless night relentlessly stewing all the possibilities in the pressure cooker of his brain. He climbed the chain link and used his coat to maneuver over the barbs. He'd chosen a spot where an old Ford flatbed had been parked for about thirty years. He left footprints in the snow and caked dirt on the hood when he stepped down from the fence.

He felt like some kind of action movie badass until he tried to flip his coat off the barbed wire. A six-inch rip down one sleeve made him go from badass to dumbass.

His boots crunched in the gravel as he made his

way to Nadine's Lincoln. They parked it between a police car with a destroyed front end (courtesy of a cow in 1988) and one of those imports with a stupid add-on wing bolted to the trunk.

Garrett went belly down on and peeked under Nadine's car. The Lincoln had bled thick black oil onto the gravel. Looked like Nadine needed an oil change as well as a new set of gaskets. More than likely, she'd never have to worry about it again.

He stood and tried to picture this dented behemoth parked in Smiley's immaculate barn. Crazy. But... if he pulled it right up to the back of the barn, the spot would be about right.

A quick glance around. The tow yard was on the outskirts of town, so very little traffic passed it. Garrett retrieved a short slim-jim from his coat and slid it between the window and the rubber seal on the driver's door. He fished around until he felt/heard a satisfying clunk.

Last chance to stop this. If he didn't break the evidence seal on the door, he could still walk away.

He cracked it and peered inside the Lincoln's cavernous passenger compartment. The interior stank of cigarettes and old lady perfume. Black powder coated every surface and there were clean square patches where tape had been used to lift prints.

There were two round clean spots on the steering wheel where they took blood samples. A little birdie named Shirley told him the car had been open when they found it, half the front seat covered in snow. There were only spots of blood on the steering wheel and a bigger spot in the carpeting of the trunk. She also told him they found a towel folded on the passenger seat, with a round impression in it. Like Nadine had been protecting the upholstery from something.

"So she wouldn't spill her pie," Garrett said aloud.

His voice sounded hollow in the quiet Lincoln. The hairs on his forearms bristled when he thought of Nadine driving along in the dark, maybe listening to her favorite radio preacher, with a warm surprise for someone on the seat next to her.

He hit the trunk release and checked it out. The entire carpet was missing. There were more of those clean spots from blood samples taken off the support arm of the trunk lid. Whoever put Nadine in the trunk of her car— Garrett was too much of a pessimist to believe she was still alive— accidentally got some blood way over there? The Lincoln's trunk was big enough to fill with water and swim laps. All you had to do was lean in and drop her. Nadine weighed about a buck-ten with her snow boots on. He hoped the blood placement seemed odd to other people, because Whit Abercrombie would never listen to him.

Missing girls but no bodies.

Missing Nadine but no body.

Standing over the empty trunk made his mind slip for a second— *A body in a trunk. Young kid, maybe thirteen, just a witness who chose the wrong alley walking home from baseball practice. Bullet holes in his face.*

Garrett slammed the trunk shut and stalked around the car, scanning the bodywork, bumpers, the grill, searching for a spec of dried blood, a scratch from a struggle, anything. He started in on the tires next. Nadine took care of her car and replaced her tires as soon as they showed wear. The treads came deep, almost like new. Mostly filled mud from the road behind the Heideman place. Whoever drove it there spattered slushy snow and mud in the fender wells Nadine kept painfully clean. A woman from her day simply did not drive a filthy car about town.

What was that? Something weird stuck inside the front left well. Covered with mud, but not shaped like a rock from the road. He flipped open his pocket knife and scraped it loose. Soft, mushy, and round. He split it with his knife and knew what it was immediately.

A cherry.

He found it highly unlikely Nadine ran over her own pie. Did she get out with it in her hands, holding it out like an offering, only to find death waiting? Someone put her in the trunk and drove her away, running over the pie in the process. Someone? He knew the answer well enough, didn't he? Damn it.

Garrett wiped the blade on his pant leg.

"Drop the knife, asshole!"

The young Sheriff's deputy outside the fence pointed a shotgun at him. Given the shaky hands on the gun, Garrett decided he would indeed drop the knife. He didn't recognize the kid, but he did recognize the forensics guy he had with him.

He smiled when he saw Garrett. "Oh hey, Chief."

"Funny story about the Chief thing," Garrett said.

***

Raw fury made Whit Abercrombie's lips turn white where they pressed together. He yelled at Garrett through the door of the holding cell. "Have you stopped taking whatever was supposed to keep you sane? You are *not* the Chief of Police anymore. Get over it. You got no fucking business sticking your nose into that case."

Whit had personally escorted Garrett to this cell when he arrived. It smelled like metal and the ghosts of piss and bleach.

"Listen, I know I've been an ass to you, and it's no secret you and I never liked each other much, but I'm going to ask you a favor here," Garrett said.

"You are crazy. I knew it."

"Please, okay? When's the last time I said that to you?"

Whit thought it over. For him thinking usually took a spell. They were alone in the holding area so the silence stretched out and out, which began to make Garrett's skin twitch. He decided to lay it out there. He'd have to sooner or later. Might as well puke it up now and see Whit's reaction. "I think... someone may have kept Nadine's car in a barn before you found it. Take your guys and a few County boys and just do a check of all the barns in the area."

He didn't want to name Smiley specifically, because he'd have to bring the missing girls into it and he knew Whit would blow it off.

"Take samples from the floors. Nadine's car had a bad oil leak. I think—"

"You think us good old boys don't know how to run a police department, right?" Whit leaned on the bars and gave Garrett a lazy smile. "Since everybody knows Nadine around these parts, the folks in the County lab hustled those blood samples for us. The stuff on the steering wheel was Bradley Wentz's. So was some of the blood in the trunk."

That struck Garrett quiet.

"What now, Sherlock? I guess they didn't teach you about coroner's reports and such in LA. We got ours back, and it says Bradley Wentz got stabbed in the heart. Once. Perfect spot. What's that tell you?"

"More importantly, what do you think it tells *you?*" Garrett said.

"Professional hit, all the way. Bradley got stupid, brought down some drug cartel on his own head. We figure they hit Bradley and when they were leaving, they run across old Nadine Pearson. Poor busybody finally stuck her nose in the wrong person's business. Makes sense they had Bradley's blood on 'em when they took Nadine and her car."

"Makes the best kind of sense, doesn't it?" Garrett said. "Except for the part about what they did with Nadine's body."

Whit thumped his can of dip and tucked a pinch behind his lip. If he had feathers, he would've preened. "We'll find her soon enough, and when we do you can read about it in the papers like everybody else."

Garrett skirted right up to the edge of telling him the truth.

"I still think... Nadine's disappearance may have something to do with the missing girls."

"Listen at you. You think everything is tied to these missing whores. You're as bad as your daddy on that thing," Whit said.

"What do you know about that?" Garrett said.

"Son, you can't dig around in other people's reports and such without people hearin' about it. Personally, I always thought maybe your old man had a bit of thing for those girls."

The red tide rose behind his eyes and Garrett wasn't really in the mood to stem it. "Of course, you never said it to his face, because he would have loosened your teeth for you."

"Tough guy, aren't you? Just like your daddy. Strutting around here talking about how his boy was a hotshot pistolero out there in LA, getting in all those shootouts, stocking up on medals left and right. I wonder

191

what he'd think if he knew it broke you, sent you home takin' pills to sleep at night."

Garrett stood up and Whit actually backed away from the dead eyes burning at him.

"I'm working real hard, here," Garrett said. "You have to cut me some slack, Whit. I need you to know something. When Mrs. Shotwell let me in Nadine's house, there was a pie in a tin."

"The missing pie thing again? I told you, we got our suspect. It's all tied to Bradley Wentz and some other drug-dealing Mexican cartel trash we'll eventually find."

"Mrs. Shotwell swears up and down all the signs point to Nadine making two pies. I think she took one to somebody the night she disappeared. And I saw a pie tin like hers yesterday."

"Where?" Whit said.

"In Smiley's barn," Garrett said. It took all he had not to break eye contact.

Whit went very still. He and Smiley went as far back as Smiley and Garrett's dad.

"You listen good, you son of a bitch. You don't go around slandering people's names in this town. Smiley Carmichael has done more for folks in Artemis than you will ever know, and he is the most gentle soul I ever met. Drug dealers killed Bradley Wentz and most likely Nadine Pearson. And now you can sit your ass in jail for tampering with evidence. Maybe we can get the County to prescribe some new medication while you're in," Whit said.

He strode away with such a smug look it pushed Garrett's inner tide too high to stop it. He should have at least tried. But he couldn't. He put his face up to the bars and called after Whit. "You can change the furniture and hang all the pictures you want, but you'll always be too small to fill his office, you soft-in-the-middle son of a bitch."

Whit slammed the door so hard the ceiling panels rattled.

***

"It's not every day I get to bail a white boy out of jail," LaSalle said. He led the way across the parking lot toward the Volvo, long leather jacket buttoned against the cold.

Garrett's teeth chattered. "Wait up, man, it's hard to walk in these."

They gave him back his coat with the torn sleeve, which kept some of the cold at bay, but his feet were already going numb in the jailhouse slippers. Whit took a bit of offense to his comment and decided to keep Garrett's boots as evidence of the break-in at the impound lot.

"I really appreciate this. Stop by the bank and I'll pay you back," Garrett said.

"I'm in no hurry. You wanna fill me in while I drive you to get some damn shoes?"

LaSalle hit the remote and unlocked the Volvo, but a black and white cruised up next to them before they could get in. Lyle Hampton rolled down his window. "Hey, Garrett. Sorry about the shoes."

"Ah, I had to give Whit a chance to earn some man-pride back," Garrett said.

"Between you and me and a knot in a tree, I bet he wishes you were still here. He can't really wrap his head around an investigation like this," Lyle said.

"Seems to have it solved. He gave me the whole cartel assassin theory," Garrett said.

Lyle glanced around and then checked to make

sure his radio mike wasn't hot. He wore a conspirator's grin. "That wasn't even his. Smiley figured out the whole thing for him."

Hot bile rose in Garrett's throat. "Come again?"

"Yeah, Smiley came rolling up to the scene and asked Whit if he needed any tracking help, you know, on account of what a good hunter Smiley is."

"Sure," Garrett said. He looked at LaSalle over the Volvo. "You've met Smiley."

"Yeah, sure." LaSalle looked a little confused, but picked up on Garrett's body language. He waited.

Garrett's lips felt numb. "Did Whit let Smiley help?"

"Didn't do any good," Lyle said. "No tracks anywhere. Smiley said there were enough signs to know another car had been there, but nothing he thought would hold up in court. Too much snow for it to leave tracks in the dirt."

Lyle chuckled. "The rest of us knew what he meant right away, but he had to explain it to Whit. A second car picked up the killer, that's why no signs of him leaving on foot. Smiley said Bradley's autopsy proved his point. The clean kill meant a pro drug enforcer came out to hit Bradley and probably ran across Nadine by accident as he was leaving."

"Sounds plausible," LaSalle said.

Garrett arched an eyebrow in his direction. Really?

Lyle went on. "Smiley figures they didn't have time to clean up since the Heideman barn was already on fire. They probably took Nadine's body somewhere else, so they could make sure they didn't leave any evidence on it."

"And Whit ate the idea up with a spoon," Garrett said.

"It was actually kinda embarrassing. He didn't run the crime scene like you taught us at all. He even let Smiley touch the blood in the trunk to see if he could tell how fresh it was."

"You're kidding me," Garrett said.

"I wish I was. I better scat before somebody accuses me of criminal conspiracy. Sorry about all the trouble, anyway." Lyle waved and drove off.

"What was that all about?" LaSalle said.

They both climbed into the car and LaSalle drove out of the lot. Garrett had to hand it to him, he had patience. He let Garrett stew for a good two miles.

"It's something I didn't want to say, because I didn't want to believe it. I still don't. But I've seen some things, and heard some things recently. I think maybe it's Smiley," Garrett said.

"Maybe what is?"

"I think Smiley's been killing girls. And maybe he's been doing it a lot longer than we're thinking," Garrett said.

19

Smiley stood outside the church in his shiny cowboy boots and string tie, shaking hands and smiling to beat the doggone band. All the old birds in town came to these Wednesday evening services, and he hadn't felt this much dry papery skin cross his palm since he first started trying to mount his trophies.

The thought of his girls sent his spirits soaring even higher. The Hunter god was among them tonight. He presided over the idiots with shiny power symbols pinned to their chests and led them down his carefully crafted trail by the nose. "Chief" Abercrombie practically groveled with thanks when Smiley put together all the loose puzzle pieces Whit held in his stupid palm.

And then Garrett Evans came to his place and took pictures of his barn. The Hunter could not be seen by mortal eyes, though. His power glowed around him while Garrett puttered around, looking but seeing nothing.

(Smiley *had* put the damnable pie tin downstairs afterward. Ignorant pride made him keep it where he could see it.)

Garrett might become a problem, though. Not

that he was smarter than Smiley, but he had a streak of his daddy's stubbornness in him. Lamar Evans had privately droned on and on about his missing whore for years. The only reason Smiley put up with it was because it excited him to hear Lamar moan about missing her, and then go down to his trophy room after Lamar left and stroke her hair in the dark.

He was firmly in control, as he always had been. None of these lesser people could touch him, he didn't fear a one. He'd waited his whole life for things to come to him and he'd always been rewarded.

Tracy Ellsworth walked out of the sanctuary and his patience was rewarded again.

"Tracy, how the heck are you?" He smiled so big it wouldn't have taken any effort at all to open a bit more and chomp her nose right off her face.

"Hi, Smiley. Haven't seen you at a Wednesday evening service in a while." She hugged him and he smelled just paint and turpentine, no perfume this time. He got a good close look at her pert little nose when she pulled away.

"I hope my barn lived up to your expectations," he said.

"Your barn?"

"Garrett told me how you were going through a barn phase. He took some pictures of my barn for you," Smiley said.

"Oh. Oh, right." She looked confused, but he could see her loyalty to Garrett lead her upstream behind him. "That is one heck of a black eye. I saw it when you walked in."

He let her swim away because he could. The Hunter could give as well as take. "Yup. Still smarts some. All these years of walkin' on ice every winter, you'd think

197

I'd have it down."

"Everybody slips sooner or later. I'm just glad you're okay," Tracy said.

"Ain't it the truth? Everybody does, don't they?"

She patted him on the arm while she talked. A toucher. "Do you remember coming out to our place when I was about eleven or twelve?" she said. "You had to pull a litter of feral cats out of the woodpile behind our barn."

"I do. Two of them little suckers liked to bit through my knuckle bone," he said.

They laughed together and he saw her white, even teeth, her pink tongue flexing and jumping behind them.

"It always meant so much to me that you took them to the adoption shelter. So many farmers in those days did terrible things to feral cats. Even some that weren't feral," she said.

"I'm sure those got some good homes," Smiley said. "I better git, I got babysitting duties tonight. Do you need a lift home?"

"Oh, no thanks. I drove myself today."

She gave Smiley another hug and he watched her say her goodbyes to everyone. He strolled to his truck, following Tracy in the corner of his eye, her scarlet hair a bright patch smeared across his peripheral vision. He imagined her kneeling at the head of his phalanx, stroking her hair in the dark, still smelling of the turpentine she used to clean her brushes.

***

LaSalle examined the photo of Lamar Evans, Smiley, and the darted bear.

"Jungle tribesmen?" LaSalle said.

198

"I've heard crazier. He very well could have missed a shot one night. And if he's taking them with tranquilizer darts, no wonder they vanish without a trace. Once they're out, he can take them anywhere, do anything he wants. No evidence left where he took them." The words felt sour in Garrett's mouth, like he tried to dry-swallow an aspirin. His dad's best friend, and the only man who'd ever really shown patience with Garrett.

"You look like you're not quite a believer," LaSalle said.

"And I shouldn't be. What, a pie tin and a weird feeling and suddenly I'm thinking a guy who was around practically my whole life is a killer?" Garrett said.

LaSalle ticked off points on his fingers. "We've got a missing girl's bracelet alongside some tracks. Same kinda tracks your old man noticed when he also had a missing girl. We got ourselves a camouflaged parking garage for a snowmobile, with branches woven by a craftsman, and a baby crib made by the same kind of craftsman. We got a guy with at least the right treads on his machine and a similar pie tin to a missing lady in his barn. As a cop what do you think of all that?"

Garrett didn't have to answer.

"Okay then, let's do it," LaSalle said. "You know what time he normally leaves for work. After he's gone, go in and check the place out."

"Without a warrant?" Garrett said.

"Last I checked, neither one of us were cops."

"Got me there. If we find something? How do we get the troops in there legally?"

LaSalle tipped his beer back and didn't set it down until it was empty. His turn to not provide the obvious answer.

"No. He has to be arrested. We're not assassins,"

Garrett said.

"And then? He gets to spend what's left of his sorry life sitting on Death Row, three hots every day, and writing letters to the victims' families?" LaSalle said.

"They fried Bundy."

"He killed college girls, not prostitutes."

"We don't know for sure Smiley killed anybody. And we can't say your girl is connected to him at all," Garrett said.

"Which is why we investigate, right?"

"Sure. And if he's dirty, he goes away," Garrett said.

"Whatever helps you sleep at night, man."

***

Smiley brushed the knots from the newest trophy's hair, taking care not to mar her scalp. The skin came out nice and supple, like they always did now. People-skin was harder to deal with than any other hide he'd processed, and it took years of frustration and failure before he hit on the kneeling body form and tanning method he used now.

This one had the silkiest hair he'd felt so far. Not quite as luxurious as Tracy's maybe, but it had a straight shimmering look favored by those skinny bitches on the magazine covers down at the grocery. He had her puffy blue coat tacked to the wall next to the red halter top his green-haired trophy wore the night she met the Hunter.

A warm summer hunt, his ribs slick with sweat, his fingers sliding over her own sweaty skin as he tied her to the sled hooked behind his ATV.

He sat behind the former owner of the blue coat in his straight-back chair. She was new, so she went first tonight and he counted a hundred brush strokes. He indulged himself by letting his rough fingers slide over the stitched areas where he repaired the marks he made on her with the hot steel and other tools.

Because she'd been on his mind so recent, he shifted his chair over behind the one who Garrett's daddy fornicated with. She had short black hair, which Smiley hardly had to brush at all. There was no wind to muss it in his trophy room, just a bit of dust he cleaned away with care.

On impulse, he pulled his jacket to his face and inhaled. Tracy's scent filled his nose from where her body molded to his during their hug. He felt stirrings, longings, an ache to be with her. Not to caress or penetrate in some foul act, but to bend to his will using sharp steel and the hard spirit of the Hunter.

The speaker mounted high in one corner *crackled* and his heart skittered so bad he had to forcefully cough a few times to get it going right again. Damn thing. He heard the unmistakable sound of tires crunching gravel. He left his beauties in the dark and hustled through the passageways, turning off lights as he went.

In the special room where he did his work with the living trophies, he checked the four monitors on his worktable. The cameras hidden under the eaves of the barn showed Misty's truck parking near the front of the house. Microphones picked up the two doors slamming and Angela chattering away to Misty.

A young fella came all the way out here from Morgantown to install those cameras and link them to screens in his house. Smiley watched close, so he could transfer the monitors under the barn after the young man left. It started with those little bastards he caught stealing Papa's old tools a few years back. He ran 'em off with a little rock-salt and gunpowder, but afterward his paranoia gnawed his guts while he was at work, made him constantly wonder if someone had stumbled across his play area.

The salesman was so happy about selling all those electronics he threw in a special little tower with a mobile Internet connection. The motion detectors would text Smiley if they were set off. Darndest thing. He remembered when only one house in town had a telephone.

Smiley shut everything down and went upstairs to greet Misty and Angela. He had a brand new gallon of chocolate ice cream just for Angela. To help her weather the tragedy of Bradley's death, and all.

***

Garrett paced the house from front of back, stopping only to refill his bourbon. Hell, he couldn't even think of it as *his* house, his dad's spirit loomed so large in every corner. The glass eyes mounted in the head of a twelve-point buck regarded him from the wall over Dad's favorite easy chair. The monster whitetail represented the first time he ever went hunting with Dad. Man, how the old man had laughed when Garrett lost his breakfast at the sight of deer guts. He put Garrett's hands in the warm muck and made him help pull out the entrails.

"Best way to face something you don't like is to walk right into it with your head up," Dad said.

Garrett carried his bourbon into his old room; it had been turned into a home office for his dad, complete with a PD line. A little plug-in exhaust fan was mounted in the window that opened onto the backyard, but it hadn't really helped. Stale cigar smoke would haunt the room forever, no matter how many times you painted.

He'd already turned the office upside down in his earlier search, nothing new here. He made sure he put *the* picture back on the upper left corner of the desk, right where he found it. Dad always kept it there. Him and Mom in a classic Hawaiian sundown picture, looking tanned and relaxed. Mom had poked him in the ribs before the shot, so the laughing smile was genuine and spontaneous.

Like the one in the other picture.

An overwhelming sadness hammered Garrett down, down. He slid along the wall until his butt thumped against the carpet. Some bourbon slopped out and ran down his knuckles—

And Michelle laughed as he spilled his Margarita on her shirt.

He shook the thought from his head so hard it made him dizzy. Levering himself upright again, he paced back to the living room. The Box popped into his head and he wanted to be anywhere but the room where the closet was. The Box sat right behind the boots she bought him.

He seriously needed to get his prescription refilled. This was not the time for cold turkey. His heart staggered for a beat when his phone rang. He nearly yanked it out of his pocket and threw it across the room. But he saw the number and answered.

"Hello?"

"Thanks for letting me in on the barn thing, asshole," Tracy said.

"Uh, I'll warn you, I've been drinking, so... What barn thing again?"

"Smiley cornered me at church and said you were taking pictures of his barn. For me."

"Oh shit." He looked up at the reproachful eyes of his dad's prize buck. "I meant to call you, I am so sorry."

"Sure, sure, but what's up with that? Why not just tell Smiley you wanted some pictures of his barn?" Tracy said.

Shit.

"Hello?"

"Listen..." He couldn't get his thoughts together. So many details, so much to think about. "I want to tell you something, but I don't want to. It's not that I don't trust you. It's just..."

Even through the phone, her voice was gentle and soothing. "I've done my homework. I know. You don't feel any situation is okay, or ever will be. But aside from the time I crushed your Popsicle stick farmhouse, you can always trust me."

He laughed at the memory and then he was talking, faster and faster, rubbing his temple, knowing she knew Smiley as well as anyone else around here and it would all sound—

"That's insane," she said. "Smiley?"

"Remember when I said I didn't want to tell you?"

As always, it was a matter of fact thing for her. "Okay, so you're investigating. Find something one way or the other, but something solid."

He felt like she just reached down and pulled him up from cold, deep waters. "I will. And thanks for listening to me."

"It's what I do. Do you mind if I do a little snooping for myself?"

"No way. You stay far, far away from this," Garrett said. *No more funerals of women I love*, he didn't say.

"Nothing dangerous. I'm curious about this arrest

for peeping when Smiley was a teenager. I'm willing to bet one of the old libraries has some papers on microfiche."

"Microfiche? We do have them Intra-webs now," Garrett said.

"Artemis, West Virginia Public Library, sweetie," Tracy said.

"Oh yeah."

"Come to my place for dinner tomorrow and I'll give you my notes if I get anything."

***

From far away, Tracy looked like a red-haired Barbie pacing back and forth in front of a dollhouse window. The Hunter's field glasses brought her into sharp relief, though. Talking to someone on the phone, twisting her luxurious red mane in her fingers.

Smiley's chest ached, but he knew it wasn't his blood pressure. A pressure of another kind welled up from deep down there, where the roots of everything tapped into the earth's blood. The Hunter felt his tendrils worming down, striking into the dirt as he lay here watching her.

He imagined he could feel the tremors in the earth as she paced and talked, each step of her delicate—*and oh wouldn't it be nice if they were bare*—feet sending a thrumming signal to the Hunter. Her Hunter.

Not now. Too many people looking and talking right now. After the black private eye left, things would cool down. Go back to normal. And then the Hunter had things to do.

20

Smiley's olive drab Jeep Willys hit the main road, turned west, and headed out toward the County Yards. He'd pick up his County truck there to make his daily rounds.

Garrett watched him go through binoculars. Once Smiley was far down the road, he started LaSalle's Volvo and followed him at a distance. He hit the button on his phone.

"LaSalle."

"Okay, we're on the road," Garrett said.

"Got it. I'm goin' in." LaSalle hung up.

Garrett got onto the highway a good twenty car lengths behind Smiley, who drove straight to the County Yards. Smiley didn't hang out, drink coffee, smoke, and bullshit like most of the other guys. He got the keys to his County truck and got on the road again.

Yes, sir. That Smiley's a hard worker.

***

LaSalle moved the last few yards through the woods and checked the GPS on his phone. He should be right on the backside of Smiley's property. He'd parked at the rest stop and made the by now familiar hump down the trail and past the hunting blind. He wore top of the line boots, but his toes were still wishing they were in a Brooklyn summer.

Emerging from the thickest brush, he saw the fence around Smiley's property line. A wood rail job with three rails, running for a quarter mile across the back of Smiley's place.

Easy enough to climb over, but something stumped LaSalle. How the hell would Smiley get a snowmobile through this fence?

He checked the fence line for a good two hundred yards in either direction, kicking himself for wasting time, but unable to let it go. If he couldn't get quick access, then it was less likely Smiley could do the things LaSalle and Garrett theorized.

On the way back to his original approach point, LaSalle examined the fence itself. The posts were put here to last, weather-sealed wood sunk into concrete in the ground. It must have taken the old fart weeks and weeks of work to make the damn thing.

Each post had been weather sealed and the fence was in great shape considering the elements it endured. A few posts were still a little rough and cracked, as if the West Virginia seasons were flipping the bird to the weather seal. He tapped each post as he passed.

The first time along the fence, he'd been hoping for something obvious, like a gate. On the trip back he noticed the fence jogged up and down with the terrain as it went. But in one spot, two posts were on dead even ground, like it had been graded special. Up close, he saw the first of the two posts had been treated with some kind of clear resin. Not just weather-sealed, but impregnated under pressure. High-end stuff. To do every post like this would have cost either an enormous amount of Smiley's time, or money. He went to the next post in line and saw the same thing. After that, the posts went back to normal weather-sealed wood.

LaSalle stood back from the two posts, about eight feet from each other. He got close and looked for signs either post could move aside, but saw nothing. He brushed snow off the top of one post. Its top was polished smooth, flawless. An adrenaline dump hit his heart as he leaned in. A barely visible part line started at the top and ran all the way down the center of the post to the ground. What the hell?

He ran his fingers around the post and felt the tiny line on the backside, too. It was like the post had been split and put back together, but with the kind of workmanship that would make a master carpenter weep.

LaSalle tugged, pulled, and tried to rattle the post. It felt like it wanted to move, but he couldn't see how to do it. Near the bottom of the first post, his fingers pushed through the drifted snow and found a sturdy eyebolt. It had nothing connected to it, which puzzled LaSalle. He tried to turn it, but it wouldn't budge. He pulled on it.

And heard a small *click* from inside the post.

With the pin released, half the post felt loose in his hand. He pushed and it slid smoothly upward about an inch, but stopped because of the crossbeams mounted to the opposite post. He saw a track system inside the post, like your kitchen drawer on steroids, expertly recessed into the post halves.

"You clever, clever, motherfucker," LaSalle said.

He ran to the other post and found the same pin at the bottom. A quick pull and half of that post came loose as well. He went to the middle and gently tugged upward on a crossing rail. The whole fence section slid upward like a conjurer's trick.

There was now an eight foot length of wood rail fence suspended about five feet off the ground. More than enough room to drive a snowmobile and sled underneath.

LaSalle felt a chill, but not from the snowflakes occasionally dotting his eyelashes. This dude was smart. And patient. Like no one he'd ever chased before. He stepped onto Smiley's property and put the "gate" back in place. Like new, just a fence. Son of a bitch.

LaSalle hiked the rest of the way with a new caution in him. He checked his phone to make sure it was still on. He didn't want to miss a call from Garrett and have Smiley roll up on him wearing the old .357 he toted around.

***

Garrett parked a good quarter mile from the house where the eviction was taking place. He had his scanner tuned to County frequencies, so he'd heard this place had a ton of dogs in the back, crammed into a barn.

Country folk don't often take to evictions kindly, and the Sheriff's Department had mounted a small army for this one. Garrett watched deputies mill around out front like uniformed ants. Red, blue, and yellow flashing lights turned the scene into a psychedelic stage show from this far back. He wished Tracy could see it.

Before long, Smiley came out with a snarling dog at the end of one of those long poles with a loop of wire. He loaded it into a cage in the back of his truck and went back in.

***

LaSalle crept up to the rear of Smiley's barn, his scalp tingling. The snow crunched underfoot, making it impossible to be silent. He made his way around to the front and checked the lock securing the doors. A Yale. Come on.

In less than a minute, LaSalle had the lock open and the kit back in his pocket.

He expected a horror movie creak from the door, but it glided open as smooth as Smiley's fence contraption. Once inside, LaSalle closed the door and again stood silent.

The first thing he saw was the snowmobile under the tarp. He pulled up the tarp to expose the drive tread. He saw the crescent shapes down the middle. A Hacksaw Trail Track, Garrett called it.

He moved on to the sled. He could already see the rails. He ripped back the tarp, not really knowing what he expected. This guy was too smart to leave blood, or hair, or anything else behind. Asking LaSalle the technical details on a sled would be like asking a rabbi what kind of bacon you should buy. This one looked pretty standard for all he knew. Something was carved into the front handle...

Hunter.

He used his phone to take pictures of the sled and the snowmobile tracks. He pulled a cloth tape measure out of his coat pocket and laid it on the floor behind the sled rails. Exact same size. He took another picture. From there, he moved to the outer walls and started a systematic search, side to side, looking for anything that didn't belong in a barn.

He saw the trash can Garrett talked about. No pie tin inside.

What he didn't see, high in the dark corners above, were the flat black motion detectors.

***

Smiley had filled up half the cages in his truck. His back ached something fierce and his knees were cussing him. All the after-hours activity was taking its toll. He'd have to retire from his County job soon. Then he'd have all the free time he wanted, until the Hunter got too weak to take any more prey.

Sharp buzzing came from his pocket. He locked a mangy Spaniel mix in a cage and retrieved his phone. The alert on the screen made him feverish and cold all at once. His motion detectors in the barn were going off.

The deputies guarding the property entrance stared at him like he'd sprouted horns when he lit out of there. The dogs yammered and howled, but Smiley planted his foot on the accelerator and shot off down the road. They had no way of knowing his barn was calling him.

Smiley had never been one of those stodgy old farts refusing to learn about computers and such. It opened his world up to new things like the bullfights sold over the Internet. He'd lived long enough to see Buck Rogers make-believe shit become reality.

He didn't even pay attention to the Volvo when it swung in behind him on the highway. He opened his glove box and took out his old Smith and Wesson. He'd left it in the truck in case it got jostled loose while he wrestled with the dogs. He holstered the revolver, but didn't snap it down. If somebody really was in his barn, they were about to see the business end right quick.

***

LaSalle felt deep disappointment. His search had yielded nothing. Just an old barn with a clean floor, not counting the oil stain Garrett thought belonged to Nadine's car, and some musty hay bales in the back. He leaned against a support beam and slid down to sit on the floor.

His tailbone scraped against something.

A small length of PVC pipe, maybe three inches in diameter, painted flat black. It came out of the floor right alongside one of the big support posts. Now what the hell would that be for?

He tried pushing and pulling it, tipping it to one side or the other. Nothing. He got down close and used his flashlight to look inside. A straight shot down into blackness.

Something familiar made his arm hairs stand on end. He leaned close to the pipe and sniffed. The mild odor of human decay.

He'd smelled it before. No mistaking it. LaSalle felt electrified. He wanted to jump up and scream. He had work to do, though. Searching for a trapdoor, some kind of access under the floor, he took one more quick trip around the barn. He wound up behind the stack of hay bales. Two bales were loose on the floor back there, but nothing unusual.

He stopped and tried to relax his mind. Quit looking for the obvious and open the backdoor to the brain. He settled onto on one of the loose bales of hay. Smiley would have another switch somewhere. Like the fence posts. Nothing obvious. No Scooby Doo coat hook on the wall, but something clever and unobtrusive.

The floor around his seat was littered with loose straw. Judging from everything else he'd seen about the man, LaSalle figured Smiley must have been in a hurry when he left. Otherwise, he would have surely swept the mess right up with the broom hung on its hook over there.

Among the scattered straw, one small bit stuck straight up for some reason. LaSalle knelt down and saw it had fallen into a knothole in the floor plank. The hole was very close to another support column. The harsh beam of his flashlight showed the edge of the hole was worn black with oils from human skin. Someone had to have put their finger here countless times to have so much discoloration.

He squeezed one of his clubby digits into the hole and his pulse throbbed in his neck. There was an eyebolt in there. He pulled it toward him and heard the slightest sigh, but nothing happened. Almost nothing. Perfect little join lines appeared in the barn floor. Those loose bales covered most of a square about three feet across.

A spark of furious energy hit him and he shoved the two hay bales away. The trap door finished opening, nearly silent on hinges seated with such care and expertise. His heart ran wild like an undisciplined hunting dog. Despite the cold, sweat ran into his eyes. Narrow stairs put together by a master craftsman disappeared into the darkness.

LaSalle clicked on his flashlight again and put a foot on the first step.

His phone buzzed in the chilly silence and he almost dropped the light down the stairs. It was Garrett. "Yeah?" LaSalle said.

"If you're still in there, get the hell out. We're almost on top of you."

"*What?*"

"Sorry, I thought he was taking some dogs back to the County Yards, but he just kept going once we got to the exit. We're close. Disappear."

LaSalle hung up and weighed his options. Whatever was down there, he didn't want a confrontation with Smiley in broad daylight over it. The law would likely get involved then.

And the law had nothing to do with what he had planned.

He pushed the door down, heard it click into place. Moving fast, he moved the hay bales back and scattered some straw. He took care to pluck the stray piece that led him to the knothole.

21

"*You want to be real still,*" Papa says. "*Wait and watch, boy. A true hunter don't ever let the animal see him.*"

Smiley sits in the blind on his twelfth birthday. He knows it's not deer season, but Papa says a man makes his kill on his twelfth birthday by God's law, and the law of man has nothin' to do with it.

Papa leans so close his lips touch Smiley's ear, and he whispers three words reeking of moonshine and Viceroy cigarettes.

"*Thar she is.*"

A doe, fat from feeding on corn at a nearby farm. Smiley raises Papa's Winchester and puts the front sight right on the pocket where the leg meets the body and up a couple of inches. His twiggy arms won't hold the rifle up for long. He squeezes.

The Winchester barks in the woods and the doe performs a graceless leap forward and to the right, crashing to the ground and never moving again. His first kill.

Smiley looks to Papa for praise.

"*Least you didn't inherit your mother's walleye.*"

Still, Papa pats him on the back and after they slice—and doesn't that feel delicious— into the skin and pull the insides onto the mossy ground at the base of an oak, Papa lets Smiley take a bite

215

out of the heart.

"Once you've tasted the heart of something you kilt yourself, you're a true hunter, boy."

***

The Hunter wore the cold mask, the one the girls saw when he took them.

Sitting below the barn in his workroom, Smiley played the video back again. The colored fella, Garrett's friend, had snuck into the barn. Damn it to hell, Smiley had only installed cameras outside, so he could watch the yard while he played downstairs. The voyeur in him wanted to know what the man did while inside the barn. He didn't fast-forward, he sat very still and watched the unmoving image of the barn door until the man came out again and put the lock back in place. Smiley had already stormed around the barn, looking for any signs the PI had found something, or left a bug device behind. Nothing seemed out of place.

The coon would damn well pay, boy. Oh, how he'd pay.

Smiley opened an Army surplus footlocker he kept behind the dentist's chair. He found an antique Russian night scope in there among the various butchering implements, scalpels, and brands. Sometimes he liked to watch the girls cry in the dark, not knowing where the Hunter would strike from next.

He planned on staying awake tonight, and calling out sick tomorrow as well. He'd guard his treasures until he could think of a way to get the black fella and Nadine together in the pit.

***

"We should try again in a couple of days," LaSalle said.

Garrett paced the ugly green shag in LaSalle's motel room. Only for high rollers, the Lazy Eight. LaSalle's laptop sat on the table. Garrett clicked through the images LaSalle offloaded from his phone. The Hacksaw style snowmobile treads. The sled with the proper size rails.

"Put this together with Nadine's pie tin and we have...jack-shit, as far as anyone else is concerned," Garrett said.

"That's why we should take another look." LaSalle didn't look at Garrett, he was too busy straightening the shirts in his closet. "And by the way, the dry-cleaning sucks around here."

LaSalle always had a way of pinning you with his eyes when he spoke to you. Was he looking away on purpose? *Or am I just paranoid*, Garrett thought.

He glanced at Tracy's painting of the collapsed barn with the tree growing through it. LaSalle had gotten the manager to let him replace the sailboat print originally in the room.

"When are you gonna ship it home?" Garrett said.

"I will, I will. I like to look at it in the mornings for some reason. Helps me get centered," LaSalle said.

"Centered, huh? I bet it'll be the first time she ever got that review on her work. You should tell her tonight. I'm stopping by her place for dinner. Good old-fashioned steak and potatoes. Wanna come along?"

"Nah. No third wheels tonight. You two need some time to yourselves," LaSalle said. He glanced at Garrett out the corner of his eye. "I'll even loan you my best Barry White CD."

"It's not like that, man. And nobody plays CDs

anymore," The seventh-grade blush creeping up his cheeks irritated Garrett.

LaSalle came over and shut his laptop. "What would be wrong if it *was* like that?"

Good question. Garrett had asked himself before. "Nothing. And everything. I think I'd just fuck it up right now. I still have Michelle running around in my head, along with who knows what else. I need to get a lot of stuff sorted out first."

"If you wait until all your problems are sorted out, you'll be dead. Trust me. It doesn't have to be perfect. It just has to be all right. People can work with that."

"You sure you're not a counselor?" Garrett said.

"Counselor? Shit, I got a PhD in Love."

They both laughed and Garrett felt good. Good. He headed for the door. "Okay, then. You're missing out, though. Tracy does a mean garlic mash."

"Bring me a doggie bag," LaSalle said.

"No promises there'll be any left."

Garrett left him and hustled through the cold to get in the Mustang.

"Hey, Chief."

Garrett turned to see LaSalle behind him, in his socks.

"The snow is gonna ruin those argyles, big man."

"I got more," LaSalle said.

LaSalle pinned him with the trademark intense gaze he hadn't used earlier. "I want you to know, I appreciate you helping me with this. I been to a lot of places with white country cops who didn't have time for me, and plenty of places, country or not, where nobody had time for some missing hooker."

LaSalle gripped Garrett's hand. "Don't listen to these assholes around here. You're a good cop, and you're a good man. Fuck these people."

The emotional swell blindsided Garrett. He squeezed LaSalle's hand and turned back to the Mustang to keep it under control. "Thanks, man. I'll see you tomorrow, huh?"

"Yeah. Tomorrow," LaSalle said.

He went back into his room and shut the door. Garrett fought down a feeling of doom at the slamming sound. He seriously needed to get his scrip filled.

***

A bloody steak and garlic mashed potatoes were really what Eve tempted Adam with. At least Garrett thought so. He finished his off and eyed the other steaks on the platter.

"I can't believe I bought all that," Tracy said.

"In your defense, you thought I was bringing a grizzly bear with me."

"Party pooper. I can't believe he'd rather go over case files than have dinner with us."

Garrett sipped some sweet tea, but she was too sharp for him. She noticed him being quiet. "What? He didn't like me? I washed most of the paint off my fingertips the night I met him," she said.

"He, uh... He had this weird idea we needed time alone."

Her cackling laugh made him dance inside. She ignored what he said and started clearing dishes. He helped her carry things into the kitchen. "Well?"

"Well what?" Tracy said.

"What do you think about what he said?"

She handed Garrett a Tupperware dish for the mashed potatoes and started foiling LaSalle's two steaks.

"Do we spend time together already?"

"Yeah. Of course."

"And is that okay with you?"

"Is it okay with me? I don't follow," Garrett said.

"There really isn't anything to follow. Is it okay with you that we spend time together? A simple question."

"Yeah, of course it is," he said.

Tracy touched his cheek, lightly, her fingers cool. He hoped she didn't feel the warmth boiling through him.

"It's okay with me, too," she said. "Very okay."

She left him standing there with a plastic dish of mashed potatoes in his hands. He put it next to the steaks and followed her into the living room.

This was the part he'd been dreading.

He had told her about LaSalle's dry run, but she forbid him to talk about anything else case related until after dinner. The conversation ran to old times, Junior High classes, big hair for her and (embarrassingly) skinny jeans for him. A red-haired force of nature, she had pulled him along in her wake, guiding them where she would, whatever sprang into her quick brain. He didn't mind.

Feeling low, he watched her spread sheets of paper on her coffee table. Time for the horrible things to take center stage again.

Tracy sat on the couch and patted the spot next to her. "Okay, come check this out."

He sat next to her and looked at the printed facsimiles of the Artemis Constitution, the oldest and only paper in town.

"It didn't mention Smiley by name, so I never would've found it if Mrs. Shotwell hadn't spilled the beans. The police blotter just says 'Local Youth arrested for peeping.'" Tracy said.

"Not much for details back then, huh?"

"Nope. I was disappointed at first. But then..."
She pointed to a particular paper.

Local Farmer Arrested for Assault.

Garrett read the first few lines. "Grover
Carmichael? Smiley's dad?"

"Yes. Again, the article doesn't mention Smiley by
name. It just says another farmer accused 'Grover's young
son' of killing a litter of puppies he had in his barn," Tracy
said.

"Holy shit. Does it say how old Smiley was?"

"No. Just that one bit. Anyway, the guy wanted
some money, Grover got pissed and beat him down in
front of numerous witnesses at Davis Hardware. Did two
days in jail."

"A lot of killers start out with animals when
they're young," Garrett said.

"This is really giving me the creeps," Tracy said.
She hugged her own chest and got up to get a sweater. "If
this is real...I mean, Smiley is a deacon at our church. No
one will believe it."

We all have our masks we put on in public, Garrett
thought.

***

LaSalle trudged through the snowy field under the
Cheshire moon, feeling like an asshole. He felt a kinship
to Garrett, even though the guy had been a cop most of
his life. It's not so much what you did for a living, but
what you did as a man in LaSalle's world. They'd both
been through some shit, and they both had their demons.
Hard as it was, he had to set the personal bond aside.

A professional does his job with calm detachment.
Gianni Lucas Santini taught a young Chester

LaSalle more than calm detachment. The old guy showed LaSalle the best place in New York to get a suit tailored, and the best place to put an icepick to make sure a guy didn't make any noise. He took LaSalle from a two-bit street enforcer to a topflight finder of men. And dispatcher of men, as well. LaSalle owed him a lifetime. Easy enough to take on the task of finding his granddaughter.

He hoped Garrett would somehow understand. After a while.

The barnyard stood empty, the gravel drive a pale ghostly snake in the darkness. Smiley's Jeep was there, parked near the front of the house. LaSalle did nothing but watch the house for twenty minutes. His feet ached and his nose felt like it might fall off, but he stood and watched for any movement.

Satisfied, he moved on. Even in the darkness, the lock was open in less than a minute. He swung the quiet barn door open just enough to squeeze inside and pulled it closed after him.

***

Despite his burning hatred, Smiley had to admire the man's discipline. He'd watched him cross the open field in the dark, probably feeling invisible in his black clothes, while in fact he glowed like a beacon in the Hunter's night vision scope. The PI stood and watched, too, exactly as the Hunter would. The Hunter gazed back from behind the kitchen window, never moving until the PI was inside the barn.

Then the Hunter picked up Papa's Winchester and went out into the cold.

***

LaSalle went straight to the trapdoor this time. When it shushed open, he caught a whiff of sickly sweet decay in the still air of the barn. He shivered and told himself it was because of the cold. He had the Browning nine millimeter in one hand and his LED flashlight in the other. He felt anything but calm detachment right now.

The stairs didn't even creak under his linebacker frame. The old coot was one hell of a carpenter, for sure. The flashlight lit up a narrow stairwell with sheetrock covering the dirt walls. Wires ran through plastic loops and bare bulbs dangled every few feet. The sheer amount of time, effort, and willpower it would take to do all this... He moved forward, finger ready to twitch and spew death into the darkness.

At the end of the stairs, he found a locked door. Solid oak, no hollow-core shit for this guy. LaSalle held the flashlight under his arm and twirled the delicate picks with his thick clumsy fingers.

Click.

He put the kit away and turned off the flashlight. He felt for the doorknob and gently opened the door, trying to stay quiet. He pushed it open and took a deep breath.

Gun up, light on.

An antique dentist's chair faced him straight away. A Victorian looking thing, with a heavy wrought-iron base, black padding, and wooden arms stained with something brown. He knew. The smell told him, but he didn't want to say it.

His feet were rooted to the ground and his eardrums *whooshed-whooshed* with the rush of his heart. He'd expected to find a burial ground down here, a crafty dump

223

for a crafty killer.

What the fuck was this crazy shit?

As he moved into the small room, LaSalle's mind kept tripping over things and rebooting to the first image from the doorway.

Was that a tray full of brands? Start over.

Was that a bone saw? Start over.

Was that a collection of painted fingernails? Start over.

Was that—Oh, Lord. A corkboard full of pictures.

So many. So many. Faded Polaroids, so ravaged by time LaSalle could hardly see the frightened girls strapped into the dentist's chair. He spotted the flier he gave Smiley tacked to the corkboard alongside a picture. He stopped and lowered his eyes. After all this time, he didn't want to see, to know for sure.

But he had to. To confirm it for her family.

The last time LaSalle cried, he was fourteen years old and broke his pinky so bad it never did get right again. He didn't cry at his mother's funeral, didn't cry when somebody shot his best friend over the name of a street. He cried bitter tears now for Britney Santini.

"Her favorite flavor of ice cream was bubblegum," LaSalle said to the dark room.

Rage. Too light a word to put a name to the thing sharpening its teeth in his chest. He yanked down the flier and the picture of Britney strapped in the chair. He'd be able to go home after this and tell her family he found her. But not like this. No.

The snowmobile and ATV upstairs had gas in the tanks. He'd take care of the whole joint when he was done with Smiley.

His flashlight swung to another open doorway. It led to a short, dark passage ending in a T intersection. Gun up again, he eased along until he had to decide to go left or right. The cloying odor of decay definitely got stronger to the left, so he went there.

After about twenty feet of narrow hallway, he found a round metal lid about three feet across. It sat on a sheet metal tube with a rubber gasket creating a seal. If LaSalle could smell it with the lid closed, he didn't really want to open it.

He went back the other way, passing his entry point and following the passage to the right. His flashlight made the camo netting on the walls cast spider web shadows. Gooseflesh rose on his arms when he saw the hand-carved wood sign over the doorway.

Trophy Room.

And then he looked inside.

"Oh Jesus, help us. Lord, no. No." LaSalle backed out. He'd seen and done some hard things in his life, but this motherfucker was beyond crazy. Beyond human understanding. And his life would end this very night.

LaSalle strode back through the nightmare rooms, burning to be out of here, feeling them behind him in the darkness. He hoped they knew he was here to avenge them.

He rushed past the dentist's chair, fighting to keep his dinner down. At the entry passage, he shut off his flashlight and mounted the stairs. Cold air dropping from above made it feel like he was climbing into a frigid waterfall, but each freezing breath made him feel better and better.

He stood over the open trapdoor, rethinking his idea of burning everything. He didn't think there would be enough gas to do it proper. Maybe after he took care of Smiley, he'd siphon the fuel from the Jeep. He'd try to save a few families the misery of seeing the horror of the charnel pit. Some asshole would eventually leak crime scene photos.

Killing Smiley would never bring Britney Santini back. Or Danielle Ortega, or Florida girl. No, it wouldn't bring anyone back, but it would douse the fire roaring in his brain. LaSalle had his special barrel on the Browning tonight. He retrieved the suppressor from his pocket.

The *BOOM* of the Winchester inside the barn sounded like the end of the world. Hot fire hit him high between his shoulder blades. LaSalle collapsed to the cold wooden planks, feeling nothing but a million volts of pain in his upper spine.

***

Smiley levered another round into the chamber. But he wouldn't need it. He knew a clean kill when he saw one. The big fella dropped like a bull elk shot through the spine.

He turned off the night vision scope on his rifle and climbed down to his trophy. Smart guy, for sure, otherwise he wouldn't have found the trapdoor.

The Hunter had been smarter, lying silent above him in the hayloft.

Smiley hit the light switch and the industrial globes overhead came on. He shook the pins and needles out of his legs. Dang circulation wasn't what it used to be. He stood over the downed man and saw he was still alive.

His eyes rolled toward Smiley, but he couldn't move anything else.

"Did you find what you were lookin' for?" Smiley said.

He took the mean blade from his coveralls.

22

He was a big man, the PI from New York. Smiley had been on more than one hunting trip to Colorado where he broke down an entire elk with Lamar Evans and old Whit Abercrombie, so he knew the work well enough. It took a while, but he got the job done. Into the pit with half of a fifty pound bag of lime. Smiley sat on his haunches and stared into the pit.

Some of the lime had puffed over onto Nadine's blue face, giving her a pristine white mask. He saw something a few years back on a science show about a tribe of African warriors who used white masks in certain ceremonies to represent female ancestors come back to guard them. He'd been so taken with the thought, he found an importer on the Internet and ordered one. He kept it in his bedroom closet. On hard nights, when the Hunter wanted to go out again too soon after taking one, when he lay twisted in the sheets, awash in his own sweat, he'd take the mask from the closet and think of Ma watching over him.

The beautiful version of Ma, before she slipped and—*Papa cracked her across the skull with a two-by-four*—hit her head on the front steps.

Smiley closed the pit. He had a job to do, and if nothing else, he'd always been known as a hard worker. He tore a small, bloody strip from Nadine's dress. He retrieved his own shirt covered with Bradley's blood from a cardboard box of incidental trophies. Nadine's pie tin was in there, as was a trucker's stolen wallet the green-haired girl had, and precisely forty-two ID cards from all across the country.

Papa had a lot of knives. It didn't take long to find a filet knife with the same profile as the mean blade. Beat up over the years, duct tape held the handle together, and he could see corrosion along the cutting edge. It hadn't been out of Papa's toolbox for forty years. With a loving hand, Smiley cleaned the rust from the antique blade. The knife had been stone sharpened so many times, its edge felt thin as a razor.

Careful, so careful now. He wet the piece of Nadine's dress enough to freshen the dried blood. Then he poked the tip of the blade through the fabric and pushed through to the haft. From this angle, he imagined being inside Nadine's chest when his own blade came through like this. The *whump-whumping* piece of muscle pierced by his sharp tip, spewing warmth and Nadine's life into his hands. He had to steady his trembling fingers in order to repeat the process with his own shirt, marking the knife with Bradley's blood as well.

Smiley took the strip of Nadine's dress and the tainted knife upstairs with him. He set the motion detectors with his remote and headed for his Jeep.

It took an hour to get out to the Lazy Eight Motel. He drove down back roads so remote even he got worried a time or two. The trusty old Jeep plowed right through the snow and frozen mud and soon enough he put his field glasses on the back side of the rundown place some folks called the Artemis Hilton.

He knew the owners, Bill and Laverne Stubbs, lived in the front. All their windows were dark, save one. He saw the white-blue glare of a TV against their bedroom glass. There were three cars in the parking lot, and it looked like the guests were spread out among the rooms for a little privacy. Perfect.

The Hunter donned a camouflage mask and got out of the Jeep. LaSalle's room key rested in his pocket, like a talisman Smiley claimed to open his enemy's kingdom.

He went on foot, treading slow and quiet, the hunting mask covering his face. Normally, he didn't wear a mask, save the one he showed the girls when they first laid eyes on him. Just the Hunter, glaring into their hearts.

Tonight he wanted to make sure nobody could say they saw an old white man sneaking into this room. He got inside quick and eased the deadbolt into place and made sure the thick curtains were drawn. Then he turned on the lights.

He'd never done this before. Been this personal with one of his kills. He stood and took in the curious thrumming silence only a motel room can present. LaSalle left his heater on, so the space felt warm and friendly.

Smiley removed his thick gloves and tugged on a pair of surgical gloves for the next part. First, he examined the things in LaSalle's room, in case he wanted another piece for his collection. The rainbow of shirts in the closet made him shake his head. New York people.

The Hunter's glittering eyes drank in pictures, maps, leftover fliers on the room's narrow desk. He took a new flier without a fold down the middle, the girl's face unmarred by an annoying line. He still had one of her broken finger bones in a cigar box under his bed.

The painting over the bed made his breath catch. He'd been to after-church gatherings at Tracy's before and remembered it hanging in her living room. He stepped up close and pulled the mask up high enough to uncover his nose, pressing it right against the painted canvas. He imagined her perfume on this piece, the oils staining her long red hair, which was bunched in his fist when the mean blade came around.

Smiley pulled the mask back down and berated himself for being distracted. The Hunter needed his discipline now more than ever. Moving fast, he took the bloody knife and opened LaSalle's suitcase. He found a pair of maroon oxford style shoes and stuffed the knife into one of them. From his inside pocket, he retrieved the suppressor off the killer's gun. He put it in the other shoe and zipped the suitcase closed again. Even Whit should be able to piece things together from there.

Next, he went to the closet and found a pair of heavy walking boots. He wet the small strip of Nadine's dress with a bit of water from the sink and used his gloved fingers to press it between the treads of a boot sole.

He put the boot back and surveyed the room again. The map. He went to it and read the pattern of dots like musical notes. Idiots. They had half of them on there at best.

Folding the map back and forth on a line to make the cleanest tear he could, he removed the piece with his property and the Heideman's on it. He put the rest in his pocket and grabbed an ink pen from LaSalle's leather satchel. Pressing hard, he circled the Heideman farm on the map over and over and left it on the desk. The Hunter paused at the door to admire his handiwork. He killed the lights and slipped out. He had a phone call to make.

As always, the fools would see what the Hunter

wanted them to see, and nothing else.

***

The morning sun cleared the fence enough to put feeble light on Garrett's work. He chipped at the frozen dirt in the backyard with his dad's shovel. It looked like he did more damage to the shovel than the earth. This wasn't the way. Besides, it did seem a little macabre to bury The Box after burying Michelle.

He decided on a Viking burial and ran to the garage for some charcoal starter fluid. He got as far as spraying the stuff on the cardboard when the weight of it started pushing down on him. He wound up sitting in the snow, staring at a stupid box dripping with lighter fluid, wondering why the hell things went the way they did, why the universe didn't leave him the fuck alone and let him and Michelle retire to Havasu like a couple of sad old cops who had nothing left to do but drink and take their ski boat on the river.

After a few high-risk warrant services, you learn to recognize the sound of several carburetors opening up, the squealing and sliding as units pull up to the location and officers jump out. He heard those sounds on the street out front.

Garrett sprinted through the house and got to the front door just in time to hear the pounding start.

"Police Department, open the door, we have a search warrant."

He yanked open the door to find Whit Abercrombie pointing a shotgun at him. Lyle and Dougie were behind him, but they held their guns low. Several Sheriff's deputies accompanied them, and they didn't have any personal ties to Garrett. They had assault rifles up and ready.

"Whoa, whoa. What the hell, Whit?" Garrett said.

"Unlock the screen and get your hands up, Garrett, or I'll rip it off the hinges," Whit said. He had the strangest look on his face. Fear and elation warred for control over his spooky grin.

Garrett opened the door and they all rushed in. The Deputies cleared the house and Whit had Garrett sit in a dining room chair. He kept his shotgun pointed at Garrett's chest.

"What is this? What have I done?" Garrett said.

"Where's your black ass-buddy?" Whit said.

"Excuse me?" Garrett felt dizzy with the red as it was, but Whit seemed intent on pushing it over the line.

"Where is he? The coon, LaSalle. He's wanted for murder."

"You're crazy. What murder?"

"An anonymous tipster called the Sheriff's, said they saw a muscular black guy in a Volvo dump a woman's body in the Monongahela last night," Whit said.

"I'd like to hear that recording. Who's the caller?" Garrett said.

"Operator said it was a male, but he called on a private line. Unrecorded."

Garrett looked around the room, wondering if there was a brain in the bunch of them. "So an anonymous tip just happened to come in on a private line so it wouldn't be recorded?"

"What of it?" Whit said. "Guy didn't want to be ID'd."

"Exactly. So he could lay it off on LaSalle."

Now came the grin. If snakes could smile, a rattler would probably look like this when it came across a baby rabbit. Whit relaxed and lowered the shotgun. A little.

"We found your friend's Volvo at the rest stop. But he was nowhere around. We also searched his motel room. Know what we found there?" Whit said.

"I'm guessing a lot of nice clothes."

"Guess that depends on your personal taste. I don't much care for alligator shoes. But we also found a filet knife hidden in a shoe, along with a silencer in the matching shoe. You know, like a pro in town to hit somebody might use? The Sheriff's lab is rushing the blood test on the knife for us. We're testing all his shoes, boots, whatever else, of course," Whit said.

Garrett knew then. LaSalle couldn't wait and Smiley somehow got the upper hand. His chest tingled and he felt short of breath. He put his head in his hands and tried to breathe deep.

"Feel stupid now, don't ya? Looks like this guy you've been helpin' out is a damn professional assassin. I'm willing to bet we find Bradley Wentz's blood on the knife, too."

Garrett wouldn't take that bet with somebody else's money. Smiley had been too damn smart for all of them. He straightened up and looked Whit in the eye. "Does this make sense to you? LaSalle introduced himself to the local Chief of Police, then killed two people?"

"His little missing hooker story gave him a reason to go traipsing around all over the place, at any hour. It's the perfect alibi," Whit said.

"I'm not sure you know what alibi means. Have Lyle show you how to Google it."

"Keep it up, smartass. You have no idea how deep you are."

"So where's the one crucial piece you're missing? LaSalle," Garrett said.

"We figure he saw us tossing his room and lit out.

Probably already been picked up by one of his cohorts," Whit said.

"Cohorts? Do you ever listen to yourself?" Garrett said.

Before Whit could respond, a deputy came in from the backyard carrying The Box.

"Found this box in the backyard, smells like it's soaked with lighter fluid."

Whit gave Garrett a triumphant dip-stained smile. "Is that right?"

"It's personal stuff I'm getting rid of. It's got nothing to do with your case." Garrett couldn't take his eyes off the Box as the deputy set it on the kitchen table.

Whit handed his shotgun to Lyle Hampton and put on a pair of rubber gloves. Garrett's heart sped up and spots of colors danced across his vision. He had to maintain here. Whit would look no matter what, but there was nothing bad in there, so bear down and make it through.

"Aw, isn't that cute, we got Disneyland wrist bands," Whit said. He pulled items out and put them on the table, but Garrett kept his eyes on Whit. Lyle and the deputy stood close to Garrett, but they were watching Whit as well.

Whit came across the picture of Garrett and Michelle at her sister's wedding. Garrett in a rented suit like a high school kid at the prom, and Michelle in a scoop-neck dress that had more men looking at her than the bride.

Whit let out a whistle. "I'll give you this. You did pick up one hot piece of ass out there."

Maybe the guys were lax because it was Garrett, or maybe he moved too fast. Garrett somehow got between Lyle and the deputy and took a looping elbow shot at Whit

Abercrombie. Whit slammed into the kitchen cabinets, a wide gash opened above his eyebrow. He scrambled and yanked his pistol from the holster, but Lyle and the deputy already had Garrett by the arms.

"Easy, Whit! You'll shoot one of us," Lyle said.

"Get outta my way," Whit said.

"No," Lyle said. He took out his cuffs and put them on Garrett, who didn't resist him.

Whit got to his feet, his gun still in his hand. Blood dripped onto the stars on his uniform collar and he glared at Lyle. "I'm gonna remember that, Lyle."

"Me, too," Lyle said.

Garrett felt an odd sense of pride in the young officer. He was a better cop than Whit and Garrett put together.

And then it was time to go to jail. Again.

23

The orange jumpsuit gave his skin a sick yellow cast in the metal mirror over the sink/toilet. Garrett had the cell all to himself last night, since he represented a major crime wave for Artemis, West Virginia.

He could see part of the cinderblock hallway, the walls painted dark blue and light blue, split halfway up. He always hated the smell of a jail. Antiseptic trying to override the stink of humans kept in a closed environment.

Clanging and creaking from down the hall told him someone was coming to see him. He stayed slumped on the metal cot bolted to the rear wall of the cell and waited. Preceded by the clomping of his heavy boots, Whit Abercrombie appeared. He had a white butterfly bandage over his eyebrow. He folded a piece of paper and dangled it through the bars.

"This guy look familiar?"

Garrett pushed off the cot and grabbed the paper. A printout of a charge sheet with a mug shot in the upper left corner.

LaSalle, Chester. Age 20.

Charge: Murder.

"He did time?" Garrett said.

"Nope. Walked on the case."

Garrett folded the paper up and shot it back through the bars at Whit. "Then that doesn't mean shit."

"Means enough when you put it alongside the knife and the blood. We got our results about an hour ago. Both Nadine's and Bradley's blood are on the knife," Whit said.

"Fingerprints?"

"I think you know better. Guy was a pro."

"Yeah. A pro who leaves the murder weapon in his suitcase," Garrett said. He went back and sat down on the bed. "You've been led by the nose all the way here, Whit. But I'll be damned if I have the energy to explain it to you again."

"Oh, right. Old Smiley Carmichael is a mastermind of crime. I forgot. Thanks for tippin' us off, he almost got away with it."

"Yeah, he almost did," Garrett said. "Why don't you ask him if you can take a look around his place and see what he says."

"Because we live in the real America here, son. Smiley's home is his own, and the government doesn't have a right to search it when he hasn't done anything wrong. I understand if that's not the L-A-P-D way," Whit said.

"Will you get off that, already? Probable cause is the same everywhere. What I'm saying is ask him. But I understand, to use your term, if you two have been ass-buddies so long you can't bring yourself to do it," Garrett said.

Whit pressed his lips together so hard it made his dip bulge out like a tumor. More clanging from down the hall made him relax a little. "Here comes your ride."

"My ride?"

Two Sheriff's deputies Garrett had never seen before stepped in front of the cell.

"You're being transported to County Jail so you can be arraigned tomorrow. You'll be held without bail until the hearing, since you're charged with felonious assault on a peace officer. Have a nice ride," Whit said. He took a set of jail keys from his belt and unlocked Garrett's cell.

Garrett let his arms hang loose as one of the deputies cuffed him. He felt numb, detached, lost in a rolling sea no one else seemed to be swimming in. At the crest of a wave, he saw where he wanted to be, solid land, emotional stability. Then he'd slide down into the trough and lose it all as he got slapped under again.

Whit led the way and the deputies escorted Garrett through the station. His face burned when he saw Shirley through the dispatch center window. He didn't know how to read her look, so he stared at Whit's back.

Outside the station, Whit halted the little procession. Smiley stood at the bottom of the steps. Although he wore a somber mask, the corners of his lips twitched upward.

"I am real disappointed you would try to bring me into this after your daddy and I were friends for so long, Garrett Evans. But I forgive you, because I know lately things ain't been right for you," Smiley said. He tapped the side of his head. "Just not right."

For some reason, that little speech recharged Garrett better than any pill could have. He straightened his spine and felt the deputies tighten their grips on his arms.

"I bet these Sheriff's boys have got some DNA swabs in their war bags. Would you like to let them swab your cheek, Smiley?" Garrett said.

Smiley began to smile. He smiled so wide he looked like a cartoon. "I don't believe I would. Because I am a law-abiding citizen," Smiley said.

"Get him out of here," Whit said to the deputies.

They escorted Garrett to a waiting Sheriff's unit and opened the back door. Before they could stuff him in, he craned his head back to face Smiley again.

"Hey, Smiley. Were you whackin' off the night you peeped in that little girl's window? Probably why Tuffy thought you would have made such a piss poor police officer."

For a hot second, the icy mask broke and Garrett felt the full heat coming from Smiley's pale blue eyes. Then Smiley relaxed again and *winked*.

"I think Tracy would be ashamed of your behavior," Smiley said.

The deputies stuffed Garrett in the car and closed the door.

***

"Smiley, watch me," Angela said.

She rolled a boulder of snow into a shape somewhat resembling a head. Smiley took it and stacked it on top of the bigger boulders he'd rolled himself, finishing off a snowman that looked like couple of drunken sailors made it. It stood next to a snow fort they dug out by Smiley's front porch.

The girl chattered away, as usual, and Smiley tried to put in the appropriate "Oh my" and "You don't say" when needed. But a furious black cloud rolled through his mind, threatening to obscure even his love for Angela.

That little shit Garrett Evans stood right there in

front of all those officers and called Smiley a peeper.

You are a dirty peeper.

Smiley cut his eyes toward the old well. But Papa wasn't there. Nobody was, of course.

"Smiley? What is it?" Angela said.

"Hmm? Nothing at all, darlin'. Just thought I saw a rabbit out of the corner of my eye."

"Did he have a pink nose?"

"Why not?"

She giggled and went back to putting pieces of charcoal up the snowman's front.

Puppy killer!

Not Papa this time. The voice of Delroy Cutler called to Smiley from the seventh grade. They all heard about it and teased him until the teachers finally made them leave Smiley alone.

Angela didn't see his face wrinkle at the edges. A crystalline memory stabbed him behind the eyes, sharp as a High Def bullfight. Papa coming home from jail after he beat up the man accusing Smiley of killing his pups. The dry, cracked skin on Papa's knuckles as his fist came arcing in from way up high.

They told everyone the old bay kicked Smiley's teeth out.

"Can you hold me up for his face?" Angela said.

"I'll try. You're getting to be so big, I won't be able to pick you up soon," Smiley said.

He grabbed Angela around the waist and lifted her up so she could put the carrot nose in place. She dug a selection of buttons from her coat pocket, her fingers red from the cold, and held up different "eyes" to gauge her favorite.

A biting breeze blew her hair into his face. It reminded him of being small, Ma holding him the way he held Angela, with Ma's hair tickling his cheek.

Mama's boy.

Smiley twitched, but didn't spin around. He didn't have to look, Papa wasn't back there.

Made you look like a fool and you did nothin'.

He took a deep breath through his nose to calm down and smelled sweet shampoo little girls use.

Told 'em about you whackin' your pecker to a little girl not much older'n that one.

A grinding sound echoed in Smiley's head. It was his dentures. He tried to relax his bulging jaw muscles.

"All done. What do you think?" Angela brushed the flying hair from her face and looked at him with those big serious eyes. She'd put in a large blue button and a small green one. The snowman looked like one of her silly Japanese cartoon characters who just ate something sour.

"I think he's about as perfect as a snowman can be," Smiley said. He put her down and she backed away to admire her work.

"He's cute," Angela said.

"Not as cute as you."

"I don't have funny button eyes," she said. She scooped up snow and flung it at Smiley.

They both laughed and pelted each other with snowballs, fighting their way back to the house. They stopped on the front porch to catch their breath. Her eyes twinkled over apple-red cheeks, her smile a thing of perfection. Weakness overcame him, and he imagined what it would be like to have a normal life. "What do you think, Angie? You think you and your momma might wanna come live here someday? You could have your own rooms."

"We couldn't do that, silly. What would Nana Emma do?"

241

Stay drunk all day like usual, Smiley thought.

"Nah, I was just kiddin'. Of course you need to take care of Nana Emma," he said.

He crushed down the rejection, packed it away with so many other things jammed into the pit of his soul. Shaking off one glove, he tucked a strand of hair behind Angela's ear. If this was all he could get, he'd take it.

At least until she got too old to be cute anymore.

***

The Hunter crept up as close as he dared.

Tracy had gone to bed an hour ago, the lights in the house winking out one by one, until only the vague yellow haze of a reading lamp shone on her bedroom curtains. The material was sheer enough to let Smiley see her, reading in bed, propped up with two pillows and covered by a thick down comforter against the chill.

Get on with it.

Looking, he was just looking. Nothing else. Not tonight.

Coward.

"I ain't," he said, so low the wind ripped the words away leaving no sound behind.

Made you look like a fool. Hurt you and smiled about it.

And Garrett would hurt for it when the time came. Not long ago, he would've worried about his urges being directed toward someone from town, someone familiar. But getting away with putting down two people right under the law's nose had been a freeing experience. He'd proven he was too smart for them. He didn't need to worry anymore.

He did worry about his lessening feelings for Angela. He'd drugged her again tonight without so much as a twinge of guilt. What if the Hunter saw her as worthy prey someday?

No. It wouldn't happen. He loved Angela. She was an innocent.

Ain't none of 'em innocent.

After they got Smiley's new dentures, Poppa had sat him down in the barn for a talk. He explained a man had to have control in his life. Over his woman. Over his money. And over his urges, no matter what they were. He never said he was sorry about knocking Smiley's teeth out.

Only later, when Smiley got old enough to have a few decades to look back on for reference, did he realize what a hypocrite the old man was. Control his urges? He was the kind of drunk you had to hide mouthwash from. And the things he did to Ma...

Smiley recognized those urges for what they were. Right down to the last swing of a splintery two-by-four.

Tracy shifted in bed and yawned. Smiley crept closer, his face inches from the glass. The light from her reading lamp would keep her from seeing the Hunter, camouflaged by the dark.

Her head nodded forward and she put the book on her lap. She yawned again and dog-eared the page in her paperback before putting it on her nightstand. Missus Crumley would send you home with a note for your parents if you dog-eared a library book. Smiley had the marks on his back to prove it.

The Hunter faded back, shining blue eyes watching Tracy turn out her light. Coward? Hardly. A smart man makes preparations before he takes his prize. Hadn't he seen Papa measuring the edge on one of the front steps? Sizing it up against a two-by-four?

Garrett would suffer the same hurt he dealt out with his nasty words. He would come to know what

Smiley knew at the tender age of eight. What it felt like to see someone you love lying dead on the floor and being too weak and small to do anything about it.

***

The jail deputies led Garrett by the elbows. His hands were cuffed in front of him and he wore the blue jumpsuit of the County Jail. He felt like they were leading him to the gas chamber instead of the visitation area. Only one person would bother driving all the way over here to see him. He had contemplated refusing the visit, but he thought she'd misunderstand the reason.

Down a drab hallway with cinderblock walls painted in nursing-home beige, through two more security doors. Here and there, the paint had flaked away to reveal an earlier generation of beige. Garrett was willing to bet the County got a bulk deal on government surplus beige paint right after World War II and they were still working their way through it.

The place even smelled beige.

Their little procession halted outside a thick steel door with a massive lock. One of the deputies produced a set of brass keys that looked like oversized toddler toys. He slotted one of those big bastards and Garrett heard the clunk inside the door.

He entered a small cubicle with bulletproof glass on one side and the door slammed shut behind him. Tracy sat on the other side, tears already welling up. Garrett took a seat and reached up with cuffed hands to grab the intercom phone.

She picked up her side. "Oh sweetie, I don't know what to say."

"Don't say anything. Just let me look at you."

Her red hair flowed in a wild ponytail, and the hand holding the phone had yellow paint under the pinkie nail.

I put glue in her hair in the third grade, Garrett thought.

"Is he gone? LaSalle?" Tracy said. She wiped tears away, but more cascaded down to replace them.

"I can't say for sure. But I think he must be. I know damn well he didn't kill Nadine, so I know what all the 'evidence' in his room means," Garrett said.

"I can't believe all this. I mean—"

He cut her off by holding up his hand. "Don't. Let's talk later. They'll arraign me tomorrow and most likely I'll be able to bail out. Feel like dinner with an ex-con?"

She wiped away the fresh tears and gave their usual banter a brave try.

"Don't you have to be convicted to be an ex-con?"

"Oh, I'm guilty, sister. You're looking at a cop-puncher."

"Since I never considered Whit Abercrombie much of a cop, I'll grant you clemency on that one," Tracy said.

"Thank you, Governor."

They both tried to smile, but nothing felt the same anymore. Seemed like his screwed up life had somehow bled over into her beautiful world of swirling colors and giggles, like a black fungus chewing away all the spontaneity and humor.

"I'll see you soon, okay?" His chest tightened and he wanted to be back in his cell, away from everything, free to turn inward and kick himself for a good long while. She nodded and touched her fingers to the glass. Before she hung up, he waved at her and motioned for her to listen again.

"Hey," he said. "Stay away from Smiley, okay?"

"Yeah," she said.

After she left, they took him to a temporary holding cell for about an hour, and then bussed him over to the courthouse with fourteen other prisoners.

Cuffed together in a line, they shuffled into the courthouse holding area. Over here the walls were painted gray. Garrett imagined the paint was once been destined for the hull of a battleship. Since they were minimum-security prisoners, they all got lumped into a giant communal cell with one metal toilet behind a narrow cinderblock outcropping.

One of the first inmates in, Garrett sat on a bench against the far wall, closest to the bars. Once they had everyone settled, the deputies went back to the intake desk. Garrett tried to relax as much as he could, but he didn't close his eyes. Most of these guys already knew he was a cop, so he'd rather not "slip and fall" in the cell while the deputies weren't around.

A muscular white dude stepped in front of him. The hieroglyphics of the West Virginia State Prison system were tattooed across his exposed neck and forearms. A lot of his size was prison muscle, but Garrett could see the guy had been big his whole life. He stood careless and unaware, flatfooted. No one had probably challenged him since he was a kid, so why would some lanky asshole who used to be a cop start now?

"Hey, piggy," the big guy said. "You're in my seat."

"Drop it. We're here for arraignment. I'm not gonna be denied bail because some peckerwood had a hard-on to show everyone what a man he is," Garrett said.

"Oh, is that right?" The man leaned down, his

thick trapezius muscles bunching, leading Garrett's eye to the base of his neck. Garrett subtly shifted his feet, gathering his power base.

"I got a hard-on for something else, and you're gonna find out when we ride back to County tonight," the big guy said.

No red tide rising. No anger. This decision came calm and cold, just like when he was in uniform working a beat. He needed to eliminate a threat. Garrett erupted off the bench and brought his right arm around in a brutal arc at the same time. He slammed the heel of his right hand into the vagus nerve on the side of the thick tattooed neck.

The big man's eyes rolled up in his head and he fell, his mass of muscle smacking the concrete floor like a beached fish. His arms locked straight and his back arched, not uncommon for someone who's been knocked out.

No one else in the cell moved, so Garrett took his seat again.

A deputy came fast-walking down the hall to check on the noise, saw the dude out cold on the floor and immediately got on his radio.

"Okay, what the fuck happened?" The deputy said.

There were fifteen people in the cell. Not one of them said a word.

Finally, an older Latino guy with a thick white mustache spoke up. He had tattoos older than the big guy Garrett knocked out. "I think the excitement of seeing Judge Dodd got to the peckerwood, Deputy. He just passed out cold."

"Uh huh," the deputy said.

They bundled the groggy peckerwood off to the

infirmary and segregated the merry little band of prisoners into smaller holding cells by race. Sure, that made Garrett feel much safer.

There didn't seem to be any complaints about his choice of seat in the new cell, though.

One by one, the prisoners were led into an elevator and taken up to the courtroom of Judge Llewellyn P. Dodd, the oldest sitting judge in West Virginia. By the time it was Garrett's turn, everyone had been to lunch. (Garrett and his cellmates had bologna sandwiches and water.) Judge Dodd looked like he needed a nap on the sofa, and Whit Abercrombie sat at the Prosecutor's table dabbing at a spot of mustard on his tie.

Garrett entered a plea of Not Guilty and the matters moved to whether or not he would be granted bail. Judge Dodd tilted his head to use the bottom half of his bifocals. "Chief—Uh, Mr. Evans, I am wary of granting you bail. Chief Abercrombie tells me not only are you aggressive toward local law enforcement, but you have repeatedly attempted to interfere with his investigation."

"Investigation? This idiot is being led by the nose to a place he wants to go anyway. That's no investigation," Garrett said.

"Young man, if you can't control yourself, I will hold you in Contempt of Court," Judge Dodd said.

"I apologize, Your Honor. I don't have contempt for this court. Just for fools in general."

"On that, we are in agreement," Judge Dodd said. He shuffled some papers and read a document. "If I were to grant bail, there is also the matter of a Temporary Restraining Order that has been filed with the Court. You are to remain at least one hundred yards away from the property and person of Jebediah Carmichael. You need to understand, Mr. Evans, if you are out on bail and violate a restraining order you will be remanded into the custody of the Sheriff's Department to be held without bail until your preliminary hearing."

"Your Honor, I have no desire to go anywhere near Mr. Carmichael," Garrett said.

Judge Dodd picked up a big file and thumbed through it. He found what he was looking for and grew very serious. "It has also come to the court's attention that you are pending a psychiatric evaluation. That, coupled with your erratic behavior and your assault on a police officer, has given the Court reason to authorize the Artemis Police Department to temporarily seize all firearms in your home."

Garrett glanced at Whit and wanted to leap over the partition and choke the smugness right out of him. Instead, he faced Judge Dodd. "That's fine, Your Honor. But I'll be filing a motion to get them back, of course, so I'd appreciate it if the Artemis PD wouldn't melt them down anytime soon."

"The guns would not be destroyed without a court order. Understood, Chief Abercrombie?" Judge Dodd said.

Whit stood up. "Yes, Your Honor."

Judge Dodd sagged in his robes, really showing his age. "Mister Evans, I understand you've been down a long, hard road the last year. I knew your father, and he is missed by this Court, and by me personally. I am inclined to take into account your record of service, both here and in California as I consider your bail situation."

A small glimmer of hope...

"I hereby grant bail in the amount of five thousand dollars."

The gavel fell on any objections.

It took three hours for the bail bondsman to get all the paperwork in order and deduct the fee from Garrett's debit account. Gates clashed and crashed and he was released into the sharp winter air in his ripped coat with his personal property in a plastic bag. He called a taxi to take him all the way back to Artemis. Tracy would have picked him up without complaint, but he didn't want her driving through the snow.

The driver tried to make small talk at the beginning, but after he got a good look at Garrett in the mirror, he stopped. They rode for forty-five minutes in silence, thoughts slipping through Garrett's mind as fast as the white stripes on the road flashed by. He didn't know what LaSalle saw in the barn. Something, for sure. Else he wouldn't have gone back on the sly.

The queasy image of Smiley winking when he mentioned Tracy rolled Garrett's stomach, threatening to give up the County's bologna sandwich. A panicky chest-tightening compulsion made him want to drive straight out to Smiley's and simply call him out. In reality, if he shot Smiley in his smile then he'd die in prison. Probably not of old age, given he was an ex-cop.

The taxi stopped outside the dark house. It reminded him of high school, pulling up out front in Mike Anderson's Fairlane, drunk as hell and hoping his parents were asleep.

He didn't have to worry about that anymore.

There was enough cash in his plastic baggie of belongings to pay the driver and give him a middling tip. He could only offer a shrug by way of apology.

Inside the house, he wandered from room to room, turning on all the lights. For some reason, it made him feel better. He called Tracy and told her he'd pick up groceries for lunch tomorrow. She wanted him to come over, but he declined. Gave her a lame excuse about needing to clean up the mess Whit's team left behind.

And then he drank.

At some point, he gathered up the pictures and other odds and ends on the kitchen table and put them back in The Box. A hint of the sweet odor of lighter fluid remained. The dried stains of it were spread across the cardboard.

Whit and the boys left The Box and its contents, but took his dad's maps and copied reports, LaSalle's flier, and all the faxed reports LaSalle ordered from other agencies. Son of a bitch had a locksmith drill Dad's gun safe when Garrett would've gladly given up the combination. It stood open and empty. They even took the boxes of ammo.

Kneeling, Garrett checked the false bottom. They hadn't found that, at least. He had put the pictures of Danielle Ortega's time back there, not really knowing what else to do with them.

He took them out to the old man's barbecue pit and sprayed lighter fluid again. This time he didn't hesitate to light it. The images of the girl who disappeared into the West Virginia night curled around the edges and slowly turned black. As they burned, Garrett held the last picture from the packet and looked at it. The one of his dad laughing, pulling up his pants. Not the greatest photo to remember him by. He put the picture in his back pocket and used the barbecue tongs to stir the burning pile. He kept at it until the photos were nothing but ash and memories.

Back inside, he went into his dad's office and closed the door. He sat behind the desk and gripped the sides like a sailor riding out bad seas. His head thumped against the blotter and he knew he'd gone over the edge of drunk and slipped right into the special phase of intoxication where time skips now and again, with hitching black spots in between.

He tried to straighten up and found himself gazing into the eyes of Master Sergeant Lamar Evans, US Army. One of those military portraits with the soft edges from the old days. His mother hung it on the wall after Dad remodeled the room. She always loved the photo. The old military cap at a rakish angle, his dark eyes offset by a jaunty grin.

There was maybe a little skippety-skip in time and then Garrett had the left hand bottom drawer open. He pulled out a bunch of manila folders with tax papers in them and revealed the wooden presentation case beneath. A little bigger than a cigar box, highly polished dark brown wood with a thick swirl of black running through it, and a tarnished brass plate on the front. Garrett focused by closing one eye and read the words engraved there.

> To: *Top Evans*
> From: The *"Bad Boys"* of *B Squadron*
> *For service with honor!*

The tiny clasp holding the box closed took a little prying. It hadn't been opened in years.

Inside, nestled in red velvet lining custom shaped for it, lay a highly polished blue steel Smith and Wesson Military and Police Model .38 Special. Not exactly a cannon, but he'd take it.

There were six ceremonial bullets recessed into the velvet. If everything went well, he'd only need one.

24

In the "Chips and Snack Nuts" aisle, the .38 tried to slip down his pant leg. It had been a couple of days since he ate anything more substantial than a County Jail bologna sandwich and his waistband had gotten a little loose. Delroy's Grocery was a pretty laid back place, but something about a .38 skittering across the tiles tended to set people on edge.

Garrett waited for a harried mother to drag her two kids out of the aisle, each clutching a bag of chips she said they couldn't have. Then he pulled the gun around tight against his hipbone and cinched his belt another notch. He didn't really remember making a conscious decision to carry it, but it felt like a good idea now that he was out here in the open.

He made his way to the meat section and picked out a couple of steaks. The spot between his shoulder blades twitched. He knew eyes followed him, quiet conversations were held after he passed. Gossip travels faster than lightning in a small town, and there was no taller lightning rod in Artemis right now than Garrett Evans.

He'd accused Smiley Carmichael of being involved in Nadine's death, some said to cover for his new black friend who turned out to be the real killer. There were even whispers about Garrett being under a psychiatrist's care when he got hired as Chief of Police.

At the checkout line, no one spoke a word, except when Sally Reeves said, "That'll be forty-six twenty-seven."

He drove to Tracy's house gripping the wheel like a tightrope walker who just slipped off the line. Heavy snow fell like volcanic ash, thick and straight down. By the time he got to Tracy's, his neck muscles were bunched like springs under a heavy load.

He made up his mind he would get through their greeting with stoic resolve.

When she opened the door, he dropped the groceries and crushed her against his chest. They stood there, her inside and him outside, until someone could talk without breaking.

"Are you... I won't say it. I'm just glad you're here," Tracy said. They picked up the groceries and closed the door against the killing winter.

She skinned the potatoes and he seasoned the steaks to give his hands something to do. They talked about LaSalle because they couldn't ignore it. Garrett laid out the old rap sheet Whit showed him, a real thing, and therefore part of who LaSalle was, good or bad. That's the way the big fella would've put it himself.

"You think he was a killer?" Tracy said.

"I think he was a tough customer who grew up on the streets. I told myself he wasn't here to track down the last guy to see his girl alive and whack him. It helped me stay involved, you know? But in the end, if I had a daughter some slimebag killed and I knew a guy..."

"Heaven forbid anyone ever had to make the choice," Tracy said. She tasted her garlic-mashed potatoes and nodded. "Let's eat."

Over rare steaks she said, "So what now?"

"Nothing, I guess. I have a restraining order."

"But I don't."

"No," Garrett said. He got up from the table and took his plate in the kitchen. He didn't know why, he wasn't close to done. He didn't want to argue with her, to let all this shit tarnish their relationship like a brass fixture touched by too many people.

She followed him. He knew she would.

"Smiley can't stay home forever," she said. "With Whit and his boys eyeballing you, I make perfect sense. Next time he goes to work, I check Smiley's place to see if I can find out what made LaSalle so hot to go back."

"Absolutely not," Garrett said. "He'll be on alert. He may have everyone else fooled, but he's worried about me, I guarantee it. If he hasn't already gotten rid of whatever LaSalle saw, he will soon. And I'm not going to risk you."

She started to argue, but he stopped her with a kiss.

He pulled away and they both seemed shocked by the development.

"Uh, sorry," he said.

"No, don't apologize. You're under a lot of stress, which makes people do things they normally wouldn't—Oh, fuck it."

She grabbed him and kissed him back.

***

Belly down, eyes to the glass. That's how the Hunter liked it best.

Smiley watched Garrett and Tracy, the two lovers

255

framed by her kitchen window and the fence beams between them and his position in the east field. He knew Garrett would be here tonight. He couldn't help himself. His world was crumbling around him and a man will grasp at a good woman during those times.

They left the kitchen and Smiley saw the bedroom light come on behind the curtains. While the animals rutted, Smiley planned. He left his position and scouted out the area around Tracy's front door. The Hunter may have been strong, but the damn bitter cold filled his knee joints with razor blades.

He spotted a likely place, about thirty-five yards away. A patch of scrub oak, its branches heavy with snow. If he wore his white camouflage, she'd never see him.

The bedroom light went out and Smiley retreated. Out past the dead garden, past the Ellsworth's barn, moving into the woods and back to his quiet little snow machine. Once he got home, he'd need to practice his sad face.

Damn shame, he'd say to those old coots outside Davis Hardware. *Poor old Garrett went crazy and kilt himself. I just wish he didn't take Tracy Ellsworth with him.*

***

Tracy put her chin on Garrett's chest, which put her eyes level with the shiny .38 on her nightstand. "You sure you don't want Daddy's shotgun?"

Garrett touched the coppery fire of her hair. "I'm sorry I put glue in your hair."

"I had to cut it out," she said. "With my safety scissors."

"I know. I would've done it for you, if you would've stood still."

She pinched his chest and he howled.

"Now we're even," she said. It was hard for her to maintain a smile for long. She went back to staring at the gun. "Seriously. He's got that Magnum."

"Doesn't matter what you're shooting if you can't hit the target. I know how to stay behind cover and move when I need to. I'll be okay. You keep the shotgun here."

They lay like the big and little spoons, and he thought only of her, his mind calm and focused for the first time in months. Finally, she got up to go to the bathroom and when she came back, he had his pants on.

"Going?"

"I should," he said.

"Why?"

"People will talk."

She snickered behind her hand, which got him going. She grabbed him and they rolled back into her warm, safe bed.

***

He'd printed all his own fliers on Tracy's computer. He loaded a stack of them onto the passenger seat of the Mustang. He'd left her nestled in the down comforter, all tousled hair and warm, sleepy kisses.

Just after the first staff member opened the gates to the County Yards at six a.m., Garrett drove right in like he was supposed to be there. He parked and carried the stack of papers over to the shack where employees signed out their vehicles. He left the fliers, weighted with a rock, on the wooden shelf outside the dispatcher's window.

He thought about picking them up and stopping this nonsense before it got too crazy. Then he thought of LaSalle. If the tables were turned, and it was Garrett who went missing, he knew the big man would have been all over Smiley.

Garrett fired up the Mustang and drove through the snow at speeds that would've made LaSalle grip the "Help me Jesus" handle. When Melvin Davis opened the doors to the hardware store at seven a.m., Garrett got out of his car and joined him. "Morning, Mr. Davis. You still carry those laser rangefinders?"

"Uh, well, yeah. Give me a minute to cut the lights on and get the heat goin'."

While Melvin fiddled with the thermostat, Garrett went past all the aisles of power tools, nuts and bolts, and gardening implements. He needed the hunting department.

The cold made the fluorescent bulbs overhead stutter for a few seconds before they came to full brightness. Garrett squatted down and perused a glass case containing high-end binoculars, rifle scopes, and on the far end, what he wanted.

Binoculars with a laser rangefinder built in.

"What do you know? On sale and everything," Garrett said.

Melvin came around and took about two minutes going through a jumble of keys on one of those retracting things hung on his belt. Normally, Garrett would have ground his teeth flat waiting for the old fart to get his shit together. But he felt free, at ease. He knew enough about himself to know that was a bad sign.

Melvin got the case open and retrieved the binoculars.

"Yup. On sale, thirty percent off. Plus, comes with a case from the manufacturer. Kinda cheap plastic, but it's free," Melvin said.

"A free case to boot? This must be the luckiest day

of my life," Garrett said.

Melvin didn't seem to get the joke. "Okay. I'll ring you up at the register."

Over Melvin's shoulder, Garrett saw a beautiful Ithaca shotgun, twelve gauge pump action, with flying ducks engraved along the barrel. "How much you want for the Ithaca?"

Melvin's eyes darted to the door and back, like maybe he was hoping someone would come in and at least increase the odds to two sane people versus one crazy.

"I'm sorry, Garrett, but I don't believe I can sell you that," Melvin said.

And he genuinely did look sorry, too. Garrett remembered Melvin being one of the first to shake his hand at Dad's funeral. Davis Hardware had sponsored every little league team Garrett ever played for. But he wasn't the gangly kid too tall to be playing shortstop, anymore; he was a grown man with drawn cheeks and a manic shine in his eyes.

"No problem, Mr. Davis. I understand. We still good for the rangefinders?" Garrett said.

"Of course. Come on over." Relieved, without a doubt, Melvin rang him up and probably was never happier in his life to accompany a customer to the door. He tried to be quiet about it, of course, but Garrett heard the subtle scrape of the deadbolt behind him.

He didn't blame Melvin one bit.

Garrett drove out to Two Trees Road, the one that led to Smiley's house. Pulling onto the shoulder, he rolled the Mustang forward, taking readings with his rangefinder binos as he went. He stopped when the laser told him he was exactly one hundred and two yards from the front post of Smiley's driveway.

He kept the motor running for the heat and... And

what? What was he doing? Trying to provoke Smiley, but why? As smart as he'd proven to be so far, surely Smiley had destroyed whatever the hell led LaSalle back.

Serial killers often collected news clippings and kept trophies, for excitement and for a feeling of control. Garrett had a lot riding on Smiley being an "average" serial killer. He knew Smiley considered himself smarter than Whit Abercrombie for sure. So maybe. Maybe Smiley's pride made him keep something, whether it was in the barn, the house, or on his property somewhere. Maybe the killer's ego wouldn't let him get rid of it.

The Mustang's interior got so warm, Garrett started to nod off. His chin dropped and he let out a loud snort, waking himself up. His eyes focused up the road and the coppery taste of panic hit the back of his throat. Smiley's Jeep Willys idled just over one hundred yards away from him.

He didn't pick up the binoculars, but he knew Smiley's icy blue eyes were glaring his way. The Jeep backed up a bit and parked. Smiley didn't get out, so Garrett knew what came next.

He left the warm cocoon of the Mustang and used his digital camera to take a few random pictures of the woods north of the road. Within two minutes, an Artemis PD unit slid to a stop behind him. Dougie Armstead stepped out and his normally cheerful round face collapsed into a frown.

"Geez, Garrett, come on. I don't want anything to do with all this," Dougie said.

"All of what? I'm just taking pictures of the woods. My friend Tracy, you know Tracy Ellsworth, right? She's a painter and I always take pictures of cool scenery for her." Garrett watched Smiley pull onto the road and head in the opposite direction, toward the County Yards.

"There's legal a restraining order. Whit says to cuff you on the spot," Dougie said.

"You tell Whit I am exactly one hundred and two yards away from the property I'm supposed to be one hundred yards from," Garrett said. He leaned into the car and picked up the rangefinders. "Wanna take a look?"

"No, I do not want to take a look. Garrett, man, I like you and everything, but I got a wife and kids to feed. I'm not gonna get fired because you think you're smarter than Whit, and the two of you wanna have a big dick contest," Dougie said.

"Which I would totally win. But I see what you mean. I don't want to make your life miserable, Dougie. I'll go take some cool tree pictures somewhere else," Garrett said.

Some of the frown came out of Dougie's cheeks. "Thanks, man. I appreciate it."

Garrett got back in the Mustang and made a three-point turn to head back the other way. He stopped in the middle of the road and took another reading with his rangefinder. He rolled down his window and said, "So there's no misunderstanding, I am now one hundred and one yards from the victim's property."

"Now you're just being a dick," Dougie said.

What could Garrett say? Dougie was right. He flipped down his visor against the morning sun and drove away, actually feeling bad about channeling his Whit-shit onto poor Dougie. The guy became a cop because he had a pregnant wife and needed a steady job. He wasn't looking to be a hero out here, he just showed up to clock in and do his job for eight hours.

Garrett made a right, drove about half a mile, then made a left on Fourth Street so he could drive past Nadine's house on the way home. He remembered her story about calling out to the trucker in the parking lot, asking him about his kids while he was picking up a hooker.

He had a feeling she'd appreciate what Garrett did this morning.

***

Smiley blinked at the piece of paper in his hands. Folks had them all over the County Yards by now. He could hear them whispering even when they weren't moving their lips.

A flier made by photocopying two old newspaper articles. *Local Youth Arrested*.

And the article about Papa's arrest. Dirty son of a bitch. Dirty, dirty son of a bitch Garrett Evans. Smiley couldn't muster so much as a grin, much less his trademark smile. He couldn't even look his coworkers in the eye. He got back in his Jeep and went home. If they called him, he'd tell them he felt short of breath and was going to see his doctor.

He roared up his gravel driveway, not taking any care to keep it neat. He leaped out of his Jeep and stormed into the house. Once he had Hank blaring on the stereo to crush out the whispering, insulting, teasing voices, he sat at Ma's kitchen table and drank for a spell.

Warmth traveled from his belly to his cheeks, but it didn't stop him grinding his teeth. He went out into the cold and took great gulping breaths. The barn called to him like a lover ignored too long. A visit to his trophies might cheer him up. At the very least he could go down there and piss on that investigator's skull. He's the one started the whole downward spiral when he convinced Garrett Evans to get involved.

Coward.

"I ain't," Smiley said. He didn't look at the well, but it didn't help. He plugged his fingers in his ears, but that didn't help either.

The Hunter is stronger than you. Always has been. You're worthless. You let 'em push you around, just like the Tunney kid.

Smiley tasted blood and remembered Dudley Tunny. Had a good twenty pounds on Smiley when they were little kids. Papa made him fight Dudley because Smiley complained about Dudley bullying him. After Dudley got in a few good licks, Smiley curled up in a ball to protect himself and Papa's lip curled in revulsion.

If you're not willing to put up more of a fight than that, how the hell are you gonna make your way in this world?

Something welled up from deep inside, an emotional festering volcano, the pyroclastic flow burning away any self-control. He covered the distance to the barn in big jerky strides and unlocked the door. Snatching the shiny double-headed axe off the wall, he used big overhand swings to hack at the remains of the ancient whipping post, sending new splinters flying, revealing shiny wood beneath the dried gray surface.

You think hacking that old post will stop it?

Smiley hurled the axe across the barn. It stuck deep in one door. "I stop it when I want to," he said. Heart hammering from the axe work, thin walls of muscle threatening to give way at any second, Smiley's gaze bounced all around the barn. Papa was nowhere to be seen, though.

Of course he wasn't. Smiley pushed him out that damn loft door right up there. Heard his neck crack and went down there to piss on him. And none of the fools who came to see figured it out. Smiley showed them the sad face he'd practiced and they hauled Papa's stinking carcass away and cremated him on the County dime.

Garrett wanted to provoke the Hunter did he? When his redheaded mistress got her brains spilled on the snow in front of him, Lamar's ignorant son would cry like a little boy. Once the tears stopped, Smiley would offer him an escape from his pain, as well.

He went back into the house, reset the needle on the record player and let Hank soothe his nerves as he poured himself a tumbler of whiskey. In the back bedroom, he kept a behemoth antique Mosler gun safe filled with rifles, shotguns, and various handguns. He sipped liquid fire and spun the dial with one hand.

He ignored his own guns. He put his drink on the top shelf of the safe and squatted down, his knees popping like those white paper snappers they sell on the Fourth of July.

He dug under a folded American flag on the floor of the safe. (Papa had served in the Army during Dubba-ya Dubba-ya Two. Stateside, but still.) Beneath the flag, he found a Colt Single Action Army .45 revolver. Second Generation model, made from the 1950s into the late '70s. Years of sliding in and out of a holster had worn the bluing down to the silver around the trigger guard and along the cylinder and top strap.

The gun once belonged to Garrett's dad.

He and Smiley went to the range and perforated some tin cans a few months before Lamar died, and Smiley took a shine to the old revolver. They made a cash deal right there on the spot, no paperwork of course.

It was still registered in Lamar Evans' name. It wouldn't be a far stretch to assume Whit's boys had missed the gun on their search and Garrett had tragically stumbled across it.

25

Garrett spun the cylinder of the old .38, watching the shiny brass circles of the casings spin into a blur of gold before slowing to become individual purveyors of death again. He closed the cylinder and heard the latch click into place. His mind pulled up an image before he could stop it.

A suicide. Guy used to be an LA County deputy back in the '70s. Got old, was constantly in and out of the hospital, and decided one last ride in, apparently. He fucked it up, angled his service revolver wrong in his mouth and cut an artery in his neck instead of blasting his medulla. Furniture overturned, curtains pulled down, the walls look like someone put blood in a paint gun and had at it.

The chirp of his phone made Garrett drop the gun on the bed like a hot coal. He dug the cell out of his pocket and saw her name.

"Hello?"

"Are you still sure about tonight?" Tracy said.

He'd half expected this call all day. "Just watching. Nothing else, I swear."

"And if you see a big bonfire going? What then?" Tracy said.

"Maybe I'll take some marshmallows with me just in case. Smiley used to love s'mores when we went camping," he said.

"Not funny."

Part of him felt remorse at what happened last night. From this point on, they'd never go back to the shoulder-bumping and cutting each other off at the knees like wisecracking friends. He may have spoiled the one pure thing he'd found when he came back to Artemis.

"Listen, I'm trained to arrest people under high risk situations. If worse comes to worse, I know what to do, and he'll be in the open where I can see him," Garrett said.

"Okay. I trust you. Just...you know."

"I'll be careful," he said.

"Call me when you start home, no matter what time it is."

"I will, I promise. Now try to relax. Bye."

"Bye," she said.

He put the phone on the bed and performed a ritual he used to do before his team served big warrants, taking deep breath and chuffing the air out in chunks, flexing his core.

A garment bag hung in his closet that Whit's boys and the assisting deputies had opened, spotted the gray suit inside, and closed right up again. Garrett unzipped it and took the suit out. It felt much heavier than any suit should. He unbuttoned the jacket, exposing the white shirt underneath. He opened the shirt to reveal a Kevlar vest, a heavy one with a trauma plate over the heart area.

He put it on and adjusted the Velcro straps nice and tight. The vest smelled of stale sweat. The last time he wore it, it had been 108 degrees in the San Fernando Valley and he'd chased what seemed like the world's fastest gangster through four blocks worth of alleys in Reseda.

In a spiteful move, Whit even took every holster he found in the house. Garrett had to put together a half-assed shoulder rig with an old belt and a cracked leather holster he found in the garage rafters. Made to hold a slimmer .45, the holster was too tight for the .38, but he forced the fat cylinder into the holster anyway and donned the rig over his vest. He checked himself in the mirror and decided he looked like an ambulatory military surplus store. It would have to do. He threw on a heavy down coat and grabbed his phone off the bed.

His gaze fell on The Box tucked back into its normal spot in his closet.

Snatching it up, he ran to the back patio before he could change his mind. He kept his plan for Smiley's place foremost in his mind so the act of spilling lighter fluid all over the cardboard talisman of his past became a pure mechanical motion.

"Shut up, shut up, shut up," he said. Soft, barely a whisper, meant to be a chant against the memories. A tossed match and it all became a blue flame that melted a clear spot in the snow on the patio. It brought to mind all the briefings he'd had on dealing with suicidal subjects. One major warning sign was getting rid of all their possessions and putting affairs in order.

Thinking on it, he decided he had no plans to die tonight. So maybe this was his way of clearing up old business for a different reason. He kicked The Box gently and it came apart at the seams. Garrett looked away from the faces curling in the flames and thought of what might be, instead of what had gone before. For the first time in more than a year, there actually was a "might be."

Satisfied the flames would claim the past, he

strode back through the house, shutting off lights along the way and locking the front door behind him.

Wet snow blew through the brilliant cone created by the Mustang's headlights. The kind of snow that stuck and piled up fast. Wonderful. He was glad he'd invested in battery-powered heated boots when he first moved back home. If he died of exposure in the woods tonight, at least his toes wouldn't be black with frostbite when they found him.

The low-slung car bucked and kicked a little going up the hill to the rest stop. He planned to follow the route LaSalle mapped out for his first scouting mission.

And his second one, too, Garrett reminded himself.

He had to admit, he hadn't felt fear like this even during the hairiest pursuit or shootout he'd been in. Smiley had somehow gotten the drop on LaSalle, who by all recent accounts seemed to have some experience taking people out.

Garrett had plenty of training, but it was of the direct confrontation type, not stealth missions and ambushes. What he really hoped was to see the old bastard loading up something nasty in his Jeep to dispose of it. Then Garrett could just call in the County boys, or maybe the Troopers. No one Whit Abercrombie could control, in other words.

***

Smiley packed the mean blade, just in case. He knew he didn't want to use it tonight, but it served the Hunter so well for so many years, he couldn't bear to leave it behind.

He had his own Smith and Wesson .357 in its

holster, but he would use the big Colt owned by Garrett's daddy for this one. He rigged a shoulder holster for it and tucked it under his white snowsuit.

He paced and paced last night, listening to Hank, sipping whiskey, and letting the Hunter think. It came to him about three in the morning. He could shoot Tracy and leave her there. (As much as it saddened him to leave his trophy of her gorgeous red mane behind.) He'd wait there for Garrett and dart him, then take him into the mountains and shoot him in the head like a suicide. Smiley knew all the game trails the predators frequented. By the time anyone found Garrett, he'd be so chewed up any subtle evidence that he hadn't killed himself would be gone. The ketamine would have broken down by then, as well, so they could 'topsy all they wanted, to quote Angela.

Inside the cold barn, he prepared the snowmobile. He'd need the sled tonight because he planned to bring Garrett back here and use the Jeep to haul him into the mountains. The quiet exhaust system smoked a bit while the snow machine warmed up. He dragged the sled across the barn floor and hooked it up. A rough fingertip traced the word *Hunter* carved into the front rail of the sled. He carved it the first time he brought a trophy back on it. Stunned, he realized that was almost forty years ago.

The Hunter was getting old.

The thought made Smiley's heart ache. He could hardly control the Hunter's urges anymore. And he knew when predators get old and weak, they hunt the sick and the young, the only prey they can still take. He closed his eyes and listened to the idling machine. The steady *duh-duh-duh-duh-duh* of the engine reminded him of hammering rabbit hearts cupped in his hands. The thready little beats before Smiley twisted the head. Same as the quick pulsing veins in Angela's skinny neck.

He curled a fist and punched the fading yellow and green bruise on his cheek, Bradley Wentz's last visible mark on the world. The pain burst bright in his mind and scattered the nasty thoughts. Zipping up his snowsuit, he opened the barn door. He pulled the snowmobile and sled forward, then shut everything up again.

His cold blue eyes took in his family homestead. The tidy little house where his Ma died, the sturdy barn where Papa took his last high dive. So many years, so much pain. So much blood, so many thrills.

A senior citizen. That's what he'd become. An old coot to be looked at with pity, his opinions meeting with rolled eyes from the new breed of gum-snapping, face-pierced kids the County hired now.

You could be famous. Feared.

"They like me," Smiley said.

Bullshit. That's your mask, it ain't what you want.

No, it wasn't. All these years of smiling in people's faces, hiding the glorious Hunter because they wouldn't understand him. They did like Smiley. Maybe some loved him. But he wanted them to know. How dumb they were and how smart he was.

You're old. Ain't got much time left anyway.

All they could do was lock him away with his memories of the Hunt, the mental images of his kneeling trophies below. Lock him away from Angela and his urges.

Smiley tilted his face up to the sky and watched the new snowflakes drift out of the starry blackness above him. After this business with Garrett was done, he'd start anew with a vengeance. He'd kill and kill and kill until they brought in one of them FBI task forces and ran the Hunter to ground. At the end, the Hunter would become more glorious than ever. People all over the world would shiver at night to think of him.

"Why not?" Smiley said.

He rode then, crossing open fields and negotiating miles of narrow tracks through the woods. He came around the backside of the Ellsworth farm and parked the machine in a stand of poplar trees. Now came the tedious part. He hooked the sled to a canvas strap system he'd made for himself. Leaning into it, Smiley towed the sled across the snow toward Tracy's house.

In the distance, he heard two horned owls hooting territorial calls to each other.

***

The owls outside had her in a wildlife mood. Tracy glanced at her reference, a barn owl Garrett photographed for her about six months ago. A little guy, peeking from a busted board in a barn on the edge of collapse. She added more gray to the weathered boards in her rendering.

She painted in the living room tonight, because the oils wouldn't like the freezing barn studio. Yeah, that was why.

She tried not to think of Garrett and instead concentrated on the huh'hoo-hoo, huh'hoo-hoo of the horned owls outside. One called from the woods east of the house and one from somewhere behind the barn. They were singing a territorial duet just for Tracy's entertainment. Or maybe a hot female horned owl's entertainment.

Huh'hoo-hoo.
Huh-hoo-hoo.
Huh—

Tracy's skin crawled at the silence. She put down her brush and turned out the lights in the front room. Her dad's old Mossberg twelve-gauge leaned against the wall

271

and she picked it up. A careful peek out the window, into the darkness.

Nothing moved out there, except snow drifting down, covering the world like God's own eraser for whatever happened yesterday. She waited and waited for the owls to resume, each quiet second tightening the muscles in her back, creeping up her neck.

She took her phone from her pocket and dialed Garrett.

***

Garrett's flashlight lit up the game trail behind the rest stop, showing him where to place his feet so he wouldn't break his neck. Hopefully.

The .38 banged against his ribs in the jury-rigged holster. Annoying, but it would have to do. Halfway down the trail, his phone buzzed in his pocket and he nearly fell on his ass. At least he'd been smart enough to put it on silent. Only one person could be calling.

"Tracy?"

"Garrett, I'm scared. I think I'm just freaking myself out, but the owls were hooting and now they're not and it's just snowing and snowing and so quiet out there."

"Easy, babe. Easy, okay?" The frightened sound in her voice twisted a dagger in his heart. He wanted to shred space and time and be there with her right now.

"Garrett?" Her voice small, vulnerable.

"I'm on the way," he said.

He ran.

Back up the trail, slipping and sliding, followed the jittering flashlight halo through the woods, cursing the fact he let himself get soft in the last year. In LA, he'd worked out five days a week, training for the violent world he found himself in. He could've run this hill at a full sprint and fought a Jiu-Jitsu match when he hit the top. Now, he felt like he'd puke at any second and he still had a good two hundred yards to go.

On rubbery legs, he made it to the Mustang. His throat burned with all the cold air his tortured lungs sucked down. Good thing he had a remote, he wasn't sure his shaky fingers would have been able to put the key in the lock. He got into the car and fired up the big V-8. The Mustang wasn't exactly a time machine, but it would have to do.

26

Smiley crouched behind the white hump in the ground that was a snow-covered scrub oak. One of the owls had been in the woods near Smiley's ambush spot and it had shut up when he passed under it, as if it could feel the presence of a stronger predator.

The Hunter sat in silence and watched the windows. He held the big Colt in his gloved hand and mentally measured the distance between his ambush spot and the front drive where Garrett would most likely pull up.

The snowsuit muffled his cracking knees as he stood and strode toward the door. He had to take care of Tracy first.

***

Tracy chewed her bottom lip and held her phone, ready to dial Garrett again. She'd had time to calm down and turn on a few lights in the house. Her courage accordingly bolstered, now she felt stupid for calling him away from the plan. He had a mission to do, something he was trained for, and she'd let her nerves screw it up. If they were going to catch Smiley dirty, she'd have to grow a set, so to speak. They couldn't do the job huddled together in her living room.

She touched the screen. *Dialing Garrett Evans.*

He answered, and she heard the Mustang growling in the background.

"Garrett, I'm sorry. I just freaked out," she said.

"Don't worry about it. I'll come check on you and then I'll go out a little later," he said.

She loved him for that and so much more. He didn't know the good man hiding under all the baggage, but she did. She'd known him since they were kids. "I'm just being a titty-baby. For heaven's sake, I live in the country. Owls stop hooting, coyotes stop howling. Big deal," she said. She propped the shotgun against the wall and opened the door to peek out at the snowy night.

A masked man clad in white was about twenty yards from her door. He had one of those cowboy style revolvers in his hand.

"Oh God, Smiley, no."

She tried to close the door— *Thunderclap* from the gun and the bullet blasted through the wood and slammed into her skull.

***

Not fast enough. The fence posts flashed by like the blades of a fan, blurring into a loose boundary in the flying snow. Garrett's throat tightened and his chest felt like someone had him in a bear hug, but he kept his right foot down and fought it. *Not now, not now, not now, not now.*

Tracy needed him.

His face started to feel numb and his heart stuttered like an engine with a bad spark plug. The panic wave rolled over his feeble mental seawall, dimming his vision. A half-mile to Bray Road, a left and another quarter mile to Tracy's driveway. If he hadn't been fighting off the panicky tunnel vision, he would have remembered to take his foot off the gas.

A split-second into the left turn, he knew he'd pushed the Mustang too far. Even in summer, with the pavement hot and sticky, he probably wouldn't have made it.

In the snow? "Probably" didn't even factor in.

The tunnel vision snapped into a crystal clear image of road signs upside down through the rectangular frame of the Mustang's windshield. And then there was tumbling. And blackness.

***

His knees were on fire, but the Hunter crouched back behind his ambush spot and waited. Tracy had saved him having to clean up footprints on her front porch. She surprised him by opening the door, and he shot her from a good twenty yards out. The rough desire to run up and bunch Ma's—*Tracy's*—red hair in his fists and pound her head against the floorboards had him gritting his teeth. He wanted to *touch hurt destroy* her.

Discipline. He had a plan to follow.

So he watched her from a distance. She lay on the floor, her feet just inside the front door. A marvelous red-black pool grew steadily from her head. He needed Garrett to see what he'd done. He needed to hear his mourning wails before he did the rest. Smiley shook off a glove and pulled out his phone.

***

Snow blew in the driver's window, but Garrett didn't remember rolling it down. He reached for the button to roll it back up and his left arm punished his lapse of memory with a lightning bolt of pain. He came to and worked very hard to understand the upside-down scenery.

Using his right arm, he unbuckled his seat beat and fell to the roof of the car. He cried out when his left shoulder hit. Most likely dislocated. He knew what it felt like. He fell out of a tree stand when he was thirteen, hunting with Dad and Smiley.

Smiley.

Garrett forced himself to crawl, squeezing out the slightly collapsed passenger window. He found himself facedown in deep snow, across a wide field from Tracy's place.

His legs felt more rubbery than after his run up the hill, but he locked his knees and stood. Blood ran down his face from something on his scalp. The drips told him it wasn't too bad. If it had been gushing, he'd be in trouble.

He actually giggled at the absurdity of that. He was nothing but in trouble. Ever. He felt the .38, miraculously still in his jury-rigged holster.

His phone buzzed in his pocket and when he pulled it out, he couldn't believe his eyes.

"Are you kidding me?" he said into the phone.

Smiley's soft drawl taunted him. "I bet Tracy would dearly love to see you about now. But I don't suspect she'll see much of anything again."

The phone went silent.

"Hello? Smiley?" Garrett said. Nothing. He threw his phone back at the Mustang and waded through the snow, his left shoulder a constant spike of pain keeping time with his heartbeat. Drawing the old .38, he approached the side of Tracy's house and peeked through a gap in her living room curtains. When he saw her, he nearly collapsed against the wall. He stumbled around to the front door, any knowledge of tactics and training gone, only her blood in his mind, so much of it, so much of it.

He knelt in the doorway and a sob wracked his body so hard it doubled him over.

But did he see that? Was he really crazy, did her chest move, did it fucking move, did it did it—

The dart hit Garrett high between the shoulder blades where he couldn't get at it. He didn't know what it was, but then again, he did. He barely felt the prick of the needle. The vest. Sharp things would pierce it, but it stopped the dart enough. He spun immediately and scraped his back across the doorframe. The dart clattered to the porch. An insane second of clarity, as Garrett thought it looked just like the one in the bear's ass in the picture.

His body swiveled, gun hand up, practiced eyes sweeping the ambush zone.

There he stood. Smiley. Admiring his handiwork with the rifle across his forearm. He had his mask up and Garrett saw the almost comic look of surprise. The front sight post of Dad's .38 was shiny and black against the white outline Smiley made in his snowsuit.

Boom-boom. A double tap.

Smiley's right leg flew back and he dropped like a penny arcade duck hit by a cork gun.

Damn it. Too low. Garrett brought his sights up... and toppled to one side, the doorframe barely catching him. The dart obviously gave him a dose before he scraped it out. He had no idea how much.

White fire bloomed in the dark out there and the wall next to Garrett exploded. Smiley had his .357 out now, no doubt about what made the booming roar.

Garrett hunched low and took cover behind

Tracy's pickup. Three solid booms in the dark and her windshield starred, *one-two-three*. Garrett didn't need to pop the .38's cylinder to check. He knew his life and maybe Tracy's—*did she move, did she move*—depended on four antique rounds from the piss-ant predecessor to the cannon Smiley had. And he'd be out there reloading.

Smiley's voice drifted in on the razor wind. "It ain't legal for a criminal like you to have a gun, boy."

Moving around out there. Changing positions.

"Problem is," Garrett yelled, "I'm all out of give-a-fuck when it comes to the law."

He bellied down and peered under the truck. His Field Training Officer, a salty bastard named Frank Holder, had taught him peripheral vision worked better at night than looking for something directly. Garrett scanned the lighter horizon, letting his eyes drift over the snow and scrub below.

A white form moved in the darkness and Garrett knelt by the truck's rear fender. In the dark, he elevated the sights until he could pick them up against the moon and then lowered them onto his target. He squeezed the trigger.

At the .38's bark, the white hump limped to the left. The magnum roared again, and metal sprayed the house behind Garrett as jacketed rounds tore through the pickup's fender.

One-two-three-four-five-six.

Smiley had been in the Army, but he was a medic. He'd never been trained not to shoot his gun dry in an active firefight. Garrett leaped up and ran at him, trying to close the gap before Smiley reloaded, wanting to be sure of his shot.

He got there in time to see Smiley snap the cylinder shut and bring his gun up.

The snowsuit made a trembling white light at the end of Garrett's tunnel vision. The way Smiley's body jerked seemed completely out of proportion to the two pops of the .38.

Blowing snow, cold against his cheeks, freezing blood on his face made a crackling sound as he opened his mouth to breathe. Garrett stood over Smiley, weaving back and forth from the drug. He saw roses of blood blooming across the belly of the white snowsuit.

The butt of the .357 stuck out of the snow and Smiley's blue-veined hand tried to pry it out, but the punishment had been too much for his old body. His arms were too weak.

He struggled to sit up in the snow and *smiled* at Garrett.

"Got me good, officer. You sure did. But you shot a little low. I figure those government doctors, they'll fix me up right as rain," Smiley said.

"And you'll spend the rest of your miserable life in prison, old man. You're done."

Smiley clutched his belly and Garrett could see the medic in him applying pressure to his wounds. "Think of all the people that'll visit me, though. The reporters, the stars of them news shows on cable. I'm gonna be the biggest damn thing that ever come out of this town. And stupid rednecks like Tuffy Baylor and your daddy will never be remembered for nothin'."

The smile absolutely blazed now. The pale blue eyes twinkled and Garrett knew Smiley was right. The killers always became celebrities in their own twisted way.

A snowflake caught in Garrett's eyelashes and he remembered his first ride with LaSalle, snow pattering against the windshield, unexpectedly opening up to the big man's soothing nature, telling him about Michelle. The story of her death and how her partner never cleared leather.

Garrett looked down at Smiley Carmichael, his father's best friend, the man who taught him how to tie a fly, and told self-deprecating stories to make a little boy feel good.

Smiley. That good old hard worker who destroyed so many lives over the years. Dozens of girls, LaSalle, Nadine, her friend Mrs. Shotwell who would sit in her empty house and think about this for what was left of her lonely life.

"As my friend Chester LaSalle once put it, the report will say you had your gun in your hand," Garrett said. This whole insane part of Garrett's life had started with three gunshots echoing over a snowy yard out at the Withers place.

Tonight, it ended with one.

27

Garrett eased Tracy's pickup into a spot in front of May's Diner. He still hadn't gotten used to parking the damn thing after driving the low-slung Mustang for so long, and it hurt his left shoulder to turn the big wheel too far.

He saw a news truck down the street, the reporter pacing along the sidewalk, wearing his serious face for the camera. Garrett couldn't imagine what there could possibly be left to cover at this point.

He and Tracy had laid low at her place in the intervening weeks. The case of the "Hillbilly Butcher," as they'd called him—*and wouldn't Smiley have hated that*—spawned a frenzy of media attention after the State Police cadaver team found the lair under the barn. Between the Polaroid pictures and newer digital printouts, they'd found pictures of twenty young women down there. From the bones in his decomposition pit, they estimated he'd killed at least a dozen more over four decades.

Garrett made sure LaSalle's remains were sent back alongside what little remains could be identified from dental records as Britney Santini. Somehow, he felt the big man would want to see her home.

He kept the painting LaSalle bought from Tracy. It reminded him of a warm friendly night that seemed a century ago.

As to the rest of what they found, Garrett didn't personally go down there, but he saw hardened State Troopers who had stood over human paste at bad traffic accidents come out of that hole looking like scared little boys whose parents lied to them about the Boogie Man. The contents of Smiley's trophy room hit Artemis like a sucker punch from a friend who suddenly turned into a mean drunk.

"Hey, Revenuer."

Melvin Davis, Earl Hunsacker, and Poor Boy Willis sat rooted to their usual spots on the bench outside Davis Hardware. No one said anything. Poor Boy peeled his old carcass off the bench and limped over to Garrett with his cane. He held out a gnarled hand.

Emotions still sometimes blindsided Garrett. It wasn't like there would ever be a miracle cure for it. He blinked a few times as he took Poor Boy's hand.

"You done what needed doin'," Poor Boy said. And that was that. He took his place on the bench again and the old boys nodded their goodbyes.

Inside May's Diner, plenty of eyes still followed him. He'd called in the order and Misty had it waiting in the service window. She brought it over with a haunted look.

"Here you go, Garrett. That'll be twenty-five even."

He gave her thirty and they shared a wan smile. Angela peeked out of the kitchen and Garrett grinned at her. "What are you doing here, girl?"

Angela glared at him in silence.

Misty said, "Eunice let me bring her to work with

me. You know, until we get our daycare situation figured out."

"Oh. Yeah. Of course," Garrett said.

Angela's hollow eyes tilted up at him and he felt the hatred boiling off her. Quiet, so quiet he almost didn't hear it, she said, "You're a mean man. You hurt Smiley."

She spun on her heel and went back into the kitchen.

"Angela!" Misty said. She turned back to Garrett. "I'm so sorry. She has no idea, and I can't even begin to explain..."

"And you shouldn't," Garrett said. "Ever. It's bad enough she'll find out when she's older. I'm a big boy. I can take it."

He drove back out to Tracy's with Angela's voice in his head. She only knew the mask Smiley wore, so he couldn't blame her. We all wear one, and someone loves us for it somewhere. Not everyone will always find out what's behind it.

The house was dark when he rolled up. He knew where she would be. He left the food in the car and went out to the barn studio.

The fact Smiley chose Dad's old Colt had saved Tracy's life. The lower muzzle velocity of the .45 Colt coupled with a pure lead bullet allowed the doorframe to break Smiley's shot up just enough. It still cut her scalp from her temple to the back of her head and gave her one hell of a concussion.

Within two weeks she picked up a brush again.

He stood in silence, watching her paint. She wore the snazzy blue beanie he bought her to cover the "Frankenstein Procedure scar," as she named it. She was stronger than any man he'd ever met.

She reminded him every day to take his pills and

made sure to post the dates of his therapy sessions on the calendar. She'd convinced him to at least check in with his LA counselor by phone once a month.

Tracy noticed him watching. She put down her brush and came to him, smelling of oil paints and turpentine, the curls of her hair caressing his face in the wind. LaSalle once told him people didn't need things to be perfect, just all right. They could work with that.

Garrett cupped Tracy's chin and kissed her.

He knew things would never be perfect, but they were a long way toward being all right.

Thanks so much for reading! If you enjoyed going on this adventure with me, please leave a review on Amazon.com.

You can find my other work on my author page at Amazon.com and follow me on Twitter @SinisterEZ.

67782609R00162

Made in the USA
Lexington, KY
24 September 2017